T0160362

THE BOOK OF EXTRAORDINARY NEW

Sherlock Holmes Stories

THE BOOK OF EXTRAORDINARY NEW

Sherlock Holmes Stories

The Best New
Original Stories
of the Genre

Edited by

Maxim
Jakubowski

Mango Publishing
CORAL GABLES

Cover Design: Gabrielle Mechaber
Layout & Design: Carmen Fortunato

For permission requests, please contact the publisher at:
Mango Publishing Group
2850 S Douglas Road, 2nd Floor
Coral Gables, FL 33134 USA
info@mango.bz

For special orders, quantity sales, course adoptions and corporate sales, please
email the publisher at sales@mango.bz. For trade and wholesale sales, please
contact Ingram Publisher Services at customer.service@ingramcontent.com or
+1.800.509.4887.

The Book of Extraordinary New Sherlock Holmes Stories: The Best New Original
Stories of the Genre

Library of Congress Cataloging-in-Publication number: 2020940958
ISBN: (print) 978-1-64250-432-3 , (ebook) 978-1-64250-433-0
BISAC category code FIC022050, FICTION / Mystery & Detective /
Collections & Anthologies

Printed in the United States of America

Table of Contents

Introduction

Ever since his most inspired creation by Sir Arthur Conan Doyle, the appeal and popularity of Sherlock Holmes has never abated and the demand for new adventures of the iconic sleuth continues to this day, helped on by the latest elegant TV series in which he is played by Benedict Cumberbatch, in the footsteps of Basil Rathbone, Jeremy Brett, and so many other extraordinary actors who have incarnated the mythical sleuth from 221B Baker Street.

Likewise on the page where a variety of writers have taken it upon themselves, first somewhat illegally, whether in the guise of pastiches or parodies, and then after the copyright expired (at different times according to the country where they lived or published) to satisfy the reading public's appetite for new adventures of the immortal detective and his cohorts. All shedding new light on the character as well as adding invaluable new adventures to the canon, many worthy of Conan Doyle himself in the process (I am thinking of John Gardner, John Dickson Carr, Nicholas Meyer, Anthony Horowitz, Michael Hardwick, Michael Kurland, to name but a few...).

Some of my favourite contemporary writers of crime and mystery have, at my request, contributed each a brand new story featuring the mythical detective (and in many cases the obligatory John Watson and even, but whisper it quietly, their nemesis Doctor Moriarty, as well as such favourite characters like the alluring Irene Adler and the familiar Mrs. Hudson, Mycroft Holmes, or Inspector Lestrade) as further examples of his awesome powers of deduction and his unerring quest for the truth, however improbable it might at first appear.

I think it makes a fitting new volume to our Mango series of mystery anthologies, which began with *The Book of Extraordinary Historical Mystery Stories*, followed by *The Book of Extraordinary Amateur Sleuth and Private Eye Stories*, and *The Book of Extraordinary Impossible Crimes and Puzzling Deaths*.

But who am I to delay your reading pleasure, so I shall cease forthwith to tease your imagination and let you get on with this treasure trove of new cases, featuring the one and only Mr. Sherlock Holmes!

The game is most definitely on...

The Adventure of the Milford Silkworms

Lavie Tidhar

Abridged from papers discovered amidst the estate of the late Dr. Watson, with annotations.

"My great-grandmother, you see, cultivated worms," the young lady said.

I had been woken far too early from a sound sleep at the insistence of Holmes, who was in turn woken up by Mrs. Hudson. I no longer asked the reason for my rude awakening—it was always a client.[1]

Holmes's clients, I had come to learn—especially the wealthier kind—had their own ideas as regards to sociable hours and the appropriate time in which to make a call. I ran a comb through my hair, dressed, and went to join Holmes in the sitting room, where a fire was already burning, and a service of coffee awaited.

As did the young lady who came to talk about worms.

"My name," she told us. "Is Constance Cornwallis-West."

She was a dainty little thing. Years later, the world would come to know and be riveted by the scandalous tales of Constance, who married and then divorced the Duke of Westminster, and of her sister Daisy, Princess of Pless. But at this time, she was yet unmarried,[2] a sweet young woman of eighteen, and troubled. Holmes poured her a cup of coffee, which she accepted gratefully, and we sat down together.

"I came by train from Milford," she said. "Milford-on-Sea, I should say. My father is trying to turn it into a resort, you see, and he felt the name change would be more attractive to visitors."

Holmes lit a pipe and listened attentively.

"We own much of the land thereabouts," Constance said. "My great-grandfather was a naval officer under Admiral Cornwallis. When the admiral retired, he moved to the Newlands Estate and, since he looked upon my great-grandfather like a son, invited him and my great-grandmother Mary to live with him. Great-grandfather

---

1 At this time, Watson appears to be staying with Holmes in Baker Street, however (see discussion of possible dates below) he would most likely have been married to Mary Morstan during this period. We will never know the exact reason—it is most probable that Mary was away for a while (perhaps for reasons related to her later illness).

2 Constance only married the Duke of Westminster in 1901, placing this tale at least some while before that date. Constance would have been eighteen in 1895, which would possibly set this some time after Holmes's return the year before.

passed away when my grandmother was but a baby. Great-grandma Mary looked after the admiral well into his old age and managed the estate on his behalf. She acquired much of the neighbouring estates and, upon the admiral's death, she and my grandmother inherited everything. Great-grandmother was, by all accounts, a remarkable woman. She managed the estate with a firm hand, but her real passion was for silkworms."

"Silkworms," I said.

"Yes."

"In England?"

"Yes. You see, she became fascinated by the possibility of raising silkworms for their silk on the estate. For that purpose, she planted mulberry trees imported from Italy, and conducted ceaseless experiments until she produced twenty yards of exquisite damask, which she presented to the queen."

"I see," said Holmes.

"I see," I said, though in truth, I didn't.

Constance tugged at a rather fetching earlobe nervously. "I am trying to give you some of the background," she said.

"Of course," said Holmes. "I wouldn't have it any other way, my dear."

I looked at him in suspicion, for Holmes, though he has many sterling qualities, can hardly count interest in entomology amongst them, unless said insects have laid eggs inside a corpse.

"Thank you," Daisy said. She took a sip of her coffee.

"My great-grandmother's interest in the silkworms led to publication of *A Manual for Rearing Silkworms in England*,[3] to this day the premier work of scholarship on the subject—"

"A rather obscure topic, in truth," I murmured, and Holmes shot me a rebuking glance.

"And to a correspondence with Charles Darwin, the scientist. Are you familiar with his work?"

---

3   *A Manual for Rearing Silkworms in England: With a Brief Notice of the Various Species of This Insect, And the Cultivation of the Mulberry Tree*, published 1848, with illustrations by the author.

"Of course," I said, "the naturalist."

"He had interesting ideas about music, as I'm sure I've said to you in the past, Watson," Holmes said. I looked at him blankly and he waved it away for another time.[4]

"Darwin asked my great-grandmother first for specimens of her silkworms for him to study. Later, he asked her to assist his research by conducting breeding experiments on her caterpillars in order to see if she could produce a strand with dark eyebrows."

"Eyebrows," I said.

"Yes. My great-grandmother complied. She separated twenty caterpillars who all exhibited dark eyebrows and bred them. And, indeed, proved satisfactorily that the silkworms in the study all inherited eyebrows from their progenitors, some darker than others but all plainly visible."

"Fascinating," murmured Holmes.

"It's all in Darwin," Constance said. "Or so I'm told. In due course, my great-grandmother succumbed. My father, her grandson, is a Member of Parliament, or was until last year. He is now firmly committed to a plan to turn the old estate into a seaside resort. My mother is not as keen. My sister, who could otherwise be relied upon to assist me in tampering my father's schemes, is recently married to Hans, the Prince of Pless, and now lives in his ancestral castle in Silesia. They are very wealthy."

"Indeed," murmured Holmes.

"I do miss her so!" Constance said.

Holmes drew on his pipe thoughtfully.

"What, exactly, did you seek me out for, Miss Constance?" he said. "I assume it is not merely to deliver this sermon about worms, as invigorating as I did find it."

The girl blushed. "No, of course not," she said. "You see, I reside in Newlands, a place which I love dearly. We still have my great-grandmother's mulberry trees... My mother wishes me to marry well, but I am yet free from the shackles of matrimony. I do not approve

---

4   Holmes does indeed mention Darwin's musical ideas to Watson in *A Study in Scarlet*.

of my father's plans for the area, but I would never stand in his way. Usually his various schemes end naturally, with no harm done. But things have gone awry in Newlands in some way. There is a...a boy, a man I mean, who lives on the grounds who I am friendly with. A Mr. Maiden, who spent some time in India and is a keen botanist. We often get such enthusiasts as lodgers staying with us. I came upon him the other night lying in the road, beaten and bloody. He refused to tell me what had transpired, but he was shook and, I must tell you, Mr. Holmes, so was I. There was a violence visited upon him, I know that much. And there is more. Strange lights at night, moving about and vanishing like will o' the wisp. And then there's the matter of the goats."

"The *goats*?" I said.

"Yes," Constance said. "They're acting strangely."

I looked to Holmes, fully expecting him to dismiss this seeming nonsense, and wishing I had had the good sense to remain in my bed.

Yet Holmes leaned forward, eyes bright and more animated than I had seen him for some time.

"How so?"

"They keep heading toward my great-grandmother's old barn," Constance said. "And they are aggressive—even more so than usual for a goat, I mean. One nearly got me the other day, and the other tenant that we have, old Mr. Hemsley,[5] has been severely bitten by them on two separate occasions. I was mortified. Newlands is a safe place from the world, a haven, Mr. Holmes. But now, I suspect that my father's plans of redevelopment have raised the ire of some local residents, who are using mean tricks as a way of scaring us off. Poor Mr. Hemsley never quite recovered from the incident with the goats and now roams the estate quite sleepless and in a state of nervous agitation that breaks my heart on seeing him. Please, Mr. Holmes. I know this mystery is barely worth your time, there is no diamond

---

5   Most likely William Hemsley, first the Assistant for India in the Kew Botanic Gardens and, later, Keeper of the Herbarium. This seems to be confirmed by later references in the text.

stolen and no murder, thank the Lord, but all the same, we are upset and baffled, and the local constable is hardly equal to the task. Will you help me?"

At such an innocent plea, delivered in such pleasing tones and coming as it did from that sweet mouth, all my previous doubts had been cast away as though they never existed.

"Well, if Holmes would not, then I would, my dear Miss Constance!" I said fervently.

She turned those big round eyes on me with gratitude. "You would, Dr. Watson?"

"Please, call me John."

"John, then," she said, and smiled.

Holmes put down his pipe.

"Well, Watson," he said mildly, "it seems you have made the decision for both of us. I am intrigued, yes, though I do believe I have all the pertinent information and have come to a preliminary conclusion based on your report, Miss Constance. But a theory is no use unless it is..." he smiled. "How would your great-grandmother might have put it? It should be *experimentally tested*. Yes. Besides, some sea air and the countryside would do us both good, don't you think, Watson?"

"You wish to go to Milford?" I said in surprise.

"Milford-*on-Sea*," Holmes said. "A change is as good as a rest, after all, Watson—as Miss Constance's father would surely agree."

If there is one thing Holmes likes it is his *Bradshaw's*. He was studying it with satisfaction long before we even left London.

"There is everything in *Bradshaw's*," he told me. "Everything!"

"It's just the train timetable," I said, "and anyhow, the train is late."

"Think how such a fact could prove an innocent man's alibi—or another man's guilt!" he said.

The Book of Extraordinary New Sherlock Holmes Stories

"But our case does not involve trains, Holmes," I said patiently. The train was finally coming into the terminal in Charing Cross, and I was only sorry Miss Constance could not accompany us. She was visiting London to see her sister, the newly minted princess, who was staying at the Langham. She seemed much more at ease after unburdening herself to us, and left with a smile, saying she would meet us the next day at Newlands.

The hustle and bustle of passengers was all about us, and a conductor blew his whistle. I wore a suit perfect for the country and quite relished our unexpected holiday on the seaside. Mrs. Hudson had thoughtfully prepared for us a picnic basket, and despite Holmes's occasional grumbling of her "limited cuisine," I thought she was a very good cook.

"Ah, here we are," said Holmes, and he closed the *Bradshaw's Guide* loudly. "Shall we, Watson?"

"Yes, Holmes," I said—following behind him with both of our luggage.

Once settled on the train, and with the pleasant views going past us, I opened the basket. Mrs. Hudson did not disappoint. Besides the cutlery and napkins she had thoughtfully packed there was a handsome meat pie, boiled tongue, ham sandwiches, a tin of sardines and the crackers to go alongside them, some hard boiled eggs, a cherry cake, and a hot flask of strong coffee.

"Now, that's better," said Holmes, after we had tucked in and spent a not inconsiderable time doing little by way of talking and much by way of filling our stomachs. He turned his twinkling eyes on me. "So, Watson? What did you make of our young client's story?"

I shrugged and refilled my coffee. "In truth, Holmes, I find there is not much in it. No doubt, as Miss Constance said, some of the local residents are resentful of the father's redevelopment plans and wish to scarper it by staging a charade. The beating of the botanist—this Mr. Maiden?—is a sorry escalation, but no doubt there is a simple answer and the whole matter can be brought to a rapid conclusion once you identify the culprits."

"Is that so?" said Holmes.

"Indeed," I said, warming up to my theme. "It is a small place. This should hardly be taxing. Why, I could do it myself!"

Holmes smiled at me. "And impress Miss Constance by doing so?"

"I wish only for her happiness," I said.

"Is that so..." said Holmes. He sipped his coffee. "In that case, I shall leave that part of the investigation to you, Watson. By all means, go amongst the people of Milford and see what you can find out. You have an honest face and an honest manner. I could not think of anyone better for the task."

I looked at him a little suspiciously, but he seemed sincere.

"And what do you make of the more puzzling elements of the tale?" he said. "This matter of the goats, for instance?"

I laughed. "Anyone who knows goats knows they need neither rhyme nor reason to get cross," I said. "Why, when I served in Afghanistan, they were a total pest!"

Holmes nodded. "You have thought this through," he said.

"You disagree with my assessment?"

Holmes shrugged. "Yours is a logical and clearly argued hypothesis," he said, not really answering my question at all. He picked up his *Bradshaw's* again, then reached for a pipe.

"Now, back to the old 4:50 from Paddington..." he said.

And he spent the rest of the journey engrossed in the timetables of British trains.

We aligned at the station of New Milton, a new, modern building[6] with nothing much beside a post office opposite it.[7] There were pleasant fields all about us, and a cab waited outside to take us to Newlands Manor.

---

6   In fact, the station of New Milton was opened in March 1888.

7   The post office, which carried a sign saying "New Milton Post Office" to distinguish it from the old post office, gave its name to the station and the eventual town that arose there.

"Mr. Holmes and Dr. Watson?"

We introduced ourselves and the driver in turn offered that his name was Joe Maiden, the botanist Miss Constance had mentioned was staying on the estate. He was quite young, and handsome in a boyish way, and he chatted in a friendly manner all the way along the road as he drove.

"Tales of your exploits have reached far and wide, Mr. Holmes," he said. "When Constance telegrammed from London to say you were arriving, I volunteered to drive you. I often help around the estate. And often I travel widely with the carriage in search of specimens. I am a keen botanist, you see."

I noticed his familiar use of Miss Constance's name. She had not mentioned an attachment between the two, but then again, she was young, pretty and unwed, and it was only natural to assume that she would have her share of suitors. I could hardly begrudge the young man his interest.

"A botanist?" said Holmes.

"Yes, sir, Mr. Holmes. I was drawn here by the old Mrs. Whithy's research in silkworms. She had imported a remarkable number of mulberry trees which remain on the estate, even though the rest of her research had long been put away and the silkworms, I believe, are long dead. My uncle, Joseph, after whom I am named, made his fame with a study of the Eucalyptus tree in Australia.[8] I hope to perhaps, more modestly, do the same with the mulberry."

"A worthy ambition," said Holmes, who had little interest in botany beyond poisons, and who knew nothing of practical gardening.[9] "And your search takes you far and wide?"

"I am interested in the local distribution of the mulberry," the young man said. "And other plants. But I fear to bore you!" he said, laughing. "Are you here for a holiday? The coast is charming this time of year and I will be more than happy to show you around. In truth there is little to do on the estate. I could take you to Milford,

---

8   Joseph Maiden (1859–1295) was a botanist and indeed an expert on the Eucalyptus who spent much of his life in Australia.

9   Watson makes much the same observation in *A Study in Scarlet*.

where there are many pleasant activities to undertake, and you could even charter a boat for the short ride to the Isle of Wight."

I looked at him in some suspicion, for had I been of a more sinister bend of mind I would have got it into my head that he wished to keep us away from Newlands. I also registered then the marks of a beating which Miss Constance had mentioned to us.

"I see you have been in a struggle," remarked Holmes, as if on cue.

"This?" Maiden touched his face self-consciously and winced. He was in the driving seat of the cart, but the horses were docile and the road all but empty, and he was half-turned to speak with us. "It is nothing," he said. "I fell in the dark. I feel very foolish, and Constance—Miss Constance, I mean—made too much of a fuss about it, I fear."

"You were in India?" Holmes said.

"Yes. For a short time only, on my quest for adventure." When he smiled, he smiled easily. "I worked as a clerk for the Royal Commission on Opium. It was not very glamorous, and the weather did not suit me, so I returned on the next ship."[10]

Holmes lit a pipe and made no further comment. We watched the gentle land roll past us. It was not long before we reached Newlands. It was a pleasant estate, very green and sedate, and as we drove in, we came upon a curious figure.

"Ahoy there, Bill!" young Joe cried. The man, who was older and wore a shabby tweed jacket with muddy boots, turned and glared at us. I noticed he was holding leaves in his hands and, as I watched in horror, he shoved them into his mouth and began chewing. His eyes were red and his manner furtive as though he was either angry or scared.

"Who goes there!" he called back.

"It's just me, Bill, old boy! Get back to your bed; you should not be wandering around in your condition!"

---

10   The Royal Commission was appointed in 1893 and released its report in early 1895, further suggesting '95 as the most likely date for this adventure.

"Nothing wrong with me!" the man cried. He stomped the ground with his muddy boot. "I have too much to do, Maiden, too much to do! Watch out for the goats!" He turned his head this way and that, then seemed to spot one such animal in the distance, at which point this otherworldly apparition gave a cry of fear or rage and ran off, leaving a trail of leaves behind him.

"Poor Bill," young Maiden said. "He has not been himself recently."

"He is a fellow botanist?" said Holmes.

"Oh, a respected one!" Joe said. "I am but a dabbling amateur. William here is the real deal, but his nerves are weak, and he was advised to come here for the rest and peace the seaside offers. I fear he is not getting any better, though."

"I see," said Holmes.

"I see nothing," I muttered at him softly, and he smiled.

"Are the goats really such a menace?" he asked Joe Maiden.

"Frightful, diabolical creatures!" the young Joe cried, and for a moment I glimpsed, underneath that handsome, boyish face, a cold dark fury I had not imagined could be there before. "They're monsters, Mr. Holmes! They eat *everything*! Try as I might to guard my specimens, these fiendish beasts get in and gobble them up without so much as a by-your-leave. Nothing is safe from these predators!"

"You keep important specimens?"

"Well, I would not say *important*," Joe said. "But important to me, yes, Mr. Holmes. Besides, you saw their effect on poor Bill. The man is distraught."

"Because of the goats," Holmes said.

"Exactly!"

"I see," said Holmes.

"I don't," I said. It seemed to me a lot of fuss about goats.

I decided not to let any of this bother me. The family, we were told, were all away that day—Miss Constance in London, and William Cornwallis-West and his wife called away unexpectedly to their castle in Wales.[11] We were shown by hospitable staff to large, roomy accommodation and were offered a more than suitable lunch from the impressive larders. Before long, I found the quiet and the fresh air to have a most invigorating effect on me until I was humming contentedly to myself.

"Stop that," said Holmes.

"I beg your pardon?"

"You're humming."

"Was I?"

"You're still doing it!" he said.

"My, Holmes, you seem as tense as that poor chap we saw earlier!" I said.

He paced restlessly.

"Why keep it quiet?" he said. "That is what I don't understand."

"I'm sorry?"

"They confound me!" he said. "They are either very dumb or very smart, Watson. But I cannot tell which."

"You make no sense, old boy," I said. "Shall we take a walk? It is such a pleasant day."

"Yes," he said. "We shall do that. I want to see what's in the old barn."

"If you wish," I said, thinking to humour him.

We donned our hiking clothes and set off at a brisk pace. I could hear birds chirping and the rustle of wind in the leaves, and the air was perfumed with flowers. I could smell, too, the sea in the distance, and thought longingly of a dip in the waters. I was about to suggest this to Holmes when we came upon the goats.

Goats really *are* mean, when the mood takes them. These blocked our way and looked quite disgruntled. They chewed on everything in sight.

"Shoo!" Holmes said, brandishing his walking stick. "Shoo!"

The goats stared at him much as young Wiggins of the Irregulars might have stared at Holmes in this situation.

---

11   Records indicate this would be Ruthin Castle, though it eventually left the family's hands and, in the 1920s, became a private hospital.

"Watch out..." I murmured.

But the goats had no interest in us. We pushed through them, though they followed us in a manner both listless and menacing as we made our way to old Mrs. Whitby's barn.

I did not know what Holmes expected, but when we got there, the barn doors were open and there was nothing inside but some rusting old machinery and freshly dug holes in the ground.

"Aha!" Holmes said. He pointed my attention to the clear prints of two sets of footsteps in the mud, and to swathes of swept earth, as though something heavy had been dragged across it.

"There is nothing here," I said.

"But there was," he said. "There was!"

"Holmes," I said. "I see no great mystery here. The young man said he fell and as a doctor I can tell you I believe him. His injuries correspond. The old man seems to suffer from some form of hysteria and was no doubt recommended the seaside as a balm for his nerves. The goats are merely goats. And there is nothing in the barn. I suspect this is all a big ado about nothing."

"What of your insistence that it was the townsfolk behind it?" Holmes said.

I shrugged. "I am happy to undertake the onerous task of visiting Milford-by-Sea and partaking of cake—I mean, making inquiries amongst the locals," I said. "Would you care to join me?"

"You go ahead, Watson," he said. "I shall continue my walk. We shall reconvene in the evening and compare notes."

"Very well, Holmes," I said, for there was no arguing with him when he was in that mood.

I left him there and though I could not find Joe Maiden I did find one of the servants who took me into town. He was a good-natured sort, a native to the area, and much attached to the family.

"Oh, no, sir," he said, upon my enquiry. "We are all excited for the work. You will see—you will hear it, in a moment."

And indeed, I did, for as we approached Milford-by-Sea I could hear the sounds of construction and industry. Men shouted, hammers fell, saws cut, beams were raised.

The man was right. The workers seemed happy at their toil—apparently Miss Constance's father paid a handsome salary—and the whole town had the smell of sawdust and fresh paint. The roads were newly laid, the shop fronts bright and colourful, and a new hotel was being erected.

"I shall drop you off here, sir, while I do a spot of shopping for the house," the man said. "You can find me at the Crown, if you don't mind, sir, when you wish to return."

I waved him cheerfully away, knowing a man who liked a tipple when I saw one, and embarked on a leisurely exploration of the village. It really *was* a very pleasant place, and one could see that Miss Constance's father invested much in this redevelopment. I decided to follow the coachman's example and visited the Gun, the Lion, and the Crown, taking a small drink in each one while chatting to the locals, who were on the whole welcoming and warm.

No, they had no notion of any trouble at Newlands. No, they were delighted with the plans for the village that Cornwallis-West had. No, there were no problems with the local goats (here they looked at me a bit strangely).

By the time I made it to the Crown I was a little bit tipsy and had to acknowledge that my initial theory was wrong. No one at Milford had cause to make trouble at the estate.

I had one more drink in the pub with its old ships' timber and merry fire, and as we returned to Newlands I was once more humming contentedly, anticipating dinner and a good night's sleep.

In both of these hopes, as it turned out, I was to be disappointed.

A strange light bobbed in the darkness toward us as the carriage followed the path through the trees. I stared, for this was evidence at last of Miss Constance's story.

"There!" I said. "Look!"

The driver tried to make the horses go faster, but in his addled state almost slipped off the cab. At that moment a tall, maddened figure burst out of the foliage, light shining forth, and the driver gave a cry of alarm.

"It's me, fool!" said a familiar voice. I stared as Holmes lowered the lamp and his face was sharply illuminated. "Come quick, Watson! The game's afoot!"[12]

"What got into you, man?" I said in alarm, for Holmes now resembled nothing so much as the old botanist we had met earlier that day, so wild eyed and fidgety he was.

"There is not a moment to spare!"

He gestured behind him, and I saw more two lights bobbing and weaving in the distance somewhere in the thicket of trees.

I jumped off the cab and followed Holmes, though I near tripped on a root and had to steady myself for a moment. Then we were off, trying to catch those elusive lights, but they kept vanishing from sight and I kept tripping and losing my bearings entirely, and the leaves brushed my face and an insect stung me.

But Holmes was relentless, and gradually we gained on the lights, for in truth they were not moving so terribly fast, and I had the sudden suspicion that they were as inadequate in the dark as we were. We were long past the old barn at this point, to the south of the estate, where the old mulberries must have grown. I had no real idea what trees or shrubs any of these were. I doubted Holmes did either.

"We lost them," Holmes said. He stopped at last, but so abruptly that I tripped again trying to halt and he grabbed my arm to steady me.

"How did your investigation in the village proceed?" he asked.

"It was as you said," I admitted. "I cannot see the locals involved in any way. *Who* are we following? And *why*?"

"You shall see," he said. "If only there was a—there!"

---

12 Holmes uses the expression again later on in "The Adventure of the Abbey Grange," though it does not otherwise appear to be something he commonly said. The term itself originates with Shakespeare, and it is unclear where Holmes picked it up. As Watson comments in *A Study in Scarlet*, Holmes's knowledge of literature was nil. Perhaps Holmes classified Shakespeare's plays under the category of "sensational literature," of which his knowledge was, of course, immense.

For a moment, I could not see what he was referring to. Then I heard a rustle in the undergrowth, and out of the darkness stepped a goat.

It stared at us without much interest and reached for the nearest shrub. It swallowed a handful of leaves, spat them out in disgust, shook its head as though disappointed, and vanished again.

Holmes sprang to action.

"Follow that goat!" he said.

In the annals of my various adventures with that most brilliant of detectives, I can recall no other more outlandish outing than that night's expedition.

Follow that goat, Holmes said!

Well, have you ever *tried* to follow a goat in the night-time?

It is not the most pleasant of experiences. Especially when you happen to step—more than once—in said goat's ordure.

Holmes paid no heed. The goat kept pushing on and soon we saw others of its kind join it on its mysterious quest. The goats kept sampling the leaves of the trees and bushes, but none was seemingly to their liking, so they kept on, guided by some otherworldly sense, until at last we saw once again, in the distance, those mysterious lights.

The lights were now stationary, and as we approached, cautiously now, I could hear two voices in conversation.

"Did you move them all?"

"I did, but the acclimatisation is sub-optimal! We are losing yield at—"

"What was that?"

"What?"

"Did you hear anything?"

"Relax, there is no one here but us."

"What of the goats?"

"They will never find it. And I put up the fence like you told me to."

There, I thought, was a man who underestimated goats—and that was to be his undoing.

Holmes hefted his heavy walking stick like a club and grinned.

"Shall we, Watson?" he said.

He pushed through the dark, following the goats. We reached a low fence, hastily erected. The goats stared at it in quiet hostility. Holmes raised his voice.

"I do not think it will take them long before they bring your fence down!" he said.

His voice boomed in the night. The two men cursed, and their lanterns were raised.

"Who goes there?"

Holmes leapt the fence.

"It is I, Sherlock Hol— Oh, dear, Watson, let me help you there."

I had tripped again, trying to surmount the fence.

"Oh, it's you," the first voice said. We stepped into their enclosure (the goats staring with intense hostility through the fence at us), and I saw the young Mr. Maiden and the older Mr. Hemsley.

"Well, what do you want?" Mr. Hemsley demanded. "We are very busy here, as you can see."

I had to admit this was not the reaction I was expecting. I looked about me, but all I could see were a bunch of green-leaf plants, some watering cans and gardening tools, and the badly erected skeleton of what could have been a glasshouse.

"The answer to a few questions, by your leave," Holmes said. "Do you know, your activities have alarmed young Miss Constance tremendously?"

"Dear Constance!" Mr. Maiden cried. "I would never—I couldn't—oh, dear. We have rather made a mess of things, have we not, Bill?"

"Nonsense, Joe. The girl may entertain you, but she will never be foolish enough to marry you."

"She would if we are successful here, Bill!"

The older botanist shrugged.

"I am ready to admit defeat," he said tiredly. He plucked a leaf from the nearby shrub, stuck it in his mouth, and began to chew.

The goats stared silently and hungrily through the fence.

"What *is* this?" I said. I was sore and tired, and my head was beginning to ache. "Mulberry?"

Holmes plucked a leaf himself and put it in his mouth. He chewed happily and his eyes grew brighter in the light of the lamps.

"Isn't it obvious, Watson?" he said. "These are coca plants."

"*Coca*?" I said.

"All the facts were there in Miss Constance's story. The two botanists, the lights in the night, the agitated appearance of Mr. Hemsley. And then of course there was the matter of the goats."

"I am getting very sick of goats, Holmes," I said.

"So are we!" said young Joe Maiden. "The fiendish beasts have developed a taste for it, you see. They have become quite addicted! They all but destroyed the plants in the old barn and we've had to move the specimens to this remote location."

"You are making cocaine?" I said. "Whatever for?"

"We are trying to raise the plant outside its native habitat," Mr. Hemsley said. "It only grows on the lower slopes of the Andes, which are beyond the British Empire's control. If we could but grow it *here*, Dr. Watson! On our own soil! Why, we could make our own cocaine—as much of it as we could possibly need!"

"I got the idea while working for the Commission in India," Joe Maiden said. "Seeing the opium production regulated and controlled by the Empire. If we could do that for opium, could we not do it for cocaine as well? It is truly a miraculous drug, a wonderful anaesthetic!"

"Of course," I said. "It was a young Viennese fellow, what was his name? Koller, I believe, who discovered its numbing properties, only a few years ago."[13]

---

13   Karl Koller indeed discovered, in 1884, that a mild solution of cocaine could deaden the nerves' sensitivity to pain, a safe replacement to the dangerous chloroform that surgeons used up to that time.

"But there is so much more!" Joe Maiden said. "Cocaine wine, such as the Italians make, could be a lucrative export, and further, some fellow in America[14] has even conceived of a sugary soda drink infused with coca leaves, a temperance drink that is rapidly spreading across America[15] and may well reach us here, too, sometime soon. We could create our own Coca Tonic, before the Americans corner the market!"

"It seems rather fanciful," I said. "And besides, I do not approve of cocaine, as my friend Holmes here well knows. It has addictive properties."

"It is a miracle drug, man!" Joe Maiden said. "If only there was a way we could make it work on a commercial scale, here in England's green and pleasant land!"

"But why the secrecy?" I said. "What need is there for these shenanigans of yours?"

"We feared competition," Mr. Hemsley said. "And Newlands is a quiet, peaceful place—ideal for our experiments. We are trying to breed a strand of coca that could grow here in England. Much as old Mrs. Whitby once experimented on silkworm caterpillars here. Read your Darwin, man! We can do it, we could breed them, given time—"

But time they did not have.

Time is a creature which devours all, and in that, I fear, it is much like a goat.

They had been staring at us through the fence for long enough. They grew restless, for the drug mania of cocaine is a fiend which at best is not dead but merely sleeping.[16] And so, they came.

They overran the fence as though it weren't even there. Then they were inside the enclosure, tearing and chewing and gulping, and all with a maniacal abandon. Poor Mr. Hemsley tried to fight them and got bitten for his pains, and young Joe Maiden was on the

---

14   John Pemberton, a former Confederate colonel and morphine addict.

15   Pemberton invented Coca-Cola in 1886, though the rights were sold to Asa Griggs Candler, who formed the Coca-Cola Company in 1892.

16   Watson indeed expresses a similar sentiment later on in "The Adventure of the Missing Three-Quarter," and perhaps it was this present episode which inspired him to change his mind about the danger of the narcotic Holmes was so fond of.

ground, kicked and stomped on by goats. I now understood fully their earlier injuries.

Holmes and I made a hasty retreat, though we got a few nicks and scrapes of our own in rescuing the two hapless botanists.

We stood well away and watched the destruction unfold.

In the morning, Holmes and I departed back to London. He had telegraphed Miss Constance, with three words only, which were *All is well*. In truth, he could have saved his money by omitting "is" from his missive, but he was always prone to a certain verbosity.

The two botanists went their separate ways after that, I believe. I do not know what became of Joe Maiden, while Mr. Hemsley went back to Kew and the pleasant gardens there. Miss Constance married and became a keen yachtswoman and motor racing enthusiast.

There are still mulberry trees in Newlands I'm told, and, in the summertime, they produce a delicious, sweet fruit.

The Lancelot Connection

Matthew Booth

Toward the end of the year 1895, a particular series of events of no significance to this narrative found Sherlock Holmes and myself in the greatest of our university towns. We were staying in furnished lodgings close to the famous circular scientific library which is so well known in that place. The sandstone buildings and the distant chiming of the college bells on the quarter hours had been an invigorating and refreshing alternative to the dark recesses and fog-shrouded pockets of London, but I could tell from his restlessness that Sherlock Holmes was eager to be back in those Baker Street rooms from which he operated his crusade against crime.

It was early in the morning that we were called upon by Professor Cavendish Fawcett, the noted literary academic. He was a small but lean man of perhaps sixty years, with the rounded shoulders of his profession, brought on by years of study. His suit was untidy, with traces of chalk dust around the lapels and the cuffs of his jacket. His hair was grizzled, somewhat unruly, and his dark, furtive eyes peered at us over the lenses of a pair of *pince-nez*. He walked into the room with a severe limp, and he leaned heavily on a Penang lawyer cane, approaching us in a peculiar shuffling gait.

"I can only thank the providence which protects us all that you are here, Mr. Holmes," said he. "You will come to understand the nervous anxiety in which I find myself all too clearly, once you have heard my story.

"Pray, state your case," said my friend.

"You may know my name, Mr. Holmes, in connection with the study of English literature. I think it is not unjust to say that I am one of the foremost authorities on Elizabethan and Jacobean drama, particularly on the subjects of Shakespeare, Marlowe, and Johnson. It is possible that you have read my rather daring dissertation on the religious intricacies of *Tamburlaine the Great*? No? It is of no matter.

"In addition to my academic work, I am a trustee of the distinguished museum of this city. At present, I am heavily involved with an exhibit of my own design, involving the evolution of drama, from the Ancient Greeks through to the morality plays of the medieval period to the Renaissance. It is a fascinating study and I would enjoy it for its own sake even if it did not, on occasion, produce some exciting and intriguing opportunities beyond simple academic interest.

"It was during the course of such researches that I came to learn of what I can only describe as one of the most thrilling discoveries of recent years. It has long been suspected that the published works of Shakespeare which we know today is but a snippet of the man's productivity. It is a theory that he produced far more than those plays which have survived but these unknown works were either discarded as being unworthy of production or else they were destroyed by accident.

"Recently, proof of the theory came into my possession. I happened to make the acquaintance of an old woman of Italian descent who had heard my name and knew of my reputation. She had something which had been passed down through generations of her family which she wished to hand to me, for she thought that I would be better placed to make the best use of it. She presented me with a small, slim package, which contained several sheets of fragile paper, scrawled over with that writing which seemed all too familiar to me as being the hand of William Shakespeare himself.

"It was a play entitled *Lancelot and the King*, a treatment of the Arthurian legend, told from the perspective of Lancelot. It is a love story above anything else, as much about the love between Arthur and Lancelot as between them and Queen Guinevere. Lancelot is the tragic hero, broken by a love which he cannot resist, whilst Arthur is the fool, cursed by his own flaw of failing to recognise treachery in those closest to him. If there is a villain, it must be the queen herself, for she is painted as a woman not tormented by fate to betray her husband but driven by her own carnal lust for two men. I tell you, gentlemen, Tennyson's *Idylls* does not come close to the play's intricacies, either in terms of being a history of Arthur's tragedy or of poetic intelligence."

Sherlock Holmes had listened to this narrative with a mounting interest. "The piece sounds fascinating and no doubt such a manuscript would be of interest to any serious scholar."

Fawcett nodded his head. "It was my intention to display the manuscript as the crown jewel of my exhibit, so I brought it back here and wasted no time in showing it to my young assistant, Mr. Laurence Maguire."

"There is no doubt about its authenticity, I presume?"

Fawcett's face paled at my companion's question. "I am in no doubt of it myself, Mr. Holmes, but a colleague of mine says he is somewhat cautious."

"May I enquire his name?"

"Zachariah Templeton, a lecturer at the university, although he is a student of the metaphysical poets rather than Elizabethan drama. Now, if I may, Mr. Holmes, I should like to proceed with my narrative, for I come to the darkest part of my own little drama. I had intended to have an early start to my day's work at the museum today, for there is much for me to do in preparation for the opening of our exhibition. I got to the museum a little after seven this morning and I went straight to the antechamber in which our collection is to be displayed."

"One moment!" interjected Holmes. "Do you have a key to the museum itself?"

"Indeed, since I am a trustee. But this morning, I was admitted by Percival Warlock, the curator. I was not surprised to find him there even at that hour. He is dedicated to his work. But Warlock's face forewarned me of disaster. He led me to the exhibits room, and I could see that one of the windows in the far wall was broken. Worse yet, the glass display case in which I had placed the manuscript was empty."

Holmes's eyes glistened with anticipation. "The play had been stolen?"

"Just so."

"Was the door to the exhibits room locked when you arrived this morning?"

"No, it was open. But the thief must have entered and left by the window, otherwise he would have been locked in the museum for the night, as the outer doors were locked. Warlock said as much, for he had to open the main door to the building upon his arrival."

"A credible deduction. Who else had keys to the exhibits room and the display case?"

"Warlock, Maguire, and I had keys to both."

"And the glass of this display case had been smashed?"

"No. The door to the case was unlocked and Maguire's own key was in the lock."

"That is suggestive."

"It is not unnatural for Maguire to have had cause to open the cabinet in order to make some examination of the manuscript."

"Perhaps not," remarked Sherlock Holmes, "but it becomes a point of interest when that same manuscript is stolen soon afterwards."

The professor shook his head with a growing disquiet. "Maguire was not responsible for the theft, Mr. Holmes. My certainty stems from a darker cause than larceny."

Holmes leaned back in his chair and drew heavily on his pipe. "I apologise, Professor Fawcett, I had assumed that it was the theft of this lost manuscript which you wished me to investigate. You have more to tell us?"

"The display case in which the play was to be shown stands on a pedestal so that it is raised some three feet from the ground. It is at the far end of the room, directly under the very window which the intruder had broken in order to gain access. At the base of the pedestal, lying on its back, there was the body of Maguire, my young assistant. The poor fellow had been the victim of a vicious attack, for he had been battered to death."

For some moments, Sherlock Holmes remained in his chair, his pipe clenched between his teeth and his grey eyes scrutinising the anguished face of his new client. At last, he sprang from his chair and, within seconds, he had thrown on his hat and coat.

"Come, Professor Fawcett, you must show us to the place at once!"

Within a quarter of an hour, we were walking through the corridors of the famous museum. We had been greeted by the curator, Percival Warlock, a man of advancing age with flaxen hair and a neatly trimmed moustache. His manner was agitated and the hands which shook ours in greeting were trembling with apprehension. He and Fawcett showed us into a large room, filled with glass fronted cabinets, some of which lined the walls and some of which were set out in a line down the centre of the room. Inside the cases were various folios and rare volumes throughout the ages of theatrical production, the treasure trove of Fawcett's exhibition, all of which might have been of greater interest to us had it not been for the dark intrigue which had engulfed us. At the far end of the room was the pedestal, topped with the empty glass case, of which we had heard. Above it, there were two broad windows, the glass of one smashed, its splinters scattered on the floor below.

Lying on the two steps which led to the pedestal, there was the body of a tall, well-made man of perhaps thirty years of age. His arms were thrown out above his head, the fingers clenched in agony. His hair was dark and luxurious, but his handsome features had convulsed into a look of shock and fear and his forehead had been terribly injured. We stared down at the savage ferocity of the blow which had inflicted the wound and Holmes, with a look of grim concentration upon his face, examined the indescribable wreck of the man's head.

"There is no sign of any weapon?"

"None."

"This broken window is how the thief made his entrance, of course." My companion moved to the broken window and stood beneath it. He was perched on the tips of his toes, craning his neck, but he was unable to see through the glass. "What is immediately outside this window?"

"A balustrade, Mr. Holmes, and a small stone balcony," said Warlock. "All the windows have them."

"They look out onto the gardens?"

Warlock nodded. "There is a small pathway between the building and the lawns, but nothing more."

"The intruder will have used this balcony to climb up to the window, of course," mused Holmes. "He would not have been able to reach up to break the glass otherwise. It might be a risky climb, but an active man would be able to jump up to this balustrade and heave himself up onto the balcony. From there, he could break the window and attach a rope to one of the pillars of the balcony, then climb down it into the room. Naturally, he left by the same means and lowered himself down the ground using the balcony, having untied the rope. So much is obvious."

"How can you deduce the rope?" I asked. "There is no sign of one."

"Elementary. If the window is too high to be reached without the aid of the balcony, it is likewise too high to make the jump from the sill to the ground. Therefore, the thief would need some means of lowering himself into the room and pulling himself back out of it."

"That is simple enough," said Cavendish Fawcett. "But what can we glean from that?"

Holmes gave a shrug of his shoulders. "Perhaps nothing more than the certainty that he came prepared for his task."

"He must have been a fairly youthful man," I observed.

Holmes raised a cautionary finger. "We must not run away with ourselves, my dear Watson. A middle-aged man in good health might have been able to perform the deed. I am certain that I could do it myself." He moved back to the centre of the room and allowed his eyes to drift around the area. "There is much to be learned. I think it would be as well if I were to have five minutes alone in this room, if you do not mind, gentlemen."

He ushered the curator and Fawcett out of the exhibit room and closed the door on them. For some moments, he remained at the door in silence, his finger pressed to his lips. Then, he whipped out his magnifying lens and began pacing noiselessly around the room, sometimes stopping, on occasion kneeling, and once lying flat upon his face at the broken shards of glass from the window. He gave a sharp gasp of satisfaction at one moment, and I watched his long nervous fingers removed a torn fragment of cloth from a ragged piece of broken glass from the window. On his hands and knees, he crawled over to a small, white object which lay on the floor. Leaning over him, I saw that it was a candle, the wax of which had fallen to the ground and hardened. At last, he rose to his feet and examined with his lens the empty case from where the manuscript had been stolen before turning to me with that look of exultation which showed that his mind was engaged fully on the matter.

"These are murky waters, my dear Watson, and the affair is a somewhat tangled one," said he. "What do you make of this piece of fabric which I recovered from the broken window?"

"A fragment of a plaid cloak, or some such garment."

"Coupled with that dropped candle over there, does this piece of cloth suggest anything to your mind?"

"Nothing, beyond the fact that the burglar must have used a candle to light his way."

Holmes heaved an impatient sigh. "Admirable, Watson, but this is not the time for a display of your blazing talent for observing the obvious."

"If the criminal dropped his source of light, he would be more likely to stumble against the window and tear his cloak, as he would be moving in darkness."

"Why should this burglar come armed with a candle and proceed to drop it at the scene of his crime?"

"He had just murdered a man, Holmes. Perhaps he was fearful of his actions."

"Possibly," remarked my friend, "but, if so, it leads us to another problem, a problem which causes me much more puzzlement than anything else. If this burglar is so terrified of what he has done that he drops his only means of illuminating his escape from the room, why does he not drop everything associated with the crime?"

"I do not follow you."

Holmes leaned close to my ear. "The weapon, Watson! Are we to believe that this criminal is so appalled by the murder that he drops his candle in fright but retains the very object with which he has committed the act? If so, he must be a very inconsistent fellow. Is it not more likely that he would discard the weapon before his candle? One would remind him of his guilt far more strongly than the other, after all."

"Where does that take us?"

"A little further, my dear doctor, but not as far as we require. Maguire had opened the display case using his own key. Did the thief come into the room and find the display cabinet conveniently open, thus allowing him to take his chance?"

"If Maguire was in this room when the burglar smashed the window, surely he would have heard the breaking of the glass and locked the manuscript away. He would not leave the case open in the face of such an obvious threat of theft."

"The alternative is that, for whatever reason, he had abandoned his post, leaving the case unlocked and the manuscript at risk of theft."

"Why should he be so careless?"

Holmes eyes were fierce with excitement. "An admirable question, Watson, and one which must surely give some pause for thought! Whatever it was must have been of some importance to the young man. We shall see. For the present, however, how about Maguire himself? What secrets can he tell us?"

Holmes leaned over the body once more, but his attention was turned to the man's pockets. His nimble fingers flew around the body, feeling, pressing, unbuttoning, and examining, all with such swiftness that the thorough nature of the inspection would hardly be credited. Finally, he examined the dead man's watch, a heavy Albert chain whose fob was a small pendant. Holmes opened the pendant by prising apart the delicate clasp. Inside, there was a lock of golden hair and a brief inscription:

"Doubt that the stars are fire,

Doubt that the sun doth move his aides,

Doubt truth to be a liar,

But never doubt I love."

"Shakespeare seems to figure prominently in this case, Watson," said Holmes. "You recognise Hamlet's assurances to Ophelia? But who is the woman who must give such assurances of her love to this young man, Maguire? Watson, we must remember this point and docket it, for we may come upon something later which will bear upon it. For now, I think our work here is done."

We found Professor Fawcett and Mr. Warlock in the latter's office and, after a few less important questions from Holmes, Professor Fawcett invited us to take some refreshment at his home and we made our way to his small but cosy abode on the outskirts of town. As we approached the house, we saw a tall fellow racing toward us. He moved at such speed that he was obliged to hold his large brimmed hat on his head with one hand, whilst the flaps of his overcoat billowed out behind him. His slim cheeks were flushed with the effort, and his dark eyes were wild with emotion. He gripped Professor Cavendish Fawcett by the hand.

"My dear Cavendish, I have just heard the terrible news," said he. "If there is anything I can do to assist, you need only ask."

"Thank you," replied the old academic. "It is good of you to say so. Mr. Holmes, this is Mr. Zachariah Templeton, of whom I spoke. Templeton, this is Mr. Sherlock Holmes and his colleague, Dr. Watson."

Templeton shook my companion's hand. "I see that Cavendish has not wasted any time in calling in the best help he could wish to have."

"Our presence in your hospitable town was entirely fortuitous," said Sherlock Holmes. "I understand that you have some concerns regarding the validity of this lost play by Shakespeare on the Arthurian legend."

Templeton was obviously embarrassed by the topic being raised in the presence of his esteemed colleague. "I was simply expressing my opinion. A man as zealous on his subject as Cavendish Fawcett can be easily swayed by his own enthusiasm."

"Men of single minds are often blinded to the truth," agreed Holmes.

"I have no wish for a dear friend to be embarrassed in public if his opinion on the script is wrong. I had no other concern than that."

"You are a noble fellow, but you need not concern yourself with the authenticity," said the professor. "We were just going for some light refreshments, Templeton, if you would wish to join us."

"I shall be delighted. I would like to hear of any conclusions which Mr. Holmes has drawn on this affair of the stolen manuscript."

We went into the house and Fawcett led us into a cosy sitting room, modestly but tastefully furnished. A woman was sitting by the window, and she rose as we entered. She was very beautiful, no more than thirty years of age, and her skin was of a gentle colour although the cheeks were tinged with passion and the bright eyes were dimmed with sadness. And yet, despite her obvious emotion, there was a delicate charm about her, and her fair hair glowed like a summer meadow in the afternoon sun.

"This is my wife, Anna," said Fawcett, going to her and taking her hand in his.

"I cannot pretend to be ignorant of your purpose here, Mr. Holmes," declared Anna Fawcett as she was introduced to us. "I trust you will do all you can to throw some light on the mystery."

We looked across at Sherlock Holmes, for he had made no reply to the lady and the room had fallen into silence. He seemed to be in another place, far removed from that quaint room in which we stood. His eyes had developed an abstracted glare and his thin lips were slightly parted in astonishment. He seemed to be entirely captivated by Anna Fawcett, but it could not have been anything approaching an attraction with him. He was a perfect reasoning machine, and his brain had always governed his heart so that such emotions as love were nothing but an intrusion into his cold, balanced existence. And yet, he was staring at the woman as though the secrets of the universe were locked within her.

"Forgive me," said he presently; "my mind was elsewhere. I hope to be able to say that I am worthy of your words, Mrs. Fawcett, but I fear that until this moment I have been nothing short of a fool. I wonder what has happened to any brains which God has given me but, as I have had said before, it is better to learn wisdom late than never to learn it at all."

"You have some clue?" asked Cavendish Fawcett with eagerness.

"It is an indication, nothing more. There is still much to be learned." Holmes walked over to the professor's wife. "Tell me, madam, are you as passionate a reader of Shakespeare as your husband?"

"I am nothing of an expert on the plays, Mr. Holmes, but you cannot be married to a student of the Bard without being afflicted with something of his enthusiasm."

"Quite so. Do you have any views on the subject of this lost play?"

Mrs. Fawcett frowned in understandable confusion. "I think it is an exciting discovery, of course, but I am not in a position to speak intelligently about it."

"You can understand why someone might wish to steal it?"

"It is no doubt highly valuable."

Sherlock Holmes rose to his feet and walked over to Zachariah Templeton. "And you, sir, do you consider monetary gain to be the motive for the theft?"

The tall academic gave a short laugh. "I would have thought that falls more within your expertise than mine, Mr. Holmes."

"There is any number of reasons, but I fancy I have grasped the correct one."

"Then for Heaven's sake, tell us!" screamed the professor.

Holmes waved a finger at him. "My friend Watson will tell you that one of my defects is that I am loath to communicate my conclusions until I am sure they are complete."

"But you must be able to share something of the truth with us," protested Zachariah Templeton.

"Perhaps I am so able, Mr. Templeton," replied Holmes. "And perhaps the best place for me to do so would be in the exhibit room where the incident occurred. However, before we make our way back to the museum, Professor Fawcett, I wonder whether I might just have a brief word with your wife alone."

After the two men had left, Holmes turned to the lady. She had risen from her chair and was standing at the mantelpiece, her head in her hands, gently weeping. Holmes was capable of extreme gentleness with women when he so desired, and now he walked toward the lady and laid his hands on her shoulders. With a soothing word, he led her back to her seat and sat down opposite her, a gentle smile on his face.

"I have the solution to this mystery, Mrs. Fawcett," said he, "but I must ask you to confirm one point for me."

"What point is that?"

"What were the relations between you and Mr. Laurence Maguire?"

"Mr. Maguire was my husband's colleague. I knew him only in that capacity."

"No, no. If you will trust me, and treat me as a friend, you will find that I shall justify that trust. Will you not tell me the truth?"

"I have done so."

Holmes gave a sigh of impatient rage. "Madam, I had hoped to spare you this by coercing you to give me the information voluntarily, but I see that I am in vain. I have opened Maguire's pendant and I have seen inside it."

Her eyes flashed a terrified fire at my companion and her lips trembled with uncertainty. She stammered some denial, but the grave expression on Sherlock Holmes's lean face was unrelenting.

"Your shade of hair is especially fair," said Holmes. "It matches the lock of hair I found in the pendant on Maguire's watch chain with the inscription from *Hamlet* offering an assurance of love. It was your means of telling Maguire that you loved him, despite your inability to be with him."

Mrs. Fawcett nodded her head and took my friend's hands in hers. "Mr. Holmes, I have been a happily married woman for so many years that I never thought anything could corrupt it. I was wrong; I had not foreseen Laurence Maguire's intrusion into my life. He was everything my husband was not and the feelings he aroused within me were impossible to resist. Just as the tides are drawn to the moon, so I was drawn to Laurence."

"And he reciprocated your love?"

She nodded. "And yet, Laurence had grown impatient with me. He wanted the truth to come out and for me to walk away from Cavendish. He had begun to interpret my inability to do so as a sign of dying love on my part. The pendant had been my way of assuring him of how I felt whilst also giving me time to summon the courage to do what my heart and Laurence begged me to do." She held her palms to her cheeks in mournful regret. "If I had not wasted time, might Laurence still be alive today? I fear that is the question which will curse me until I too pass. Laurence loved me as I loved him, but he was unable to wait any longer to declare his love publicly."

"Mr. Maguire threatened to divulge your secret to the professor?"

"He said it was best for the truth to be told. He was an honest man, Mr. Holmes, and the duplicity of working with the very man whom he was betraying with me had begun to corrode his soul."

"Did you go to the museum last night in order to convince him otherwise?"

"I went to beg him to reconsider. I had told him I would sneak out once Cavendish was asleep."

"You pleaded with him not to speak out. Did he agree?"

Between those choking sobs, Anna Fawcett forced out her words. "He did not. He could wait no longer, he said, and he was to tell Cavendish this very morning."

Holmes was silent for a moment, those austere eyes glaring at the woman. "What did you do?"

"I could do nothing. He was adamant that his course of action was the right one. I ran home, my eyes stinging with tears and my legs barely able to carry me."

"Did Mr. Maguire lock the main door after you had fled?"

She nodded. "I heard him do so. The closing of the door felt like the final toll of the bell for our love and my happiness. I cried myself to sleep, but I had resolved to tell my husband before Laurence had the opportunity. I would have that decency if nothing else."

"But when you awakened this morning, you found your husband had left the house already?"

"Later, he sent word to me, telling me what had happened. My eyes have not stopped weeping since that terrible revelation."

"And yet, it must be said, that the man's death has saved you the hardship of your confession. It has preserved your secret."

She understood the veiled accusation. "Do you accuse me, Mr. Holmes? Do you think I murdered the man I loved to safeguard my own shame?"

Holmes shook his head and rose from his chair. With a gentleness which I have rarely seen, he touched her cheek and raised her gaze to his. "I do not, madam. I fancy the matter was taken out of your hands by another. I fancy this cycle of death and forbidden love makes you more a Juliet than a Lady Macbeth."

In reply, Mrs. Fawcett simply lowered her head and sobbed into her hands. I touched Holmes on the arm and gestured to the door. He gave a last look at the woman, urging her to speak, before submitting to my entreaties to leave her in peace. It was not until we were in the hallway that he turned to me with that familiar look of exultation on his face which spoke of his assurance of success.

"I have the threads in my hand, Watson, and the matter is as clear to me as if I had been there. Come now, we must return to the museum."

We made our way back to the museum to find that the sinister occupant of the exhibit room had been removed to the mortuary. Holmes strode into the room and made his way to the pedestal which housed the glass case where *Lancelot and the King* had been displayed. I remained by his side, whilst Cavendish Fawcett, Mr. Warlock, and Zachariah Templeton sat before us like students in a criminological lecture in which Sherlock Holmes was the tutor.

"The misapprehension about this case was that the theft of the manuscript and the death of Laurence Maguire were cause and effect," declared Holmes. "It is not too much of a stretch of the imagination to forge a connection between a theft and a death which occur in close proximity to each other, but in this instance, the events were independent of each other.

"I shall deal with the theft first. I have already explained that the burglar must have gained access to this room through the window. Likewise, I have detailed how a rope must have been used in order to gain such an entry and how the intruder must have scaled the outer wall with the aid of the balcony which adorns the window. Clearly, Professor Fawcett could not have made that climb. His lameness would have prevented him from executing the athletic steps required to break into the room. What is more, he had a key not only to the museum, but also the exhibition room, and the display case. He would not need to break into a building to which he had unlimited access and nor would Mr. Warlock. The breaking of the window indicated an external culprit and it was not too much of a difficulty for me to name the thief as you, Mr. Zachariah Templeton."

All the eyes in the room turned to the tall academic, whose head was bowed and his cheeks flushed with shame. "Say what you must, Mr. Holmes."

"I suspect you came prepared to break the glass of this case, but you were fortunate enough to find that the door to the cabinet was open. I doubt you pondered this happenstance for a great deal of time; rather, I suspect you took the script and made your escape."

Fawcett had gripped his friend by the shoulder. "But why, Templeton? Why?"

Sherlock Holmes spoke before Templeton was able. "He had doubts about its authenticity, as he told us, but his alleged concern over fearing you might ruin your reputation was a blind. If the play were genuine, it would be highly valuable. I fancy he took it in order to confirm its veracity and then see about selling it. Academic work is fulfilling but hardly profitable."

Templeton nodded his head. "It is as you say, Mr. Holmes. I saw at once the significance of the play and I saw the opportunity to make money from it. I broke in, as you say, and I found this room empty but the case open. I grabbed the play and fled. It was not until I examined it at home that I discovered it was as I feared. I am sorry, Cavendish, but Shakespeare did not write that play. It is skilfully done, no doubt, but it is a forgery. It is exceptionally well done, but some of the phrasing is off and, in a few instances—not many, I grant you—the metre is wrong. It seems to be from the correct period, but whether it was a prank or the work of a lesser scribe seeking to use Shakespeare's name to further his own career, it is not a genuine Bard. Maguire must have known it too, so I cannot imagine why he did not tell you."

Fawcett's hands went to his temples, and he gave a cry of despair. "I must form my own opinion. Where is the manuscript? What have you done with it, you fiend?"

"It is still in my house."

"It could be nowhere else," said Holmes. "Once you had discovered that your burglary had been for nothing, you returned at once to the museum in order to replace the manuscript. By doing so, you would leave a case of forced entry but no theft. There would be no investigation in all probability if nothing was stolen and you were not allowing yourself to be the subject of a police enquiry for the sake of a forgery.

"When you got back into this room, however, you discovered a corpse. In your initial shock, you dropped your candle on the floor and, in your haste to escape, you tore the fabric of your plaid cloak on the broken glass of the window. You see, Watson, the importance of my deduction about the absence of any weapon? The answer to the problem is that the intruder did not drop the weapon of murder in his panic because the intruder was not the murderer.

"But now Zachariah Templeton has a difficulty. He knows that the theft and the murder will be connected, and he has in his hands the manuscript itself. He cannot get back into the museum to replace the manuscript for the police may be present. So flustered was he by discovering the body of Laurence Maguire that all thought of the play went out of his mind and, as a result, he was forced to retain possession of the one piece of evidence which might implicate him in a murder which he had not committed."

Templeton raved in the air. "It was maddening to find myself in that position. I had been such a fool and my penance was to live in fear of losing my life for a murder I had not committed. I shall return the play, but my assessment of it is correct. It is a hoax. What is not a fraud, Mr. Holmes, is my innocence of the murder of that young man."

Holmes nodded. "I am aware of that. The murder was not connected to the play, save in the most indirect and ironic fashion."

"I do not understand," said Mr. Warlock.

"The play concerned the forbidden love of Lancelot and Guinevere," said Holmes. "At the centre of this mystery is a similarly forbidden love, one doomed to tragedy and death. Three points about this case struck me as vital: that Maguire had left the open display case unattended; that his watch bore an inscription offering an assurance of love; and that there was no sign of the murder weapon.

"The first of these points suggested very clearly that something of the utmost importance had prompted Maguire to leave the manuscript vulnerable in that careless fashion. The nature of the quotation and the lock of golden hair suggested a romantic affair. You will recall that I was silent for a few moments when I was introduced to Mrs. Anna Fawcett. I was marvelling at my own stupidity, for it was at that point that I realised that the murder and the theft were not connected. Her hair was of such a striking blonde that the lock of hair in the pendant on Maguire's watch chain could only have been from her head. Thus, I began to see that the reason for the man's death was his love for Mrs. Fawcett and not his interruption of what can only be described as a clumsy burglary."

Fawcett was on his feet. "That is a monstrous accusation, Mr. Holmes."

Holmes remained at his authoritative best. "No doubt, but your wife has confessed, sir. She came to the museum last night to plead with Maguire not to say anything of the affair to you. Her arrival was the reason for his dereliction of duty in leaving the display case open and unguarded. His mind was occupied with more personal and important matters. Of course, you know this, because you followed her to the museum and witnessed their altercation on the doorstep."

The old man's eyes glared with spite. "That is a lie!"

"The lie is yours, professor, not mine," said Sherlock Holmes. "The final point which interested me was the absence of any weapon, as I have said. Once I had identified you as the murderer, the question was answered. The weapon was removed simply because it had to be removed."

"What do you say?"

Holmes lowered his voice, pointing to the professor's Penang lawyer. "You require the weapon in order to aid you to walk."

"I have heard enough of this nonsense!" spat the old academic, making for the door.

"There are four men in this room, Professor Fawcett," announced Holmes. "Do not for a moment think that their combined efforts will not detain you here until the police arrive. Once it is proved that the theft and the killing are not related, the focus of the mystery shifts. The love affair between Maguire and your wife gives you a motive to dispose of him. Your possession of a key to the museum gives you the opportunity to enter the building after Maguire had locked it when your wife left him last night. There is no escape."

The old man remained at the door of the room; his eyes turned in hatred on Sherlock Holmes. "That young jackanapes stole everything from me, Holmes. Anna was the only girl I had ever truly loved. My curse was that I met her in my twilight years, whilst she was still blooming. I never hoped to be everything she needed, but I tried my best for her, and she never complained. Not until that Romeo walked onto our stage. I did let myself back in and I came into this very room. I found him, young Maguire, mad with fear and rage. Rage at Anna, no doubt, and fear that the play had been stolen."

"I think not," said Holmes. "I fancy that Templeton is right. I suspect Maguire had determined that the play was a forgery but had kept silent. If Anna would not leave you for him even after he had exposed their infidelity to you, he might well have the opportunity to have revenge in your public humiliation at the unveiling of the fraudulent play."

Fawcett was nodding his head. "It is something the little snake would think of, I am certain of that. But the theft of the play was nothing to me in that isolated moment. All I could see was betrayal; all I could hear were mocking lies in my ears; and all I could smell was deceit. I struck him down like the coward he was, but I must tell you that I remember nothing of the deed. For that, at least, I am ashamed."

We said nothing after he had spoken as Fawcett began to weep silently. After some moments, Holmes dispatched Mr. Warlock for the police inspector. The old academic made no movement: to his mind, he was alone in the room, save for his guilt and his shame.

"If he was guilty of murder, why did he consult you at all, Mr. Holmes?" asked Templeton. "He must have known that your investigation into my own crime would reveal his."

Sherlock Holmes chuckled gently. "He found himself in a similarly invidious position as you, Mr. Templeton, in having circumstances force him into checkmate. A theft and a murder had been committed, and here was none other than Sherlock Holmes on the doorstep. Fawcett could not possibly have ignored my presence. Any failure to consult me in such circumstances would have aroused immediate suspicion. Perhaps I am being conceited in imagining it to be the answer, but I confess that I am a man who cannot agree with those who rank modesty amongst the virtues."

Bloody Sunday

Bev Vincent

D uring his early years as a consulting detective, Mr. Sherlock Holmes came by most of his cases via referrals from police inspectors who had reached their wits' ends, a condition which Holmes often said was easily achieved, or by way of recommendations from satisfied clients. On a few occasions, I recommended him to patients I encountered at my practice, as with the adventure instigated by an engineer's severed thumb. As his reputation grew—in no small part due to my accounts of his more unusual problems—people sought his assistance directly.

The affair which transpired on the day that came to be known as Bloody Sunday is the only instance I recall where Holmes decided, without any tangible evidence, that a serious crime had been committed somewhere in the city and went in search of it.

I returned to our sitting room on the afternoon of November 13, 1887, exhausted from my adventure, to discover Holmes still trying to perfect Caprice No. 23. After hearing the same passage some five and twenty times, I had fled our rooms before lunch, despite the chill wind.

As I was removing my overcoat, he set aside his violin and said, "I trust that your patients will all survive?" Seeing the look of consternation on my face, he continued. "Come, now, Watson. You are intimately familiar with my methods. The moment I explain, you will deem my deductions perfectly obvious. The knees of your trousers are creased and soiled, telling me that you have been in a position not generally adopted by a man who is merely out for a walk to escape his roommate's violin playing. There is a stain of what can only be iodine upon the index finger of your right hand. The handkerchiefs protruding from the pockets of your greatcoat are stained with blood and, from the way the pockets bulge, a number of other such rags keep them company. If only a single patient were involved, I fear he could not have survived. No, it is more likely that you successfully treated several injured parties. And, by the glimmer in your eye, I perceive you have a story to tell. Sit, my dear fellow. Sit."

He was in an uncommonly good mood, despite having been idle for some days. I poured a glass of brandy from the flask on the table next to the bow-window, lowered myself into my armchair, and began my tale.

I'd had no fixed destination in mind when I entered Baker Street a few hours earlier. The dull, mud-coloured clouds did not inspire a visit to the botanical gardens, and I had little interest in seeing who was taking advantage of the Park Regulation Act to stand on a soapbox and prattle on in Hyde Park.

My attention was drawn to a notice plastered to a brick wall on the opposite side of the street which announced a demonstration against the Irish Coercion Acts planned for that very day. Organised by the Irish National League and the Social Democratic Federation, the demonstrators intended to demand the release of William O'Brien from prison, where the Member of Parliament from Cork was being held without trial for incitement during a rent strike.

While I had no particular sympathies for the Irish Home Rule movement, I was curious to see what might transpire. Trafalgar Square had, of late, become a gathering place for the disgruntled unemployed, who saw it as the symbolic border between the city's East and West Ends. At the very least, I thought it might make an interesting story to report to Holmes over dinner. He was as ignorant of contemporary politics as he was of the earth's place in the solar system.

With my overcoat buttoned to the neck, I leaned into the wind. The magnitude of the crowd once I reached Piccadilly Circus astonished me. On any other Sunday, with all the shops shuttered and closed, I would have encountered only a few people out for afternoon constitutionals or taking in matinees at one of the theatres on the Strand. It soon became apparent that the gathering at Trafalgar would be impressive.

People seemed in high spirits, smiling and joking; however, the peaceable mood soon changed. Word passed from person to person that the police had banned the assembly, and that a ring of officers two deep had formed inside the square. A regiment of mounted guards approached from the rear, ordering the crowd to keep moving. I had a notion to turn back, but the surge pushed me onward.

As we approached Trafalgar, military officers charged into the crowd, waving batons and truncheons, and throwing fists indiscriminately. People grew frightened and scattered in all directions. Some were driven against the shutters and iron railings of the shops. Many of those who regained their footing entered the fray once again.

The police, some two thousand strong, as I later learned, and reinforced by foot soldiers and mounted Life Guards, were massed at Trafalgar. Before the National Gallery, the Grenadiers and police had formed a gauntlet, shoving, kicking and punching members of the crowd to drive them through. Guardsmen slammed their rifle butts on the toes of anyone who came within reach and threw punches with great vigour.

"I tell you, Holmes, I felt like I was in back in Afghanistan. Only by staying in the centre of the throng was I able to avoid being assaulted. A mounted constable dragged the man next to me away by the collar, and another was hauled off by his hair while officers kicked and punched him, even though he already appeared quite unconscious. Constables bashed people in the head from behind without cause. The crowd responded with bricks and stones. Blood flowed from the heads and faces of dozens of men within my sight."

Holmes listened attentively, offering sympathetic interjections whenever I mentioned an incident that left me in fear for my safety and nodding approvingly as I detailed my efforts to minister to the injured while avoiding the cruelties inflicted upon those around me.

"Eventually, the police drove everyone away—those who could walk that is—and sealed off the area. I heard reports that at least one man died from his injuries, though I did not see it myself."

"You were indeed fortunate, Watson," he said at the conclusion of my story. "All manner of miscreants take advantage of riotous situations, from the most determined anarchist down to the pettiest of thieves. Based on your account, it would appear that the authorities behaved unwisely, provoking the crowd." He broke off. His narrow features grew sharper and his eyes blazed. "Kindly be so good as to summon Mr. Lestrade," he said. He leaned back in his armchair and fixed his gaze at a spot on the wall.

Though I was taken aback by his reaction, I complied. For a few shillings, a Hansom driver agreed to deliver my hastily scrawled message to Scotland Yard. When I returned upstairs, Holmes was poring over a newspaper plucked from the stack on the floor beside his chair.

"Whatever are you looking for?"

"A peculiar message in the agony column in yesterday's paper. At the time, I did not recognise its import."

"I've never understood your fascination with that chorus of groans," I said.

"It is a most valuable hunting ground, Watson. These messages are one means by which criminals conduct business, and there have been several significant items of late." Seeing my sceptical reaction, he read aloud a request from a generous man seeking an agreeable lady. "Do you think he is searching for anything other than a woman of ill repute?" He dragged his long index finger down the column. "And this message from someone who claims he has fallen on hard times and wishes to discreetly sell certain valuable heirlooms. I wager a sovereign that he acquired these items by illicit means."

"And the police allow this to continue?"

"It is to their advantage," Holmes said. "And frequently to my own. The press is a valuable institution if one knows how to use it. But these are just common thieves and disreputable men. There is something far more sinister going on within these pages. Ah, here it is. 'Reward offered for information concerning the whereabouts of Edward Mortimer of 18 Lark Hall Lane. Last seen on Friday evening in the company of an unknown caller, with whom he departed his home. His wife and children are distressed by his failure to return.' I suspect there is a fascinating story here."

At that moment, Mrs. Hudson brought in our tea. Holmes ignored his plate, which earned her disapproving glares when she returned to clear the cloth. He had a peculiar notion that the process of digestion diverted blood from his brain, so he often fasted when on a case. I returned to my armchair and perused the latest issue of the *British Medical Journal.*

A short while later, he said, "It would be most useful to know where he was employed."

"Who?"

"Mr. Edward Mortimer." Seeing my blank look, he indicated the newspaper. "The man whose wife and children are so desperate to locate him. After we speak to Lestrade, I believe I shall call on the anxious woman. Will you join me?"

Though I had no idea what made him so interested in this woman's plight, I knew better than to doubt his intuition. "With pleasure."

Holmes drew his long legs up in the chair until his knees nearly touched his nose and pressed his fingertips together. His eyes grew vacant. The black clay pipe clenched between his teeth produced thick clouds of smoke. When he picked up his violin again, instead of playing Paganini, he produced a series of atonal sounds that seemed to represent his anguished state of mind. I cracked open a window to reduce the miasma and returned to my journal.

Within the half hour, Lestrade barged into the sitting room with Mrs. Hudson close on his heels. She was accustomed to the detective's regular visits, yet she liked to stand on formality and was distressed by anyone who breeched decorum. "Thank you, Mrs. Hudson," Holmes said, which placated her. She left us to our business, though her foot was somewhat heavy upon the stairs as she descended.

"I received your message and here I stand, hat in hand. It's not as though we didn't have enough to keep us busy at the Yard, but a man who knows a thing or two about the world does not reject a summons by Mr. Sherlock Holmes."

If Holmes detected sarcasm in Lestrade's speech, he gave no sign. "I was hoping you could enlighten me as to any crimes of a singular nature that took place this afternoon."

Lestrade's brow furrowed. "Other than the twenty thousand anarchists hurling bricks at coppers in Trafalgar Square? The whole area is cordoned off while the damage is assessed and repaired."

Holmes waved a dismissive hand. "That is of little consequence."

"Some are calling it Bloody Sunday." Lestrade snorted. "If the papers get hold of that, it will stick. Those thugs are accusing the police of brutality, sullying the reputations of fine men who put an end to a deliberate attempt by the criminal classes to terrorize the city."

"Watson has brought me thoroughly up to date on the matter. No, I was looking for something else."

"What would Dr. Watson know about a socialist meeting run amok in Trafalgar?" Lestrade asked, with a perfunctory glance in my direction.

"I happened to be there," I said, taking a draw from my pipe.

"Did you, now?" Lestrade fixed his steely, rat-like eyes on me. "I would never have taken you for a sympathizer, Doctor. I would be most interested to hear your account of events."

"You might not like what I have to say," I replied coolly. "If anyone behaved riotously, it was the police."

"Ha!" Lestrade replied. "One man I spoke with, a newspaperman no less, said that if he'd been there, he would have shot the whole lot of them. Socialists, anarchists, and criminals. Men with no honest purpose or serious convictions, who love disorder and thought there might be some plunder in the chaos, turning a fine Sunday afternoon into a carnival of blood. A threat to public order, that's what they were," Lestrade concluded.

"We have more important matters to consider, Lestrade."

"Indeed? And what might they be?"

"At the moment, I do not know. That is why I asked you to call. Be so kind as to tell me what else transpired this afternoon."

Lestrade pulled a notebook from his pocket and leafed through its pages. He recited a litany of crimes that exposed the city in all its shabby glory. Assaults, burglaries, threats, brawls, public drunkenness, and indecency—it was enough to make a man forsake all hope for humanity.

When he was finished, Holmes looked up. "Is that all?"

"Shall we call it a slow day, then, Mr. Holmes?" Lestrade said, with a dark grin.

"There must be something else that has not yet come to your attention. Thank you, Lestrade. I had hoped you could be of help, but it seems that is not the case."

"What's he going on about?" Lestrade asked me, as if I were an interpreter of the strange utterances of my friend.

"I have no idea," I said.

"How long has the public known there would be a manifestation today?" Holmes asked, adopting the tone a man might use when attempting to extract information from a dim-witted child.

"They've been going on about it for weeks," Lestrade said. "Gave the commissioner ample time to prepare."

"Well-publicized?"

"Notices plastered on just about every hoarding and wall in the city. Our men tore them down, but they went up again just as fast."

"You anticipated a large crowd."

Lestrade shrugged. "We were prepared."

"Expected to be disorderly?"

"Never did see a group bigger than a handful not get up to some manner of trouble."

"So, if you were a mastermind looking to pull off a daring crime and sought a time when the eyes of the city might be focused elsewhere?"

Lestrade again shrugged. "I suppose. What mastermind might that be?"

"Don't be thick, Lestrade. You know who I mean."

Holmes had often spoken of a brilliant but twisted man who he believed sat at the centre of London's web of crime. Though this master criminal still seemed like a work of fiction to me on that day, Holmes claimed that virtually every unlawful enterprise within the city paid this man a percentage of the take. I would later come to know the name Moriarty and suffer at great lengths on his account before his reign ended and his network was disbanded, but at that time, Holmes refused to identify him in my presence. "You might accidentally mention him in one of your chronicles," he told me once. "And that, my friend, could be the undoing of us all."

"You're not on about him again, are you?" Lestrade said. "We've looked him up one side and down the other. I know you sometimes pick up on little things we miss, but you're on your own on this one, Mr. Holmes. Can't have you libelling the name of a perfectly respectable gentleman."

Holmes snorted, as much, I suspected, at Lestrade's understatement of his mental prowess as at his assessment of Holmes's nemesis. "Thank you, Lestrade. If something does come to light, as I'm sure it will?"

"I'll drop everything and come straight over."

"That would be most appreciated," Holmes said.

Lestrade glared. From a larger man, it might have been a daunting look. He turned, nodded briskly in my direction, and stormed out.

"Why do you think something else happened?" I asked.

"I do not think it—I know it. How many times have we handled cases where a person has been given a task under a pretext meant to keep him occupied while something nefarious took place at his home or place of work?"

"Surely you don't believe someone caused the riot to cover up another crime."

"The way the authorities reacted is suspect, and I am convinced that this man's reach extends even into the ranks of the police. It has not been so long since the Turf Squad scandal, n'est-ce pas?" Holmes said. "No, this is a most sinister affair, Watson. Before we go out, please summon the troops." He waved his hand toward the bow-window.

After our years together, I knew what he meant. I descended the stairs once again, stuck my head outside, and whistled. A ragged urchin named Simpson, one of several who loitered on Baker

Street, came running. "Mr. Holmes has a task for you. Mind your boots, or Mrs. Hudson will have your hide stretched out next to our bearskin hearthrug."

Simpson sniffled and dutifully wiped his filthy feet on the mat inside the front door before following me upstairs. When we reached our room, Holmes was pacing. Brightening at the sight of the boy, he reached into his pocket and withdrew some coins. "Assemble your colleagues and head to Trafalgar. Stick your noses in the air and put your ears to the ground. Dig up any rumours of suspicious activity in the area this afternoon. Pay special attention to the Strand." He handed over several shillings. "Each boy who tells me something different will be rewarded."

Simpson tipped his hat and scampered off on his mission, pockets jangling.

Holmes placed his revolver in his pocket, which told me he anticipated serious business. I retrieved an old overcoat from my room to replace the soiled one I had worn earlier and pocketed my own revolver before joining him on the street, where we hailed a cab and asked to be taken across Vauxhall Bridge to Clapham.

The house at No. 18 Lark Hall Lane proved to be a dull brick affair. After telling our driver to wait for us, Holmes tapped on the front door with his walking stick. A woman of not more than thirty greeted us. She wore a dark dress, as one in mourning might. Despite her puffy face and red eyes, she was pleasant in appearance, and some colour returned to her cheeks once she discovered the identity of her uninvited callers.

"Mr. Holmes," she said as she escorted us into the drawing room. "This is unexpected. Do you bear news of my husband? Even if it is bad, I must hear it."

The room was warm and comfortable, furnished with several well-stuffed chairs. A thin carpet covered the floor and tapestries adorned the walls. "No news, Mrs. Mortimer, only questions," Holmes said.

"Please sit. I've been on my feet all day. Pacing mostly. I am at a complete loss as to where Edward could be."

"You had a caller on Friday evening."

"Edward did."

"Someone you didn't know."

She shook her head. "I sensed that Edward didn't know him, either."

"What did this man look like?"

"Perhaps your age," she said, indicating Holmes. "And around your height," she continued, indicating me this time. "Well-dressed. A black frock coat with a silk facing. Grey trousers. He carried a cane and wore a top hat."

"Tell me what transpired."

"After a brief exchange, Edward said he had to go out, but would be back before long. He put on his good coat, the one he wears to work, and gave me a peck on the cheek. I haven't seen nor heard a word about him since." Her eyes brimmed with tears, but she maintained her composure. "Whatever do you suppose happened?"

"I have insufficient information at the moment. Where is your husband employed? Somewhere near Trafalgar?"

"Why, yes, he works for Firmin on the Strand. He oversees the uniform orders."

"Aha," Holmes exclaimed. "Now we approach the truth. You have been most helpful," he told the distraught woman.

"Do you know where my husband is?" she asked.

"At present, I do not. I will report back when I know more."

We returned to our cab with orders to head for the Strand after stopping to send a wire to Scotland Yard. "Something nefarious is afoot," Holmes said as we jostled toward the bridge.

When we reached Cockspur Street, we were forced to abandon our cab because the area was still cordoned off. Lestrade was waiting for us at in front of the offices of P V Firmin & Sons, near the construction site of a new hotel next to the Savoy Chapel, and not far from the private hotel where I stayed when I first came to London. Lestrade looked displeased. "I should be enjoying my dinner about now, Mr. Holmes. What's this all about? My men have checked the place over front and back. There's no sign of forced entry."

"A man with a key would not need to force his way in," Holmes said. He glanced at the pavement but shook his head. "It would be useless to search for clues here. The entire city has stampeded up and down this street. No, we must gain access. Did you summon the proprietor?"

"That should be Mr. Straker now," Lestrade said. He indicated a tall, gaunt man approaching from the direction of Charing Cross." He had grey whiskers and the bearing of someone with military experience.

"Mr. Holmes thinks your establishment may have robbed," Lestrade said.

Straker gave Holmes a questioning look but said nothing. He produced a ring of keys from his pocket and inserted one in the front door. He was about to proceed inside but Holmes held him back.

"Permit me, Mr. Straker. There may be clues that I would not wish to have obscured." Holmes produced his magnifying glass and entered the front room, which was in darkness. He struck a match and lit a lamp inside the door. After a quick but thorough appraisal, he summoned Straker. "Prey tell me if you see anything amiss but disturb as little as possible."

Straker went from room to room, thrusting his lamp inside each and muttering to himself. At the third door, he stopped and tugged at one of his great whiskers.

"What have you detected?" Holmes asked.

Straker indicated a garment rack. "Uniforms are missing. At least a dozen." He opened a series of drawers and cabinets in rapid succession. "And all the associated regalia."

Holmes turned to me. "You observed a significant complement of uniformed soldiers this afternoon, did you not?"

I nodded. "Yes, both mounted and on foot."

"Can you recall who first entered the fray?"

I closed my eyes and pictured the scene. "We were herded along Pall Mall by mounted guards. Just before we reached the National Gallery, several soldiers waded into the crowd and started hitting people."

"Wearing uniforms like these?" Holmes asked, indicating the remaining garments on the rack.

"Yes," I said, confident of my memory.

Lestrade stepped forward. "You mean to say that the first ones to strike a blow today—"

"—were scoundrels dressed as soldiers." Holmes finished. "Violence in a crowd spreads like a disease. It would not take much more than a dozen men in strategic locations to start a riot."

Lestrade uttered a sentence with several vivid adjectives and summoned a constable from the cordon. "What does this fellow Mortimer look like?" Straker provided a detailed description, which the constable took down. Lestrade sent him to Scotland Yard to distribute a bulletin.

"Wouldn't someone have noticed that they weren't real soldiers?" I asked.

"Emotions were running high," Holmes said. "In any case, who looks closely at a man in uniform? So long as all the regalia were in order, a man would assume that a stranger was new to the unit or on loan from some other division."

"Was Mortimer behind this scheme?" Straker asked. His face had turned the colour of cigar ash and his voice quivered.

"I believe he was brought here under false pretenses. His visitor lured him with news of a break-in, or a tale of something afoul with the bookkeeping. An urgent enough excuse to draw him away from his family on a Friday evening."

"Seems like extraordinary lengths to go to," Lestrade said, "when all they had to do was smash a window."

"If someone detected the robbery too soon, their devilish plans might have been jeopardised," Holmes said.

"How would they know to involve Mortimer?" Straker inquired.

"I suspect that a military officer was behind this scheme," Holmes said. "Someone familiar with your business. The second most dangerous man in London, unless I'm mistaken."

"Whoever do you mean?" Straker asked.

"Colonel Sebastian Moran, once of the first Bangalore Pioneers in Her Majesty's Army. When he retired after a splendid career, he came to London and took up evil pursuits. He is chief of staff and the right-hand man of the master criminal who has you all so buffaloed that you still deem him a respectable man."

"You're not going on about that again, are you, Mr. Holmes? What would be gained in starting a riot? Where's the profit in that?"

"It is the magician's trick of distraction. Suppose you wanted to rob a place where the valuables were locked inside a steel vault. What would you require?"

"A sledgehammer and a strong man," I suggested.

"You get before yourself, Watson. Any group of men could easily run a ram through a door, barred or otherwise. But the trick is to get in undetected, leaving ample time to open the safes and lockboxes. And, of course, escape with the loot." Holmes waved in the direction of the Strand. "Today's riot provided the necessary diversion to allow them access to a place where their activities would otherwise draw unwanted attention. In fact," he said, a look of realisation crossing his face, "the robbery might still be in progress. The thieves may not have anticipated your cordon. If we're sharp about it, we might yet foil their plans. Tell me quickly, what businesses are close at hand that might bear sufficient riches for a scheme of this magnitude?"

"William Mansell, the jeweller," Straker said. "Across the street."

Lestrade summoned another constable and ordered him to check out the building. As the constable was leaving, Simpson slipped in through the open door. "Go on, get out of here you little rascal!" Lestrade roared. "There's nothing for you to steal in here."

"Wait. I know this boy," Holmes said. "Do you have something to report?"

The boy's wide eyes regarded Lestrade with trepidation.

"Speak, lad. Speak," Holmes said.

Simpson drifted beyond Lestrade's reach. "One of me mates saw a bunch of shifty men hanging about behind the bank up the street. Up to no good, he says."

"Coutts & Co.," I said, picturing a brick building a block away.

"My word," Straker said. "That's where I make my deposits on Friday afternoon."

"No doubt many other businesses do the same," Holmes said. "A plum ripe for the plucking. Well done, my little friend." Holmes ruffled Simpson's hair before filling his hands with coins.

Lestrade summoned several officers. Holmes and I followed them up the Strand, revolvers at the ready, accompanied by Simpson. The street was far emptier than when I had last been here, so it took but a few minutes to reach the bank. A group of urchins who had slipped past the cordon lurked in the alley across the street. Simpson gave a sign and a boy crossed over to provide an accounting of the situation.

"Take note, Lestrade. You'll find no better intelligence anywhere." He drew himself up to his full height as he spoke. "Six men have installed themselves behind the building. They are well armed and appear to be waiting for the police presence to diminish before making good their escape. Five are bearing large duffel bags, probably filled with money and valuables from safe deposit boxes. The sixth man, according to my agents, is restrained. I have no doubt that we will discover that this is none other than Mr. Edward Mortimer, who the thieves have held captive lest he raise the alarm. Make certain that your officers do not mistake him for a villain. These rogues will not hesitate to use him as a shield."

Lestrade organised his men and dispatched them behind the bank via several routes, cutting off every possible avenue of escape. Holmes rewarded his irregular forces and sent them on their way.

From behind the bank came yells and the sounds of gunfire. Lestrade emerged several minutes later with his men and, in shackles, four dangerous-looking miscreants in dark clothing and soft-soled shoes. Two of them were wounded, though not seriously. A fifth man, with a bruised face and torn clothing, proved indeed to be the missing Edward Mortimer. His heart was racing when I checked him with my stethoscope. I tended to his wounds, which on closer inspection proved to be minor, and bid him see his own specialist once he had finished providing testimony to the police.

"A busy day for your practice, my dear Watson," Holmes said amiably.

"And for yours," I replied. "Your alertness has foiled a major felony. The owners will be grateful that you have saved their coffers and preserved their customers' possessions."

Holmes made a dismissive gesture. "I see only four prisoners," he said.

"Perhaps the lad miscounted."

Lestrade approached. "They didn't give up without a fight," he said. "One managed to slip away by scaling a drainpipe and leaping across the rooftops. My man gave chase, but one of the chasms was too wide to risk leaping. His prey was daring to take such chances."

"A man with whom I am familiar, I suspect," Holmes said. "A known associate of Colonel Moran. Slippery devil, but someday he may attempt a leap beyond his ability."

"Bank officials have been summoned," Lestrade said. "They will want to shake the hand of the man who prevented a great blow to their business."

"I would prefer, Lestrade, if my name did not come up in association with this affair. You are free to shake their hands and spread the credit among your men as you see fit."

"Are you certain? This would be a fine feather in your cap."

"It would look better in yours," my friend said with a wry smile. "As I have often said, the work is its own reward. Watson and I shall take a leisurely stroll back to Baker Street, where I hope Mrs. Hudson has prepared something hearty for our dinner. Good evening, Lestrade."

"And to you, Mr. Holmes." Lestrade said. His beaming smile betrayed his anticipation of favourable headlines in the morning's newspapers.

When I entered our sitting room the next day, I found that Holmes, though still wearing his mouse-coloured dressing gown, had already completed his breakfast—no great surprise, considering the late hour. He was an early riser by habit, and the exertions of the previous day had taxed my constitution greatly, so I had slept well past my normal waking hour.

I poured a cup of coffee and took my seat across from him. A moment later, Mrs. Hudson arrived and placed a plate before me. While I buttered a slice of toast, Holmes read an account of the evening's events.

"A fairly accurate rendering, wouldn't you say, Watson? All the pertinent facts without unnecessary embellishments."

"Except for the obvious omissions," I replied.

Holmes shrugged. He was filling his first pipe of the morning with the plugs and dottles of the day before when an express messenger arrived, bearing a letter addressed to Holmes. He scrutinised the penmanship for a full minute before carefully slitting open the envelope and withdrawing a cream-coloured card of expensive bond.

"Ha!" he said, tossing the card on the table dismissively. "I had hoped to evade his notice."

I picked up the card. In a strong elegant hand was written a single word, below which appeared only an initial for a signature:

BRAVO!

M.

The Case of the Cursed Angel Tears

Ashley Lister

S herlock Holmes asked me not to write about the Case of the Cursed Angel Tears. His detractors, and there had always been many, insisted this reluctance was because it was one of those rare cases that he filed under the heading of "unresolved." They argued his ego was too great to tolerate any written account that showed him to be fallible or suggested that his logical approach to a case could prove flawed. However, my own feelings were that Holmes had personal reasons for wanting to keep the details of this case off the public record. Consequently, I am writing this account for my own satisfaction and not as one of the narratives intended for publication in *The Strand*, which Holmes always insisted were sensationalised accounts of his investigations.

"This is a most remarkable series of events," he told me one morning over breakfast. He was examining a lengthy letter that Mrs. Hudson had placed on the tray. He pointed idly at the contents with his butter knife whilst finishing off a slice of crisp golden toast.

In an effort to emulate his deductive reasoning, I had already glanced at the letter and seen it was handwritten in a small, neat print on a scallop-edged page that resembled watermarked vellum. Other than thinking the author was a fussy individual because of the preciseness of the writing, and exceedingly verbose because the letter looked to consist of four or five pages of closely scripted text, I was able to deduce nothing that I considered of value.

"Most remarkable," Holmes mused thoughtfully.

"Is it a case?" I asked.

"Possibly," he laughed. "Although, if Countess Pleasington is accurate in her supposition, it's a case that will involve our exploring worlds we've never previously needed to examine."

I frowned, unsure at the source of his amusement.

As Holmes tucked into another slice of toast, he said, "Would you care to consult that copy of *The London Journal* on my desk and tell me what it says about the Star of the North? It's open at the article."

I climbed from my chair and examined the open newspaper. The Star of the North, it transpired, was a sizeable diamond that had been mined in the early 1850s from a site owned by the Pleasington Mining Corporation in South Africa. "The diamond is remarkable for its size and clarity," I read aloud.

Holmes nodded.

"But it is more remarkable for the bloody history that has plagued it since it was unearthed," I told him. "According to this article, on excavation, two miners fell into a fatal dispute over which of them had first found the stone. A fist fight resulted in one man being beaten to death and then his killer was hanged for the crime. The mining company took ownership of the diamond and, within twenty-four hours, a group calling themselves *Umkosi Wezintaba*, I believe it translates to the *Regiment of the Hills*, made an attempt to steal the stone. Twelve people died during the attempted robbery, including three of the assayers, seven of the *Umkosi Wezintaba*, and two Kommandos who were trying to intervene in the name of justice."

"Fascinating," mused Holmes. His eyes were glassy, as though he was bored, and he stared blindly out toward the window that overlooked Baker Street. "One could genuinely believe that the curse was real," he murmured.

"The Pleasington Corporation sent the diamond to London to be auctioned, but a further tragedy struck when the packet-ship on which it was being transported sank just off the coast of Plymouth. Only one passenger survived and, when he was dragged to shore, he was found to be clutching the Star of the North."

"Truly remarkable," Holmes said softly.

"There were three further attempts to steal the stone, two of them resulting in mortal injuries and one which left the would-be thief crippled for life. There was also a fire at the auction house where it was on display which destroyed a Botticelli and a Titian but left the Star of the North unscathed."

I paused, expecting further comment from Holmes, but he said nothing. After a moment's silence, I read the concluding remarks from the journal. "The stone was eventually divided into two pieces, both of which were polished and shaped into identical marquise cut gems, each weighing a little over twenty carats, and mounted on white gold as a pair of earrings. Because of this distinctive cut, and because their colour and clarity are so perfect, the stones are now referred to as the Angel Tears."

"The *Cursed* Angel Tears," Holmes corrected. "The Countess Pleasington regaled me with the more recent history of those damned earrings in this letter."

"Is this a case you're thinking of accepting, Holmes?"

"It would be difficult to refuse this one," he admitted. "The puzzle is so neatly couched in notions of the supernatural that it reads like some gothic novella written by Horace Walpole or Bram Stoker. The Countess Pleasington tells me that the Star of the North was returned to her after the fire at the auction house. She was the one who commissioned the stone to be fashioned into earrings and she tells me that the jeweller took his own life shortly after completing the commission."

"Good heavens," I muttered.

Holmes leafed through the pages and said, "She goes on to mention further examples of tragedy and misery surrounding the earrings, but the most recent development happened yesterday. Her husband, Count Pleasington, collected the earrings from the jeweller's executor first thing in the morning, and then he died the same afternoon in a hunting accident."

"That is a remarkably tragic chain of events," I admitted. "It's almost enough to make one believe in the terrible power of supernatural forces."

Holmes laughed again, this time with an edge of bitterness to his tone. "If you subscribe to the notion of *post hoc, ergo propter hoc*, then I'm sure it's more than enough to make one believe in the power of the supernatural."

I blushed, more than a little irritated by the way he dismissed my credulity. "Are you saying there's no relationship between the tragic history of these earrings and the supernatural?" I snapped. "Are you trying to suggest that all these events associated with the diamonds are merely coincidence?"

"I'm saying that, as with so many of the other cases that we see, this can all be resolved with the careful application of observation and deductive reasoning."

"And there's no influence from the supernatural?" I asked.

Holmes smiled blithely. "Would you care to accompany me this afternoon when I visit Countess Pleasington?"

"You're taking her case?"

The chiming of Mrs. Hudson's clock in the room below, striking the hour, made him pause before responding. Holmes shook his head as if to indicate his reply could wait and said, "My client says she will have a brougham outside for us at half past the hour. I think it will make a better impression if I meet her wearing my ulster and cravat rather than my pyjamas and smoking jacket. Hurry yourself along, Watson. The game's afoot."

⁕

It was a brisk autumn day, the city streets littered with rust-coloured leaves that had been shaken by impending winter from the local deciduous trees. We sped toward the outskirts of the city where the detritus of the season became more colourful with red and gold leaves plastered wetly to the surface of the rain-slick roads. On Holmes's instruction, the driver of the brougham dropped us at the gates of the walled Pleasington estate.

Holmes set off briskly up the winding driveway that led to the manor house. I could see his shrewd glance was taking in every detail from the small copses of hazel, maple, and hawthorn, through to the barking cries of game birds as they cawed laconically at each other.

A weasel-faced man called for us to stop, and I was somewhat surprised to see Inspector Lestrade of Scotland Yard bearing down on us having emerged from an overgrown coppice. His cheeks were ruddy, and he sounded out of breath when he spoke. "I'm surprised to see you here, Holmes," he gasped. "I didn't think this would be your sort of case at all."

"You do me an injustice," Holmes laughed. Despite the brisk pace he maintained, there was no suggestion of breathlessness in his voice. "I thought you understood I have an interest in any puzzle that goes beyond the natural."

"Yes," Lestrade agreed. "But this touches on the supernatural, doesn't it?"

Holmes graced the policeman with a condescending smile, before shaking his head sadly and striding onward to the distant doorway of Pleasington Manor.

"Why are you here, Lestrade?" I asked.

He gave me a gruff grin and shook his head as his irritated gaze followed Holmes. "Protocol," he explained airily. "Count Pleasington was shot yesterday. Even though we're sure it was an accident, I've had to conduct a cursory investigation, so we have a record of what happened."

"And what did happen?" Holmes asked. He was still ahead of us and called the question idly over his shoulder.

Lestrade offered me a sympathetic expression. "It was one of those accidents that looked like it had been waiting to happen. The Pleasingtons were having a shooting weekend. Two parties were engaged in separate hunts and, when pheasants were beaten from one copse, both parties shot at the birds from different sides of the same bush. Count Pleasington got caught by a stray shot intended for a startled game bird."

"How unfortunate," I offered.

"Not unfortunate," Lestrade said darkly. "The Countess Pleasington tells me this misfortune was all brought on by a cursed piece of jewellery that she owns."

I considered him doubtfully. "Do you believe that's a plausible explanation?"

"I don't believe the supernatural is always an answer," Lestrade said defensively. "But I think it's fairly conclusive that the uncanny has been at work here. There have been deaths associated with these earrings and the stone they were cut from. Count Pleasington was just another unlucky bystander."

"A very unlucky bystander," Holmes laughed drily. "The coroner tells me that the shot penetrated his heart as though it had been fired by a marksman."

"When did you get a chance to talk with the coroner?" Lestrade asked indignantly.

"I happened to be passing his offices yesterday evening," Holmes explained. "When I was out for my evening constitutional. The coroner is always happy to discuss any *cause célèbre* that has the misfortune to visit his office. This one struck him as remarkable because of the way the shot looked almost as though it had been planned."

"Good God," Lestrade cried. "Are you suggesting Count Pleasington was deliberately murdered?"

"Why would I suggest such a thing?" Holmes replied airily. "I thought you'd already established that this death was brought about by supernatural means. He took possession of a pair of mystical earrings. Isn't that what the coroner should be putting on the death certificate?"

Whilst Lestrade blustered at Holmes's sarcasm, I asked, "Do you have any idea who would want Count Pleasington dead?"

"I have several ideas," Holmes admitted. "But you know I don't try to fit facts to a theory. I need a little more evidence before I make up my mind on this, and I think we'll find our answers inside the manor house."

We had reached the door and Countess Pleasington had personally come outside to greet us.

"Mr. Holmes," she gushed enthusiastically. "I am so grateful that you've agreed to take this case."

"It interests me greatly," Holmes told her.

Lowering her voice to a conspiratorial whisper, she asked, "And you're unconcerned by the danger the Cursed Angel Tears present?"

He laughed softly. "I think there are more corporeal things that should be causing me concern." His sharp gaze flitted briefly over her, and he said, "Count Pleasington wasn't your first husband, was he?"

"He was my third husband," she admitted.

"And the marriage wasn't proving to be as happy a union as you'd initially envisaged?"

"Holmes," I hissed, indignant on behalf of the widow. "Please be a little more circumspect."

"Circumspect?" he echoed, sounding dumbfounded by my use of the word. "The woman's husband died yesterday and yet there are no signs of tears or upset and there is certainly no suggestion of mourning. I can't think why you should think I'm not being circumspect because I state the obvious fact that this woman's relationship had proved distinctly unsatisfactory."

She glared at him and, for a moment, I didn't think she was going to respond.

"Regardless of how satisfactory, or otherwise, our relationship was proving," she began frostily. "I'm not sure how that has any bearing on your presence here."

A young woman appeared at the countess's side and placed a reassuring hand on her arm. From her sombre manner, well-groomed appearance, and air of insouciant confidence, I assumed she was a member of the family. "Is everything alright, Mother?"

"This is the count's daughter, Marianne," the countess explained.

"From the count's first marriage?" Holmes said, taking the young woman's hand and kissing the knuckles lightly. When she scowled at him, clearly puzzled by his knowledge of her family's history, Holmes said, "You are the very image of your late mother. I remember seeing her photograph alongside her obituary fifteen years ago. At the time, I commented on her striking beauty, didn't I, Watson?"

I agreed he had, although I had only the vaguest recollection of the exchange.

Marianne looked both surprised and mollified by Holmes's explanation. "What are you doing here, Mister Holmes?"

"Mister Holmes is here to take on my case," Countess Pleasington told Marianne.

"Your case?" Marianne asked uncertainly.

"Those cursed earrings," the countess explained. "They've brought us nothing but ill-fortune. Tragedy and death follow them wherever they go. Mister Holmes has kindly agreed to act as an agent, take them to an auction house, and broker a reasonable price for them."

"This isn't your usual sort of case," I told Holmes quietly.

"No, Watson," he agreed. "But there's little that's usual about this case and these circumstances."

"Why are you acting as the countess's agent for a jewellery sale?" Lestrade asked bluntly.

"I'm doing it to assist the countess," Holmes explained. "She doesn't feel as though she can sell the jewellery herself for fear of jeopardising the safety of the auction house or the life and happiness of any prospective purchaser."

"But she's alright jeopardising your life?" Lestrade asked doubtfully. He considered this for a moment and then said, "I can relate to that attitude."

"The countess contacted me because she's aware that I have a reputation for rationality and give little credence to notions of cursed jewellery. She's read accounts of my dealing rationally with the supernatural in cases such as *The Hound of the Baskervilles* or *The Sussex Vampire*. The countess is of the opinion that my pragmatic involvement will help to break the chain of misfortune."

I nodded acceptance of this explanation, but it still struck me as odd that Holmes was wasting his time on such a frivolous distraction. Given his caseload, I would have thought he couldn't spare the time for such an indulgence. It was only as an afterthought that I realised he was agreeing to act as her agent, so he had an opportunity to investigate such a singular case.

"Were you going to tell Countess Pleasington that her husband's death was accidental?" Holmes asked Lestrade in a conversational tone.

Lestrade frowned, as though he didn't like to have his proclamations pre-empted, and then nodded reluctant agreement. "Everything happened exactly as was described by the gamekeeper," the inspector explained. "I've interviewed the head of each hunting party that was out yesterday, and it seems clear that this was just an unfortunate accident, potentially influenced by the curse on these earrings."

"Ha!" Holmes barked.

"You think the inspector's conclusion is erroneous?" Marianne enquired softly.

We all stared at her. There was something odd in the coolness of her tone that made me think the young woman could be a powerful adversary if pushed.

Holmes seemed to have missed the steel in her voice. His reply was offhand and almost indolent. "I think it's accurate in some areas, and thorough in most of its detail, but the inspector's conclusion fails on some relatively important aspects."

"Such as?" Lestrade snapped. His cheeks were turning the colour of freshly pulled beets. His eyes were narrow and sharp.

In a bored tone, Holmes said, "Your conclusion is missing out the detail that Count Pleasington was deliberately murdered so that his benefactor could inherit his estate without having to tolerate his interminable company any further."

The countess clutched at her breast in shock. Marianne fixed Holmes with a scowl as she went to comfort her stepmother.

"These are outrageous accusations," Marianne exclaimed.

"Indeed, they are," Lestrade agreed.

"And you permit him to make such slurs?" Marianne demanded of the inspector.

Lestrade shrugged. "It's been my experience that, even though I don't like some of the things that Holmes says, he's frustratingly accurate when he makes a pronouncement of foul play."

Holmes smiled warmly at the inspector. "Thank you for that, Lestrade."

"And do you have any evidence to support these accusations?" Marianne asked.

"Certainly," Holmes said. "Perhaps, if we could make ourselves comfortable inside the manor house, you'll allow me to explain what has taken place?"

⁕

A maid provided us with tea in front of a warm fire. After the cold wind and driving rain that had pummelled us along the estate's driveway, it was a relief to be sheltered indoors and enjoying the vibrant orange warmth that came from the crackling logs.

"All the evidence for this murder points toward Countess Pleasington," Holmes declared.

Marianne and the countess both exclaimed loudly. Lestrade blustered a response that sounded like an inarticulate denial before he said, "I've seen no evidence for this being a murder case, Mister Holmes. I've certainly seen nothing to indicate Countess Pleasington's involvement in the death."

Holmes shook his head. "I suspect," he began, "you have seen everything, but simply failed to observe."

The two women, sitting side by side on a chaise longue near the fireplace, shifted their gaze from Lestrade to Holmes and then back to Lestrade, as though they were watching a lawn tennis rally at Wimbledon.

Stiffly, clearly aware of the scrutiny the two women were giving him, Lestrade said to Holmes, "Kindly explain yourself."

"Very well," Holmes agreed. "There are two reasons why I believe this is a murder investigation," he began. "The first being the deliberate shooting of Count Pleasington yesterday afternoon—"

"Accidental shooting," Marianne corrected.

Holmes continued as though there had been no interruption. "And the second reason being the death of the stable hand."

"What?" demanded Lestrade.

"How did you know about this?" asked Marianne.

"It's the curse," Countess Pleasington moaned. "The Cursed Angel Tears have claimed another victim."

"You'll need to explain this second death to me, Holmes," I told him. "I wasn't even aware that a stable hand had died."

"This is the first I've heard of it," Lestrade scowled. "And I don't appreciate being kept in the dark about such matters."

"The stable hand's body was found yesterday evening," Holmes said easily. "It was believed he was the unfortunate victim of an accident that came from him being trapped in a stable with an agitated horse."

"An accident?" Lestrade echoed. "Like the accidents that have plagued everyone associated with those cursed earrings? Surely, that's just another coincidence, isn't it? I thought you were of the opinion that coincidences don't happen, Mr. Holmes?"

Holmes shot him a withering look that was half-irritation and half-pity.

"Coincidences do happen," Holmes admitted. "But this isn't a mere case of coincidence. This is premeditated murder."

Countess Pleasington paled. Marianne, sitting beside her, clutched tight at the older woman's hand.

"The police don't yet know who was responsible for the fatal shot that killed the count," Holmes explained. "There were four shooters in each party, and Inspector Lestrade has closely examined the guns of the party that accidentally fired on the count."

"That's correct," Lestrade admitted. He fumbled through a notebook and added, "There are no ballistic similarities between the injuries sustained by the count and the guns being used."

"But you haven't checked the guns from the count's own party, have you?"

Lestrade clustered. "There didn't seem a lot of point. The second party would have no idea where the count was, so it seemed prudent to check their weapons. However, the count's party would have known exactly where he was, so they wouldn't have discharged their weapons in his direction."

"Unless," Holmes pointed out, "one of that party wanted him dead."

"But why would anyone want my husband dead?" asked the countess. Her voice was strained with the frustration of not understanding. "I admit, I didn't care for him in the same way I had when we first married. But I didn't want to see him dead."

"I suspect financial gain was the motive," Holmes admitted. "It so often is in cases like this. The estate of the dead count goes into the hands of his benefactors and, if no one suspects foul play, the villain gets away with their heinous crime."

The countess shook her head. "That can't be correct," she explained. "I was the only person likely to gain from his death."

"Which is why you are our primary suspect," Holmes declared.

Countess Pleasington shrank back in her chair. "You don't mean that."

"Holmes," Lestrade gasped. "You can't go making such serious accusations without proof."

"It looks like you paid the stable hand to join in with the shooting party," Holmes told Countess Pleasington. "He was given strict instructions to shoot the count at the vital moment when the two parties *accidentally* came face-to-face." He placed a knowing stress on the word *accidentally*, letting us all know he thought the timing was anything but accidental. "The stable hand did as he was instructed and came into this very room to receive his payment for committing the murder."

"And how do you deduce that?" Lestrade asked tightly.

"Look at the dusty footprints leading from the French windows," Holmes told him. "Those are prints that have come directly from the stables. They're too small to belong to the count, and none of the other party guests would have had reason to enter this room."

"And you're accusing me of giving payment to this hired assassin?" Countess Pleasington asked indignantly.

"The stable hand wasn't merely paid whilst he was in this room," Holmes admitted. "This is also the room where he was poisoned."

"Poisoned," Lestrade gasped.

"The coroner had no intention of examining the body for poisoning," Holmes said. "The hoof marks to his face and chest looked like self-evident indicators of the cause of death. But I noticed a touch of cyanosis around the lips and a fragrance of almonds lingering at the nostrils, so I asked the coroner to be a little more diligent."

"What makes you think the stable hand was poisoned in this room?" Marianne asked him.

Holmes raised an eyebrow. "It's really quite elementary," he smiled. "On the sideboard, you have three decanters, two of which are two thirds full whilst the third is empty."

Marianne, Countess Pleasington, Lestrade, and I all turned to study the three decanters. The cognac and brandy decanters were each two thirds full of clear golden liquid. The third decanter was empty and sparkled in the crackling flames from the fireside.

"That proves nothing," Lestrade said.

"Agreed," Holmes admitted. "But think about what it indicates. That decanter is not just empty, it has been washed and wiped clean, as though the person who emptied it wanted to remove every drop of liquid from inside. A member of the serving staff would have taken the empty glassware away and kept it in the kitchens or replenished it with liquor and replaced it. This suggests, to me, that the cleaning was done by a member of the household who wasn't a member of the staff."

"But why does it matter if a member of the household cleaned the decanter?" Lestrade asked.

I had followed Holmes's reasoning, and could have supplied an answer, but I thought it best to let me friend explain.

"Why would someone want to clean a decanter so thoroughly?" Holmes asked Lestrade. "Because they wanted to disguise the fact that the contents of the decanter had been deliberately poisoned."

"I would never—" Countess Pleasington began.

Holmes spoke over her. "You'll notice that one of the crystal glasses is missing from the collection, and I suspect it broke when the victim consumed the poison and then succumbed to the typical convulsions that are symptomatic of cyanide poisoning." He pointed toward the hearth and said, "There's a shard of glass sparkling in the flames, and I'd bet good money that was once part of the broken glass."

Lestrade knelt in front of the fireplace and retrieved tweezers and a small envelope from his pocket. Gently, he picked the shard of glass from the hearth, dropped it into the envelope, and then placed the envelope in his pocket.

"This is outrageous, Mr. Holmes," Countess Pleasington wailed. "My husband and I were a trifle distant, but I can assure you I had no desire to cause him any harm."

Holmes graced her with a winning smile. "I'm aware of this, Countess," he said affably. "I know you aren't responsible for these deaths. I only said it looked like you were responsible. The person behind the murders is your stepdaughter, Marianne."

Lestrade and the countess gasped.

Marianne glared at Holmes with a vitriol that looked murderous. "Are you able to support that statement?" she asked, a low rumble of menace at the back of her throat, "or should I use that line as part of my case against you for defamation of character?"

Holmes laughed and shook his head as though dismissing her threat. "You wanted your father's money," he told her. "Your father had little time for you with each new wife he claimed and, eventually, you realised he was making no provision for you or your future."

"This is all speculation," Marianne growled.

"The final straw came when his mining company unearthed the Star of the North and he refused to give it to you. It must have been so frustrating to see the diamond was being given to your ungrateful stepmother, a woman who was fatuous enough to buy into the superstition attached to the stone."

"Really!" exclaimed Countess Pleasington.

Holmes waved a hand in her direction and mumbled, "No offence intended."

"And that was when you began to plot a story behind that diamond that would make everyone think it was cursed, and therefore responsible for the spate of deaths you were planning."

"You can't prove this," Marianne snapped. "You can't prove any of this, so I'm not sure if there's any point in you continuing with this tirade."

"I can't prove that you arranged for the stable hand to shoot the count," Holmes agreed. "And I can't prove that you laced the decanter with cyanide. But I know, when we've interviewed the kitchen staff, one of them will be able to tell us that you purloined some of the cyanide intended for the rat traps and I suspect we'll get an admission from your coconspirator, the gamekeeper, when we ask if he helped you to take the stable boy's body into the stables."

Marianne fixed Holmes with a look that was the epitome of hatred.

"The gamekeeper?" gasped Countess Pleasington.

"You're going too swiftly for me, Mr. Holmes," Lestrade complained. "What's this development?"

Holmes and Marianne ignored them both.

"How do you know about my relationship with the gamekeeper?" Marianne asked him.

"Only the gamekeeper could have given the signal for the stable hand to shoot the count," Holmes explained. "Otherwise the timing of that fatal shot would never have been so perfect. The gamekeeper couldn't have been working alone because he would gain nothing from the count's death. The gamekeeper could only have been working with someone who would profit from such a tragedy and I believe, if Countess Pleasington had been convicted for the murder of her husband, the estate would have fallen into your delicate hands."

"How did you piece all of this together?" Marianne asked tersely.

"It was obvious from the moment I read your article in *The London Journal* about the colourful history of the Cursed Angel Tears. There was no wreck off the coast of Plymouth according to the coastal records I studied. And there was, therefore, no last survivor clutching a cursed stone. Those were all fabrications, weren't they? There were no robberies by the *Umkosi Wezintaba*, and no subsequent deaths. Those were acts of dissimilitude, created by you, so you could obfuscate the deaths you were planning with stories of supernatural mystery."

"They weren't all fabrications," she told him. "The majority of those stories were true."

"And is it true what Mr. Holmes says about your involvement in the death of your father and the stable hand?" Lestrade asked softly. "Is the gamekeeper your partner in this crime?"

She hung her head and looked deflated. "Yes," she admitted. "It's true. I organised my father's murder and, together with William, I poisoned the stable hand and then made his death look like an unfortunate encounter with one of the horses."

"Marianne!" the countess cried in disbelief.

Marianne glared at her as Lestrade approached and placed cuffs on her wrists. "But you'd better be careful," she told the countess. "Because the curse on those earrings is very real. They were brought into this world with deaths, and they'll continue to inspire more tragedy and upset to everyone who handles them."

It was a week later when Holmes reminded me of the case and asked me to keep the details away from the public record. "Ordinarily, I wouldn't ask," he apologised. "But it's the most curious thing."

"Go on," I encouraged.

"Countess Pleasington still wanted me to act as her agent for disposing of the jewellery," he explained. "Because she genuinely feared the curse that Marianne had described in her article for *The London Journal*. Even though I'd only taken the case so I could get closer to the murderer, I felt obliged to take the earrings to an auctioneer I knew and get him to organise the sale."

There was something unnerving in his tone that I had never heard before. "What happened?"

"The auction house burned to the ground last night," he said quietly. "Some valuable paintings were destroyed in the conflagration, as well as a handful of irreplaceable antiques. Only one lot managed to survive the fire without being damaged, almost as though the item was cursed."

"Which item?" I asked, although I suspected I already knew the answer to the question. "Which item survived?"

He fixed me with a stern, solemn frown and said, "The surviving lot was the Cursed Angel Tears."

The Case of the Air that Was Taken

Keith Brooke

I should have known that, like any good idea I claimed for my own, my proposal for a recuperative break by the sea was not in fact mine, but rather a seed that had been planted by my friend, the inestimable Sherlock Holmes.

"You're looking a trifle peaky," I told him as we sat in the parlour of the Baker Street flat we had once shared. Holmes drew on his favourite oily clay pipe while I poured the tea Mrs. Hudson had deposited seconds before. "Don't you think so, Mrs. Hudson?" The good lady was yet to retreat downstairs, instead loitering in the doorway, a sure sign that she too shared my concerns. We both knew that Holmes was not one to look after himself even at the best of times.

"And your reasons for drawing such a conclusion?"

I drew myself up in my chair, straightening my waistcoat. As a medical doctor, I felt sure of myself on this topic, even under the scrutiny of one so insightful as Holmes.

"A certain sallowness of complexion," I told him. "Dark shadows beneath the eyes. A lacklustre spirit and, even by the standards of one normally so aloof, an even greater disinclination than usual for any sort of society. My conclusion is that you have been working too hard, and a restorative break would be of great benefit."

For a second, Holmes allowed me to preen myself on my analytical powers, and then he gave a slow, withering single shake of the head. "Sallowness of complexion is normal when one has been working undercover in the opium dens of the East End," he explained. "As too are shadows beneath the eyes and a lacklustre spirit, when one considers the normal hours of operation of such establishments. It is now slightly more than a day and a half since I last slept, and so my demeanour, and the symptoms you describe, are to be expected, and not a sign of 'peakiness,' as you say."

"And your case concluded successfully?"

"It did, which explains my disinclination for the trivialities of social concourse of any kind."

That was true, at least: Holmes always tended to withdraw from those around him when the thrill of the chase had passed.

Chastened by the unravelling of my logic, still I clung to the argument. "If your case has concluded, then now is the perfect opportunity for that restorative break," I said triumphantly. "A breath of sea air is my prescription for you, Holmes. I'll hear no more objections, for I have already made arrangements for my absence with my good wife, and a locum has been appointed to cover my practice for the remainder of this week."

⁂

Having gone our separate ways for what remained of the morning in order to arrange luggage, I spotted Sherlock Holmes again pacing up and down the platform at Liverpool Street station, his tall, gaunt figure made to appear even gaunter by the flapping of his long grey travelling cloak.

"Frinton-on-Sea, you say? What is there to engage us in a place such as Frinton-on-Sea?" Holmes asked, renewing our conversation of two hours ago as if uninterrupted.

"Nothing," I told him, which was entirely the point of my selection. "It is a genteel and refined seaside town, removed from the grime and bustle of the capital, with nothing to vex us beyond the choice of whether to turn left or right when reaching the promenade for our daily perambulation."

Holmes did not look convinced. In truth, my old friend would probably have found it easier to relax in some rough and tough dive in the East End than in the genteel surroundings of my chosen destination, but I would have none of it, and for once he seemed to recognise that I would brook no argument.

We secured seats in a compartment unoccupied except for a spinsterish woman in her late forties who sat staring fixedly out of the window. Holmes greeted her with a remarkably polite nod and a "Good day, madam," before seating himself and quite openly studying her from head to foot, much to her discomfort. When she turned her gaze on him again, challenging him to look away, he merely smiled and said, "I trust that you will enjoy your excursion to the seaside to visit your sister's family, madam, particularly with so trying an employer overseeing your filing work and taking unfair advantage of your desire to improve yourself."

The woman's jaw visibly sagged, then she gave a great big huff, gathered her things, and moved to another compartment.

"I say, Holmes, wasn't that a trifle—"

"Effective?"

I knew better than to ask, but nevertheless did so. "How could you tell such things at the merest of glances? No wonder people accuse you of the black arts."

Holmes shook his head, and for a moment I thought he was disinclined to explain, which in itself would be a sure indication that he was out of sorts. Then he told me, "Really, Watson. I sometimes think I am the only one who can see."

"See what? All I observed was a lady hoping to complete her journey without undue and unwanted interactions."

"A lady who has come to the train direct from her place of work, as witnessed by her outfit—that of an office worker, a bookkeeper or filing clerk, I'd warrant, which was confirmed by the indentations of pince-nez on the bridge of her nose and the orderliness of her travelling bag. She dresses above her station, trying to impress. Her employer clearly takes advantage of this desire to improve herself and is trying and demanding, if he makes her work a half day before she can get away to catch her train to the seaside."

"And her family?"

"She travels alone, with no wedding ring, and so is clearly a spinster, for a widow would still wear her ring. She has presents, which suggests she is visiting family, but her age suggests surviving parents are statistically unlikely, so visiting a sibling is more probable—a sibling with children, judging by the presents—and with all the best will in the world, a sister is generally more welcoming of visits than a brother."

I shook my head. With the woman now gone, it would be impossible to confirm Holmes's deductions, but it was clear from her reaction he had at least hit close to the mark. Once again, I felt myself to be an inferior species of man to my companion.

We passed some time in contemplative silence, as the outer reaches of the capital peeled away to either side of the track. Sometime later, when I glanced away from the window, I saw that Holmes had produced a crumpled newspaper clipping and was studying it closely. Immediately, I experienced the sense that I had fallen a step behind.

I sat patiently, sure he must be aware that I had noticed what he was doing. Finally, he looked up and feigned surprise at my interest. I raised my eyebrows, trying to make both my resignation and my curiosity evident.

"Just a trifle to entertain and divert us while we are away from home," he explained, making a very poor show of dismissing the subject.

I reached out and, after a slight pause, he handed me the clipping.

" 'Notorious Art Thief Found Dead Weeks After Release from Gaol,' " I read aloud. When Holmes gave no reaction, I skimmed the story. Art thief Ronald Taylor had been found dead in his room near to the fish quay in Whitstable, Kent, of natural causes, namely asthmatic lung disease, only five weeks after his release following eleven years at Her Majesty's pleasure.

Holmes was studying me closely now, and I knew I had missed something that was, to him at least, obvious.

"You're going to have to give me a clue," I said.

He shook his head, and instead of a clue, merely gave a long sigh. "I wonder," he said, "don't you find that, in many people, education reaches beyond the scope of the intellect?"

It took me a moment or two to realise he was referring to me: educated, yet still unable to see what, to Holmes, was blindingly obvious.

"An old case of yours, I presume?" I said. When there was no reply, I went on. "Ah yes...the Taylor boys. They stole fine art to order, didn't they? So slippery, no one could ever pin them down."

"No one but me."

"Eventually."

"Eventually," Holmes conceded. "Ronald and Thomas Taylor taught me a lot. One might even regard them as mentors in teaching me the workings of the criminal mind."

As was so often the case, there was a significant element of respect in the way Holmes talked of a certain class of criminal.

"Brothers in crime," I said.

"Brothers, and yet they hated each other, and always did. That's why I acquiesced to this little trip. If Ronnie Taylor has dropped dead, then no matter how innocent it may appear, I suspect the hand of his brother in it."

Even now, my brain was racing to catch up. Events of the day needed reordering in my understanding as I came to suspect that, far from this trip being my own unprompted idea, it must have been something Holmes had in some way suggested.

"But... But this report talks of Whitstable and we're heading for Frinton-on-Sea, fifty miles away across the Thames estuary. I don't understand."

"Isn't it obvious, Watson? We're going to Frinton-on-Sea because that is where Thomas Taylor has been living since his release from gaol. Do keep up."

Frinton-on-Sea... Not only had Holmes somehow sown the seed of a break by the sea in my unconscious so that I might think it my own idea, but he had even selected our destination!

Now I glanced at the top right-hand corner of the newspaper clipping and saw that it was dated two days before I had even had the idea of this trip...

I looked up at Holmes, but already he was in his thinking repose, with his eyes closed and his fingers steepled before him, and I knew the opportunity to dig deeper had passed.

I found Frinton-on-Sea to be a charming little town, comprising several streets of terraced houses and imposing villas clustered along the top of a steep grassy drop down to a row of white-painted bathing huts that formed an orderly line along the promenade.

The place was genteel and restrained, no bawdy drinking establishments or music halls to disturb the peace. Even the railway station was set discreetly, back half a mile from the sea front. The town's peaceful disposition could not have been farther removed from the noise and smell and general bustle of the capital.

We took rooms in a four-story guesthouse on the Esplanade, with views out across the steely grey expanse of the North Sea. It was after four o'clock by the time we had established ourselves, and I was inclined to ask the housekeeper to draw a bath, but Holmes's spirit was revived—whether by the sea air or by the intrigue of his renewed acquaintance with the Taylor boys, I could not tell.

"Let us take a stroll," he told me, already dressed again in his travelling cloak and close-fitting cloth cap.

I acquiesced, of course, knowing that exercise was the last thing on my old friend's mind. Sure enough, when we emerged from the guesthouse, instead of directing ourselves across the greensward to the promenade, we turned left, and then left again, along the town's main thoroughfare.

"You have an address for Thomas Taylor, of course?" I enquired of him, for it was obvious even to me where we were headed. I had already noted that Holmes had chosen to walk with a cane—one he was wont to also employ as a weapon, should the need arise. For the first time, I realised the danger of our situation: we were heading out to confront a hardened criminal, freshly emerged from gaol and suspected of murdering his brother in crime. I wished, rather belatedly, that I had thought to pack my service revolver.

The surviving Taylor brother lived in a basement room situated on a side street off the town's main road. In a town so refined, this little row of buildings seemed out of place, shabby and unloved, with boards over the windows and ragged urchins playing in the street and eyeing us for the strangers we were.

Holmes rapped sharply on the cracked wooden door with his cane, and when there came no response, placed his face close to the boarded window and called, "Tommy Taylor? I'd like a word. It's an old acquaintance. Sherlock Holmes."

I heard sounds from within, the clearing of a throat followed by a hard cough, then, "Holmes? Well I'll be..." followed by more coughing.

Holmes reached for the door, pushed, and stepped into the basement's gloom.

Following my friend, it took a moment or two for my sight to adjust.

"Leave the door open," croaked a voice from the dark interior. "I want light to see you by, Holmes... Well, I never."

Taylor, if it were him, sat on the room's one wooden chair in a corner of the room. By the window lay a sorry-looking straw mattress and a wadded bundle of bedding. A jug and a tin mug sat on a wooden stool by Taylor's chair, along with an unlit candle.

I recalled that by all accounts, the Taylor brothers had lived well at their peak, but that lifestyle had clearly been lost to Thomas upon his release from prison.

"I'd get up, but..." The man shrugged, as if to indicate his own incapacity.

"This is my friend, Dr. Watson," Holmes explained. "We came to express our condolences upon the loss of your brother."

Taylor laughed. "Yeah, of course you did," he barked. "I cared for Ronnie about as much as you do, and that's not much at all. You don't have any feelings of condolence or otherwise to express, Holmes. You never did. So, what do you want?"

My eyes better adjusted now, I studied Taylor more closely. Grey of hair, and overweight, he exhibited difficulty breathing and no doubt suffered other ailments, aged far in advance of his sixty years or so. The man was clearly in no condition to have made the arduous journey to Whitstable, found a way to murder his brother, and slipped away scot free.

"I had the notion you might know something about the nature of your brother's demise," Holmes said. He had clearly reached the same conclusion as me.

"You thought I did for him, didn't you? Never one to accept natural causes when you see the chance of intrigue, were you? Well I'll tell you, the old sot died of his chest, just as I'll die of mine one day. There's nothing for you there, Holmes. And I certainly didn't go down to Kent to see him off. I can barely get out of this chair, these days."

"Perhaps," Holmes said. "But you're well enough, at least, to take your daily stroll along the promenade."

Taylor stared, startled at my friend's insight. Alert to Holmes's methods, I followed my friend's gaze to the corner of the room, where a pair of stout boots stood, the toecaps frosted with giveaway traces of sand.

"That's about my limit," Taylor admitted. "It's as much as I can do these days to get to the prom and back, let alone take my daily walk. There's no way I could get to Whitstable."

"You knew Ronald resided in Whitstable, then," said Holmes, "even though you didn't stay in touch?"

Taylor shrugged. "Course I did. Didn't want to end up accidentally taking my retirement in the same seaside town as my brother, now, did I?"

I could see where my friend's reasoning was leading, but so too could Taylor, who went on to add, "And if you think I sent someone down there to take care of things, then you're over-estimating my reach, I can tell you that." With a shrug and a tip of the head from side to side, Taylor indicated his modest surroundings. "I have neither the finances nor the contacts to have people going about on my behalf these days. Believe me when I tell you, it's the quiet life for me; just glad not to be looking at the sky through iron bars, I am."

Holmes remained unconvinced; I could see it in his eyes. We both knew that a man like Thomas Taylor had ways to influence others beyond the financial. He had a lifetime of favours to call in, and I didn't doubt he still had plentiful contacts in the underworld, should he choose to use them.

"You want my advice, Holmes?" We waited for a coughing fit to pass before the villain could continue. "If you're really convinced Ronnie didn't die of natural causes, you talk to Bertie Donahue. If anyone bore a grudge against Tommy, it's Bertie."

❧

Outside, the late afternoon sunshine was dazzling after the gloom of Thomas Taylor's basement room.

"You believe him?" I asked, as soon as we were out of earshot of the man.

"It is mine neither to believe nor disbelieve," Holmes responded, in typically tangential manner. "You observed the sand on his boots?"

"Explained by his daily perambulations."

"And that is all it tells you?"

I remained silent as we made our way back to the High Street.

"Rarely can so few grains of sand offer such insight into a man's character," Holmes said eventually. "A man who makes great show of his incapacity, and yet who is able to undertake a daily walk that takes him to the beach. How far would you say that is? A quarter of a mile to the promenade, and then enough of a walk to make it worthwhile. Added to that the very physical descent from the promenade to the sandy beach, it suggests a far greater physical capacity than he would have us believe."

"You think he murdered his brother?" Those grains of sand showed the man to be a liar, but it still seemed to me a great leap from being able to undertake a daily walk to being able to travel to another county via London and perpetrate that most heinous of crimes.

"I do not think that at all," Holmes corrected me. "I merely gather the evidence in order to build a picture of the man as he is, rather than how he would have us see him."

We had reached the Esplanade now, the wide road that ran the length of the seafront, above and parallel to the promenade and separated from it by a steep grassy slope. A paved path ran down to the lower level, and we took this. At the bottom, a few stalls sold pies, pickled oysters, and ginger beer.

Holmes lingered here, and the grumble in my belly reminded me that it was some time since tea and Mrs. H's plum duff at Baker Street.

"Cockles and whelks?" bellowed a young vendor, his intrusive tenor earning himself a glare from his older rival whose pickled oysters Holmes had been perusing.

Holmes didn't even deign to answer, and so I gave the two vendors an apologetic smile before rushing to catch up with my friend.

"So tell me, Holmes, who is this Bertie Donahue that Taylor mentioned?" We were walking along the paved promenade now, a few feet above the level of the sandy beach.

"Albert Donahue," Holmes said. "An accomplice of the Taylor boys on some of their heists. He was the buffer between the two brothers, stopping their fighting from ever getting too much, smoothing things over. They gave him the runaround, exploited him, and so he was probably closer to each Taylor boy than the brothers themselves."

Holmes's words confirmed my own assessment of the Taylor brothers: that while they fought and often hated each other, the sibling ties were just as intense. "So Donahue was like a third brother?"

"Indeed. The oil that smoothed the workings of their criminal machine."

"But why would Thomas Taylor accuse Donahue?"

"Because when the chips were down, they turned on him. When Lestrade finally called me in to put together the pieces of the case against the Taylor boys, some eleven years ago, the brothers turned on Donahue when the trap closed on them. In truth Donahue was only ever on the periphery of their operations, and when arrests were made, he should, by rights, have got away with only a few months in gaol."

"But the Taylors put the blame on him?"

"They did indeed. When the three went to trial, each blamed the other in equal measure, and the judge had no way of apportioning responsibility, so all three received the same sentence. Eleven years, and Donahue left a sickly young daughter threatened with life in the poorhouse."

"Little wonder Taylor thinks Donahue would be vengeful!" I paused for thought, before continuing. "So Frinton-on-Sea has been a wild goose chase?"

"Never," Holmes snapped irritably. "The process of deduction is founded on building a picture from the smallest items of evidence. There is no such thing as a negative result, or wasted time, if that process helps firm up the *true* picture."

I should have known not to even hint that Holmes may have pursued the wrong thread, let alone suggest he had been mistaken.

"Well, anyway," I huffed. "Perhaps now we can put this diversion aside and concentrate on the real reason for our visit to this fine town: the taking of some fresh sea air."

"Indeed, we shall," concurred Holmes, much to my surprise. "And then in the morning we will renew our acquaintance with the Great Eastern Railway and go to visit Mr. Albert Donahue, wherever he may reside."

I should have known Holmes would not give up his pursuit of the puzzle so readily. "How do you propose to track him down?" I asked.

Holmes paused, and indicated the façade of a building with a nod of his head. Our perambulation had taken us back up through the town to the High Street, and now we had stopped outside the post office.

I was still puzzled until Holmes explained. "I will use their telephone to place a call to Lestrade at Scotland Yard. If anyone can rapidly locate the whereabouts of Albert Donahue, it is Lestrade."

A short time later, however, the puzzle had deepened.

Holmes emerged from the post office, his features dark as only on those rare occasions when events had taken a turn unexpected even to the great man himself. I knew better than to ask immediately, for I saw on his face the look of intense cogitation that I had long ago learned never to interrupt. Instead, we walked in contemplative silence back to the Esplanade and then along to our guesthouse.

Finally, outside the front door, Holmes fixed me with narrowed eyes.

"It would appear that Taylor is mistaken in his assertion that Albert Donahue is the man to investigate," he told me. "Because Lestrade tells me Donahue is dead."

"Dead? Murdered too?" My mind raced, wondering if Thomas Taylor had been so cunning as to deceive us over *two* deaths.

"No, I don't think so, for Donahue died of a heart attack earlier this year while still detained at Her Majesty's pleasure. I don't think even Thomas Taylor could have murdered him while he was still in prison, do you?"

"Not directly, perhaps," I conceded. "But he could be orchestrating things from afar." It was not at all beyond the realms of possibility that Taylor had used contacts in the prison world to dispose of Donahue as well as his own brother.

"If one was inclined to leap to conclusions then that might be an obvious one," Holmes said. "But I prefer to gather evidence until the conclusions jump out at *me*."

Chastened, I asked, "So what next?"

"Next I propose a good dinner of locally fished seafood, and an early night, before we pay Thomas Taylor another visit in the morning. And now…" Holmes produced a clay pipe from the depths of his cloak. "I have some thinking to do, and I think this is at least a three-pipe problem."

Bright and early the following morning, after a breakfast of locally smoked kippers, Holmes and I made our way back through the town to the side street where Thomas Taylor resided.

Immediately, we were confronted by the sight of a young constable standing guard outside the villain's basement door. After introductions, Holmes asked what was amiss.

"It's the gentleman who lived here," said the constable, and immediately I noted his use of the past tense. "Died in his sleep. We've sent for a doctor, but I'd hazard we're about twelve hours too late."

Holmes muttered a most ungentlemanly curse, then gathered himself. "My friend here, Watson, is a doctor, and we both work closely with Scotland Yard. Make haste and allow us to examine the victim, for I fear all is not as innocent as it appears."

Startled, the constable stepped back, allowing us entry into that gloomy basement room.

Thomas Taylor was still in the chair where we had seen him only the day before, but his frame had slumped, and his head lolled to one side, a trail of spittle glistening on his stubbly chin and neck.

I went to him immediately, but he was cold, and rigor mortis had set in, indicating a time of death at least six hours previously, and in my estimation probably, as the constable had guessed, about twelve hours before.

"Cause of death?" Holmes asked, as he stalked around the room, no doubt searching for any evidence missed by normal eyes.

"Asphyxiation," I told him, my conclusion informed by the blueness around the victim's mouth.

"Suffocation? Smothering?"

I shook my head. "Natural causes, I'd say. He suffered chest disease, as we saw yesterday, probably obstructive pulmonary disease. There is no bruising around the nose and mouth, and the eyes are not bloodshot, as they would be as a result of smothering. There are no marks to the neck to indicate strangulation, no sign of a struggle, and no defensive injuries."

Still, Holmes paced, pausing only to root through a crate Taylor had apparently used for refuse.

"It's my fault," Holmes said, eventually. "All my fault. I should have seen!"

"Seen what?" As so often, I felt myself left far behind by the workings of my friend's brain.

"Come, before we're too late." Already Holmes was at the door, and I hurried to follow in his wake.

"Too late for what, Holmes?" Then, as Holmes ignored my question and was already striding away, I hurried to catch him. "Where are we going?" I asked.

"To catch the perpetrator!" As he passed the constable, Holmes clapped a hand on the uniformed arm, before adding, "Come with us, young man. We are in need of your services. The body can stay here—it's going nowhere—for we have a murderer to apprehend!"

The constable resisted briefly, staring wide-eyed at me for assistance. I shrugged, then nodded, indicating that there was nothing to do when Holmes became like this, other than to follow.

Together, the three of us strode rapidly back to the High Street and then headed toward the promenade.

"Think, Watson," Holmes told me, as we walked. "Tommy was a man of limited routine. What did he do every day other than sit in his basement room?"

"He walked, to take the sea air. He described it as a daily walk, to the promenade and along the beach."

"And we made that same walk yesterday. What did we see? What stood out as unusual?"

I couldn't for the life of me see where Holmes's reasoning was leading. "Bathing huts," I said. "Families disporting themselves on the beach. People strolling the promenade. Sellers of cockles, oysters, pies, ginger beer. Seagulls." In short, all the things one would expect to see in an English seaside town.

"And not one of those struck you as out of place?"

I shook my head, still floundering.

"Both Taylor brothers died of breathing difficulties," Holmes said now, taking a different tack. "Neither was suffocated, but what else can cause such symptoms?"

I refrained from pointing out that both suffered lung disease, for Holmes had clearly dismissed that explanation. I thought hard before answering. "Poison?" I ventured, after a time.

"Poison," Holmes confirmed. "That staple of the murderer's trade, throughout history. Tell me what you know of poison as a murder weapon, Watson. What cases do you recall?"

We were crossing the Esplanade now, the promenade ahead of us, and beyond it the grey expanse of the North Sea. I wracked my brains. "Socrates?" I ventured.

"Sentenced to kill himself by drinking hemlock. That doesn't count. Think more recently. Murders."

"Well there was Mary Ann Cotton..." Known in the newssheets as Britain's Mass Murderess, the poisoner of no fewer than four husbands. "And the strychnine murderer, Christiana Edmunds. And...that nurse in Oxford, what was her name?"

"The name is not what matters most," Holmes interrupted, exasperated.

"Then what is?"

"The gender," Holmes explained. "Poison is a woman's murder weapon, a tool that overcomes the otherwise unequal balance of physical strength required by any other weapon of murder. It is subtle and sinister, and far too clever."

"So the killer is a woman?"

"Albert Donahue had a daughter," Holmes told us. "A sickly child, abandoned to the poorhouse when Bertie went to gaol. Daisy Donahue grew up from the age of ten only ever knowing her father from very occasional visits to see him in prison, and she was no doubt raised with a distorted prisoner's view of justice and revenge. When her father died shortly before his release, after serving a sentence made far more severe by the betrayal of his two accomplices, she must have hatched her plan."

We had reached the point on the promenade now where vendors were setting up for the day.

"Look around you, Watson, for the killer is near."

I was lost now. The pie seller, the oyster man, the cockle seller, the purveyor of ginger beer... Each of them most evidently male, and not the daughter of Albert Donahue.

"Tommy Taylor came this way every day. A Londoner, fond of his traditional foods and refreshments. What would he buy, do you think?"

"Pie and mash?" I ventured. "Jellied eels?" I eyed the pie seller closely. Was he our man? But why had Holmes made a point of the murder being of the gentler sex?

Holmes shook his head, frustrated at my slowness of wit. "I repeat my question: what is out of place?"

I still failed to see.

Finally, Holmes chose to explain. "This town," he told me and the young constable. "It is like that lady on the train: genteel and proper, dressed above its station, aspiring to finer things. Frinton-on-Sea has no drinking establishments, and only deigns to allow vendors such as these here on the promenade and not in the town itself. Frinton-on-Sea thinks of itself as a refined place. Its shellfish of choice is the Mersea oyster."

Then, with a grand wave of the hand, he indicated the other of the two seafood sellers, before continuing. "Not the working man's cockle or whelk. Whitstable is famous for cockles and whelks, is it not? And the East End. And if you'd paid more attention at Thomas Taylor's dwelling, you would have seen the debris of his predilection for a punnet of cockles!"

I stared, as did the young constable, at the young shellfish vendor, and finally I saw through the disguise. A young man, smooth of chin, with a pageboy haircut and a high, tenor voice— and no doubt a tightly bandaged chest to disguise the more feminine features.

"Meet Daisy Donahue," Holmes said. "Daughter of Albert Donahue, and self-appointed executioner of the Taylor brothers."

There followed a brief interval while the four of us exchanged looks. Donahue was the first to move. She pushed her stall, tipping it so that the three us had to dodge back out of the way. Shellfish tumbled in a fountain around our feet, and as we moved to avoid them, she ran—for now I could see clearly that it was, indeed, a she.

What followed was almost too fast to see, and only pieced together in hindsight. I thought Holmes had fallen, skidding on the carpet of spilled shellfish, but instead, he had dropped to a low, hunter's stoop, drawn his arm back, and then hurled his cane like a spear.

The stick flew fast and low, hitting the paved ground just behind the fleeing murderess before passing directly between her feet. As her trailing foot swung forward, the cane caught between her ankles and she faltered, her upper body continuing under its own momentum even as her feet caught on the cane. She tipped forward and landed heavily, face-first on the promenade.

Holmes straightened, brushing himself down, before turning to the constable. "I assume you can handle matters from here?" he asked, before turning to me and continuing. "I believe we came here to take the air, did we not? In which case, I believe I am just about ready to do so."

With that, my friend turned and strode off along the promenade as if nothing untoward had occurred and I hurried, once again, to keep up.

The Chandelier Bid

Rose Biggin

From the private papers of Irene Adler. Undated; from its tone, possibly intended for posthumous publication. It is in that hope, in any case, that we reproduce it here.

The first time I dramatically left London I had sworn, quite fervently, that I would never return. But such resolutions, broken once, are easily again; especially when one works in the arts. The Imperial Opera of Warsaw was once more touring to London, and I found myself drawn by the promise of hearing applause in a familiar language. I was in my dressing room gossiping with a countertenor when a knock came upon the door. It was a smart knock, a series of clean raps with a cane; the knocker was either very confident or had steeled himself to be.

A man in a bowler hat and respectable grey suit, and an even more respectable moustache, stuck his head into the room.

"Pardon the intrusion," he blustered, as the countertenor stood and hastily bid me goodbye. "I've a message from an old friend and not much time."

He looked into the corridor quickly as if to check he hadn't been followed, then closed the door carefully. I wondered at his high level of caution. He removed his hat and bowed, holding the brim tightly in one hand, and coughed politely as if not sure how to begin. I gestured toward the chair the countertenor had so recently vacated.

"I shan't keep you long," he said. He walked to the chair, with a slight limp steadied by his cane. "Congratulations on a triumphant performance, by the way! Marvellous."

I nodded to receive the compliment, maintaining what I felt was a suitably dignified silence. He sat down heavily in the chair.

"You may not remember me, of course," he said. "I don't believe we really spoke..."

I smiled. "Dr. John Watson," I said. "I suppose we've never had the pleasure of a conventional acquaintance but, rest assured, I know you."

Watson breathed out heavily and rubbed his hands together as if to warm them. I always kept it warm enough in my dressing room, believe me; quick changes or no. I therefore determined that he was unsure whether to be relieved or concerned by the news that I, most certainly, did recall him. And I will confess, this is not the best of me, but I let him sit in that uncertainty for a few moments more.

"Well then, Dr. Watson. What brings you to the theatre this afternoon? As much as I'm pleased to see you're well, I'm unsure why you've chosen to renew, or even begin, an acquaintance between us now. And I'll confess I didn't take you for a matinee-goer."

"Then I'll come straight out with it, Miss Adler. My primary reason for visiting was not to watch your performance; although I would wish it known that it was a very pleasant way to spend the time, and I wish my purpose could have been solely one of cultured leisure. You're aware, of course, of my ongoing collaboration with Sherlock Holmes, you know of his detective brilliance. I know there is, there must be, a certain quality of...bad blood, between the two of you. He isn't here with me now, by the way, do rest assured about that: and I think he would be adamant against my seeking you out. Hence my concern on entering just now, for I have been trying to get away to see you in secret. I think I just about managed it. I told him I was headed to the market for tripe and onions. Researching a folk remedy for treating the gout," he added.

"Watson," I said, "I thought you were going to come straight out with it."

"Of course, my goodness; apologies. Miss Adler, I've come to ask you to pay a visit to Holmes and myself at Baker Street this very evening."

"I understand your desire to widen his social circle, but why?"

"He's in need of your eye. We're working on a case at present that's proving fiendishly tricksy to him. Earlier today I caught Holmes loudly declaring his wish for—specifically, a woman fluent in matters of artistry, if you'll pardon me—with whom to discuss an issue. By chance, I had seen your name on the playbills and knew you were only briefly scheduled to be in town, so I thought I might seize the chance. If you chose to honour myself and Holmes with your presence, he'll be able to fill you in on the nature of the mystery."

I looked up at the chandelier above my dressing room mirror and spent a moment watching the playful movement of dust around it. It could be amusing, I thought, to illuminate an issue that was confusing Sherlock Holmes, of all people. And where else, I reflected, would such an opportunity arise?

I took Watson off from the hook upon which he was dangling and told him I would call directly after the evening's performance. Or not quite directly; I said I would be late, as I was obliged to mingle backstage with some influential patrons before leaving the theatre. Which wasn't true, but created an appropriate sense of my being in demand.

❦

The lamps cast steady glows across the rain-glinted cobblestones as I left the Hansom cab at Baker Street. To my surprise, Watson himself answered my knock at 221b, and breathlessly beckoned me inside.

"Do come up," he said, as I dropped my umbrella into the stand beside the door.

We ascended the stairs, the strains of a violin growing louder as we approached. I confess a certain trepidation. I had been to the front door, of course, but only briefly; and I had never gone inside.

Watson ushered me into the drawing room, where a familiar back stood by the window, one arm moving to draw a lump of rosin across his violin bow. He spoke without turning around.

"Ah, Irene Adler. How very good of you to come." He replaced the rosin and began fiddling with the strings, retuning the violin with small plucking noises. "I'm delighted you're joining us after your performance—" *pluck* "—I'm sure the opera tour is proving is a triumph—" *pluck* "—although I hope you didn't have a difficult journey in the cab—" *pluck* "—given the traffic difficulties at present in—" a high-pitched *pluck!* "—Goodge Street."

Watson gave a cough of surprise and alarm and muttered something like "Well *really* now, Holmes," too quietly to necessitate a reply.

I took it in my stride and did not take a seat I had not been offered. "We took a detour," I said, "but I'm glad to have arrived. For my part, I'm grateful you've received me; especially given that your housekeeper is away taking the Derbyshire water cure."

He spun around to face me, and, for a moment, my gaze was locked with his.

He did not look much different from the last time. That same studious air, the utmost confidence in his shoulders. But in that moment, his eyes had the coldness of ice.

Watson coughed again, with a spluttering laugh. "Well I must say," he said, "if you're *both* going to be doing this I'll find myself completely lost at sea. Two of you at it…"

Holmes's expression relaxed into what I took to be an attempt at hospitality.

"Quite right, Watson," he said, still looking at me. "Let us all sit down and set about the mission for which we are gathered." He gestured for me to take one of the chairs beside the fire, which I did. Holmes and Watson settled down too, although not before Watson had placed several thick slabs of fruitcake onto the table.

"I hope you're enjoying your return to London, by the way," said Watson.

"Oh, very much," I said. "Less eventful, so much more enjoyable, than the last time: I'm afraid I ended up participating in a botched diamond theft at a high society ball."

A look of surprise flashed over Holmes. "So that was you! I recall reading about the caper in the papers. I thought at the time it had something of your nature about it."

(*I hadn't been acting alone then, of course. Professor Moriarty and I had led each other a very merry dance, and in more ways than one. But of this adventure I have already written.*) I picked up a piece of fruitcake before Watson ate it all.

"Let's hear your reasoning, at least," he said to Holmes through a mouthful of cake. "How did you guess about Miss Adler's journey going via Goodge Street?"

Holmes shrugged. "An arrival at this late hour must mean joining us after the performance, and there's only one theatre grand enough to house the Imperial Opera. It was little work to calculate the most likely route between there and here."

Watson turned to me. "And how the devil did you know about Mrs. Hudson?"

Holmes flung one leg over the other and tapped his long fingers impatiently upon the side of his chair. "It is very simple," he said. "Miss Adler saw the coffee stains on my right jacket-sleeve, forming the distinctive splash-pattern of a sudden burst of boiling liquid, and correctly surmised that I have been lately forced to tackle that awful stove-top pot on my own. Hideous temperamental thing," he added.

Watson turned, again, to me. "Is that so?"

"In fact, it was that postcard pinned to the wall," I said. "*Greetings from the Wholesome waters of Matlock Bath*. And it was you who let me in, Watson—although that could have been to keep my arrival secret, I suppose."

"Speaking of attempted secrecy," Watson gaped again at Holmes. "How did you know I was bringing Miss Adler here in the first place?"

"Simplicity itself!" cried Holmes. "First, I read that the Imperial Opera of Warsaw is scheduled to perform several dates in London. I adore classical music, a fact of which you're well aware, Watson, since we discuss it all the time. Or at least I rhapsodise about it, and you kindly indulge me...but suddenly, it is as if the topic is banned by the Lord Chamberlain himself. The opera is never on your lips, in fact you go out of your way to change the subject when I bring it around. I conclude there must be a reason this particular repertoire makes you nervous around me. A theory forms. I complain loudly during breakfast about the lack of a suitably artistic female accomplice for my present conundrum, and, that very afternoon, you slink off to the theatrical quarter muttering about onions. It seemed not only natural, but inevitable, that I should find myself sitting face-to-face with Irene Adler before the day was out. And here we are."

He turned to me. "Does that sound about right, Miss Adler?"

"Perhaps," I said. "By the way, now that you've mentioned it, I should point out there is coffee staining on your lapel as well as your cuffs."

Watson dropped some cake crumbs onto his plate.

"That damned pot, I ought to throw it out. Let's dispense with these pleasantries," said Holmes. His face settled into an expression of keen concentration and he laced his fingers together. "Miss Adler, you might help me to unravel a mystery of peculiar nature. It's a matter of taste; I seek to take advantage of your artistic eye. Do you know W. Bart?"

"Not personally, though I know his paintings sell very well at auction."

"We were recently visited," said Holmes, "by his former art tutor."

"Oh?" This already sounded like a suitable intrigue for me.

Holmes never touched his cake, nor even his tea, as he spoke of the visit.

"She had decided that she simply must come and see me. She has picked up many students, as you would imagine, in the wake of Bart's success.

" 'I know that I should be proud,' she said. 'My former pupil's paintings so highly sought. But I spend entire days wondering, frankly, what his collectors see in him—and I cannot for the life of me puzzle it out!'

"I asked her to clarify the nature of her confusion.

" 'His paintings, Mr. Holmes...they leave me completely perplexed. I am confounded they can be sold at all.'

" 'I suppose some *do* like his work, even if you personally can't see its value,' I had said. At this point, Miss Adler, the whole thing seemed little more than professional jealousy and certainly not any problem of mine, and Watson put in a reminder that aesthetic preference can be a thoroughly subjective business.

"The art tutor sighed and said: 'Normally I would agree with you, of course; I realise this situation is out of the ordinary, Mr. Holmes! I suffer such guilt for taking on students in the wake of Bart's success when I cannot understand how it is possible. Others agree with me about his work: my friends; fellow artists.' "

At this point, I intervened in Holmes's telling. "If Bart's work is the fashion," I pointed out, "that could be enough to make someone desire to buy one. Especially if the purchase looks to increase in value."

"True," said Holmes, "but that only defers the question, it does not answer it. Something has to have made his paintings the fashion in the first place."

And he continued the story.

" 'I was taking a student today,' the art tutor told me, 'and she spoke of Bart's new painting and had I seen it? When I said I hadn't, she showed me its image clipped from the paper. Mr. Holmes, this brought my anxiety to a head. Either through my years of study and expertise I had learned absolutely nothing, or this was a particularly unremarkable painting. I simply had to come here. I have brought a few images of his work, so you can agree for yourself.'

"Watson and I duly poured over the images, and presently, Watson said that we should agree to take on the case. So, there you have it. This could be a unique mystery with all manner of foul play to uncover, or it could be the mad ravings of an art tutor."

I replaced my piece of cake on the plate and looked for a moment at the firelight glinting off the currants. "I still don't see why you need my assistance," I said.

"I need another opinion," said Holmes. "Watson said, on looking at Bart's paintings, that the tutor is quite right about the artist's work. But in truth my difficulty begins where everyone else's seems to end. I cannot go on Watson's word alone. I need someone who has impeccable taste when it comes to the arts, and a good eye, someone with refinement—"

I noticed Watson's shoulders were slumping a little as he stood and went to the bureau.

"—to confirm this beyond question of doubt, in order to *properly* begin on this case. To be perfectly honest Miss Adler, I do not understand much of contemporary art, and when I saw the images, I could not make head nor tail of them. My question to you therefore is: *are these paintings bad?*"

Watson presented an array of documents, a collection of facsimiles of Bart's oeuvre, torn from newspapers and auction catalogues. I looked over them quickly, then took a few moments to make sure I was certain about what was being asked of me. I looked up again at Sherlock Holmes.

"I can't tell."

He shook his head.

"Not from these alone," I said, calling on all my airs of professionalism. "Works of art need to be seen as they are intended. It simply isn't helpful to draw conclusions from newspaper facsimiles. One must be in the presence of art to have any real sense of it."

Holmes leapt up and stood beside my armchair, craning his neck to look again at the pictures. "You're sure?"

"To really know would take seeing them in person, therefore I cannot yet agree with the tutor."

Holmes nodded, accepting my judgement, but at the same time he frowned a little, as if he still couldn't quite understand it.

Watson came to the rescue, saying brightly, "We do have a chance to see one in person. Tomorrow, Langford's is having a large auction of contemporary works, the centrepiece of which will be Bart's *The Scene.*"

Holmes stabbed a finger onto the pile of facsimiles. "That is *that* one," he said, squinting at it.

The following day had suddenly become much more eventful and so I rose to leave, promising that I would see them promptly at the auction to confirm my judgement of the painting. I looked forward to attending in any case. It's quite enjoyable to watch things grow steadily more expensive.

⁂

The auction house stood imposingly on the Strand and a high wind whipped the canvas banner that hung across the large entrance doors, grandly advertising the day's business. I chose to take its wind-bashed rippling as fortuitous, since it put me in mind of a curtain rising. Along the road horses stamped their feet in readiness to get going, as the cabs dispatched their passengers into the blustery street.

I arrived with plenty of time before the day's proceedings, as had most visitors, for it was an additional pleasure to wander through the exhibition hall, where the items were on final display. W. Bart's *The Scene* had pride of place at the head of the gallery and a crowd was already bunched in front of its imposing frame, looking at it in careful silence.

As I contemplated the painting, a gallery official sidled up to me in a smart overcoat with brass buttons, peering awkwardly through thick-lensed pince-nez. For a moment, I really thought I was going to be informed that the gallery was closing, or that I was about to be accused of trying to steal one of the sculptures.

"Well, what do you think of it?" said Holmes, for of course it was he.

I wanted to laugh at the familiar voice coming from such an unrecognisable visage. Really, it was a dreadful shame the two of us had never appeared on the stage.

"The art tutor is absolutely correct," I said. I looked solemnly at Holmes. "It is not a good painting. I had considered that something may have been revealed in the presence of the object itself, telling us some profound truth that the clippings could not. But this has not happened at all."

Holmes nodded curtly, listening.

"I have acquaintances across the spectrum, Mr. Holmes. Life-long experts, practiced virtuosos, keen new-money hobbyists, dedicated amateurs, critics at both the professional and dinner-party conversation level, artists and patrons of art; I even know a few who are utterly disinterested in anything to do with it. I am in no doubt that not one of them would pay anything for this."

Holmes looked again at the painting, craning through his pince-nez over the shoulders of its current audience.

"It's bad," he whispered, speaking mostly to himself.

"Unquestionably," I responded, firmly. I wanted no ambiguity on this point.

Holmes turned to me with the air of one making a final decision. "Now we have confirmed beyond doubt that the painting is bad, let us stay to watch the auction. We will learn much about these perplexing sales if we witness one."

As if in response, a great gong now shimmered out across the building. Excited conversation broke out between people as they headed toward the auction room.

"I am putting a lot of trust in you, Miss Adler," said Holmes as we walked along. "If that painting turns out to be good after all, I will not be best pleased."

We went in separately: I arrived at the auction through the main entrance, and Holmes took the staff doorway at the back and dropped off the uniform as he went.

I took a seat near the back and waited for the sale to begin. Soon Holmes joined me, no longer in disguise; he stood out instead in the dignified dark suit of his own unmistakable self. I began to hear whisperings at the sight of us together; I heard my name. It seemed the auction was already, to some, slightly scandalous.

The auctioneer sauntered into the hall when the tension of waiting had reached its highest point, a piece of timing I admired. The clerk sat efficiently behind his desk and a row of handlers in white gloves were clustered together. Lining the wall were writers from the newspapers with their notebooks, and photographers with large wooden cameras on tripods, ready to capture the event.

Holmes cast a careful eye over people taking their seats. A respectable gathering, the attendees were easily as interesting as the paintings they were seeking to buy.

Holmes spoke quietly to me.

"Once the sale begins," he said, "keep an eye on the crowd, see how they take it. We must try to deduce the *nature* of people's desire for the painting. If what you've told me is true and this painting is as bad as you say it is, we could be looking at multiple crimes, of a very shocking nature, going back many years."

"I understand," I said.

He looked at me, surprise flashing over his features. "My apologies," he said, recovering. "Usually I'm speaking with Watson, and that's not a response one usually receives from Watson."

The auctioneer announced the first piece (a portrait of some Lord or other's niece), the bids duly arrived, and we were away. Holmes and I did not speak throughout all this. He was looking about at anyone and everyone, and I settled into my seat. The reader will understand that I am not generally one to dabble in the art market myself. Huge paintings become difficult when one is on tour.

The auctioneer announced he would now take bids for W. Bart's new work, *The Scene*. Whispers broke out in the audience as the handlers brought the painting out. It looked particularly incongruous in the auction room, this space dedicated to informed value judgement in gilt edging and dark wood.

The starting price for *The Scene* was higher than for any of the other paintings, but nevertheless opening bids came quickly from the crowd.

I cast my gaze around the hall as bidding settled into a steady rhythm. The price was rising smoothly as bids passed at a clip.

Sherlock Holmes held up a long finger.

"New bid from the gentleman at the back there: £----!" said the auctioneer. People craned to look.

Holmes was quickly outbid by someone near the front. He waited a second, giving the impression of deep thought. Then he bid again, and once more was countered.

There were more whispers of my name around our seats as people recognised me from the theatre. I wondered whether I had the chance to become a *maker* of taste—even with a painting as nondescript as this one. A fun diversion, I thought, having never to my knowledge set a fine art trend, and I raised my arm into the air.

"New bid: lady in the opera gloves," proclaimed the auctioneer. "£-----!"

Holmes glanced at me.

Another bid came from a woman in the top balcony.

Holmes raised his finger once more, then I bid again. I was glad of my choice to wear opera gloves; an affectation, perhaps, during the day, but they made my bids strikingly visible and dramatic. Holmes grunted, and bid again himself.

My actions had worked; my name was whispered with a new urgency. A line of women in silk dresses and smart hats, who had not yet bid on anything, joined in now, bids passing across them in a long line. After that, more came from the balcony. Then I bid again. Then Holmes.

His face was etched with annoyance. "Miss Adler, would you please desist bidding!" he hissed. "You are throwing my experiment off."

"I'm conducting one of my own," I said. "I never knew I had such influence."

We had reached a new band of bidding increments: the price was going up by much larger amounts each time, now. The auctioneer was practically leaning over the lectern to search out new bids from the floor.

Holmes bid again. Then, I did.

Heads turned to look at us; feathers in hats bobbed. I have already said that I believe my own celebrity inspired some to commence bidding; but to this day, I like to think it was the sight of the two of us together—Holmes's apparent wish for *The Scene* as well as mine—that inspired the real excitement. For suddenly, it was as if someone had pulled the stopper from a bottle and released a wave of enthusiasm over the room. Hands shot into the air, one after another. The clerk scrambled to note the numbers of all these potential buyers.

I bid again and made a quick mental calculation. If I bought the painting now, I would certainly have to change my hotel; give up the top-floor en suite and take cheap digs in Soho until the tour moved on to Prague.

Another bid came assuredly from the balcony.

I bid again, £------. I would have to secure several more patrons to keep up expenses.

"Will you stop this, Miss Adler!" hissed Holmes, raising his finger once more.

I shot him a sweet smile as I bid again, and there was another flurry of bids around the room. I would have to give up the charitable salon performances that I so loved. And no more lobster dinners between now, I thought, and Christmas. Quite possibly next Christmas.

The auctioneer held his small wooden gavel high in the air.

"Surely there are no more bids!" he cried.

But he was wrong, for Holmes made one and then plenty more burst from the audience in its wake. The doors burst open and more journalists entered the room, summoned by their colleagues. The audience cheered, glad to be witness to this piece of art history.

I heard Holmes say quietly: "*Enough.*"

He raised his finger again, and in a clear, steady voice, declared a price.

There were gasps, and everyone in the building turned as one to stare in our direction. The auctioneer was shocked into stillness, his small hammer paused at head-height. Holmes had put in a bid that soared beyond the highest number we had reached; in truth, he had uttered a greater amount of money than I thought possible. The power of it coursed through me as if I were finally accepting a bouquet after a dozen encores.

£--------. The bid was as grand and unreachable as a chandelier glinting at the very top of the tallest ceiling.

The silence was broken by the soft puffing sound, with the bright flash, of a photograph being taken of Holmes as he performed this triumphant final bid.

Then the auctioneer brought the gavel down onto the wood with dazed finality, and the auction house descended into uproar.

Holmes rubbed his forehead with his hand.

"The good news," he said, his eyes closed, "is we can say the mystery presented to us by the art tutor is solved. The more... inconvenient news is I appear to be saddled with a painting for my troubles, and a bad one at that, and with no thanks to you, Miss Adler, for driving up the price. Watson?"

The good doctor had appeared beside us, still looking quite agape at this recent turn of events. "How can I help?" he managed, shouting over the chaos.

"Run outside and summon the first policeman you see," said Holmes. "We have the necessary information to make an arrest. And while you're out—I fear, Watson, you ought to do this first—go to the telegraph office and send a message to my brother." He sighed, then spoke with a voice of flat resignation. "I'll need to request some funds."

⁂

The auction room was much emptier now. Chairs were askew and the floor was scattered with torn-out pages from the catalogue. Before us, the painting leaned heavily against the lectern. It was now officially the most expensive piece of art Langford's had ever sold. Watson was examining it with his hands on his hips.

"Can't think where we'll put it," he said. "So, putting aside what you've *spent* today Holmes, what's the answer to the mystery? What will we tell the art tutor?"

Before Holmes could explain, we were joined by the auctioneer, his hair still plastered to his forehead with the sweat of all the excitement. Standing beside him, looking like the cat who had obtained access to an entire dairy, was a confident-looking young man in elaborately patterned crimson trousers.

"I had to tell him the news personally, and he wants to meet you," said the auctioneer. "May I present W. Bart. This is Sherlock Holmes, he's the new owner of your painting."

"Mr. Holmes, I cannot thank you enough," said the artist, bouncing along on a tide of happiness and unaware of the graveness of Holmes's countenance. "This is the utter high-point of my entire life's work, and it's all down to you." He held out his hand, but Holmes did not shake it.

"I'm glad you're here, given what I am about to say," said Holmes. He waited a moment to ensure he had our attention. Then he declared: "That you are less the artist and more the criminal!"

The auctioneer looked embarrassed at this turn of events. "Yet another surprise from you, Mr. Holmes," he said. "What on earth is your basis for such an accusation?"

Holmes ignored him and spoke directly to Bart.

"I have been...made aware," said Holmes, "that no one of taste, not even those with questionable preferences, ought really to show interest in you art."

The painter stared at Holmes. The shine in his eyes at the recent sale softened at this judgement on his work. The auctioneer did not leap in to defend it, but stared blankly at his own shoes, willing a professionally awkward moment to swiftly pass.

"I'm sure a life devoted to art is difficult. But let me tell you, sir, that nonetheless, you have acted very wrongly by pursuing the hideous practice of blackmail!"

Although I was prepared for what Holmes was going to say, I still felt a prickle at the mention of blackmail. It is a crime for which I have particular revulsion.

The painter looked somehow smaller, and less stable, as if half the air had been let out of him. "Art is my very being," he said. "And patronage is an acknowledgement of that. Years of tireless dedication and the Academy continues to refuse me. How else could I secure an endorsement in my position?"

"Of course!" cried Watson. "The painter who forces his patron's hand! The art world is made up of high society clientele, plenty of incriminating information swilling about. So the blackmail itself was secondary to an elaborate ruse to sell your canvases."

"If my theory was correct," continued Holmes, "I knew that somebody would want the painting more than anyone else. But only when the auction began did the scale of the crime become clear. One victim is bad enough. But a double blackmail! And there you sow the seeds for a thrilling auction. The Viscount of Marle (near the front, on the left) and Lady Déricourt (up in one of the top balcony boxes) treated the auction with great importance and bid with assurance. Marle revealed a tendency to fiddle with his cravat-pin, which he did with ever-increasing fervour; from changes in her stance, I saw that Déricourt needed to win the auction. Once I'd identified the victims, I decided to bid myself, to see how far they would go, confirming my hypothesis and timing my bids to gauge their reactions."

The auctioneer was looking at Bart with a face of utmost betrayal.

"What I was *not* expecting," admitted Holmes, "was that everyone else would start bidding also." He avoided my gaze. "It complicated things considerably."

"But think what I found out," I said. "It seems many would look to us, Holmes, for the question of how to decorate their drawing rooms. I certainly didn't intend to knock your concentration," I added, and Watson caught my eye and winked. We both knew that if Holmes wanted to focus, even the auction house catching on fire would not have stopped him.

"I never sought money for its own sake, you must understand," said Bart. "And if the Academy had given me a chance, I could have developed myself through more noble means."

"To make a piece of art itself both ransom note and hostage," muttered Watson. "Incredible."

"We have summoned the police," said Holmes. "They have been waiting for you."

Watson signalled off into the shadows, and a pair of constables joined our group. They stood either side of Bart, who didn't pay them much mind. Presumably, he was still thinking about how his painting had sold in a particularly thrilling manner; if the crime itself was simply a means to an end, no doubt so was being caught.

He turned to me. "Might I sketch you someday, for inclusion in a future work?"

I made do with arching an eyebrow at him.

"Not to worry."

The constables clapped their heavy hands onto his shoulders, and we watched as he was dragged from the hall. The auctioneer made some small excuse and left us.

Holmes broke the silence. "I shall write to Marle and Lady Déricourt directly," he said, "and assure them the bribe has been voided and their secrets are safe."

Then he sighed. "For now, however, Watson, let us summon a cab. I suppose we must get this thing home."

I saw no more of Holmes after that day and proceeded to continue my performances with the Imperial Opera of Warsaw. For a week or so, the headlines shouted about the hullabaloo of the auction, and the jailing of the disgraced painter; but soon that news, as all news, was replaced by something else, and in time, given my own occupations, I thought only rarely of the adventure. On my final day in London, however, I received an urgent summons.

COME AT ONCE, the telegram read. *BREAKTHROUGH*.

Naturally, my interest was caught, and I put my plans for various romantic *au revoirs* aside and visited Baker Street en route to the station, leaving my trunks in the Hansom.

When I arrived into the drawing room, I was surprised to see that W. Bart's *The Scene* had in fact been hung. It covered almost all of one wall, dominating the view as soon as one entered. Holmes was pacing to and fro in front of it. Watson was sitting in his armchair, trying to concentrate on the paper; well-worn marks in the carpet revealed that the chair had been recently rotated to an angle that faced further away from the painting.

Holmes spun around to face me.

"I have been staring at this painting since I bought it," he said. "I can tell you the company that manufactured the pigment, and the country where it was mined; I know the artist is left-handed, suffers a minor tremor when deprived of sleep, and used to own a piebald dachshund. I can identify the colourman who supplied the paint to the factory, and I know he lives near Green Park in spite of his hay fever. This painting was finished on a Wednesday and stored in an attic that contained a stack of leather-bound bibles damp with mildew, a woolen blanket in rare Highland tartan, and with a hole in the south-facing roof. Miss Adler, using my powers of deductive reasoning, I have learned everything about this painting that I can. But I cannot, after all this time, tell you *why*, as you say, as the tutor said, as even Watson here declares, the painting is bad. I am baffled, Miss Adler. I have spent an unthinkable amount of my brother's money on this. And I haven't the faintest clue why this painting is worse than the next. Perhaps it is because of…this bit? No, never mind!"

I approached Holmes and the painting. "Developing a tasteful eye," I said, "is the work of a lifetime."

"Forget it, Miss Adler! I sent that telegram to declare to you that as of today I am utterly defeated. Never mind refilling Watson's teacup now, Mrs. Hudson!" For the housekeeper had just come in and was waving cheerily to me with one hand, holding a teapot in the other. Holmes motioned for her to put the teapot down.

"Mrs. Hudson, please have this painting removed and stored in one of the darkest and remotest cupboards of the house. I cannot bear to look at it a moment longer."

"Finally!" she said. "I must say I've never liked it."

Holmes covered his face with his hands.

He was still ranting about *The Scene* as I bid goodbye to Mrs. Hudson and Watson, who were both grinning widely as they waved me off at the door. As the Hansom juddered me across the cobbles to the station, I could still hear his cries of frustration, and I knew the housekeeper and the doctor would already be halfway up a stepladder, relieving the picture-rail of its cumbersome occupant.

The Recalcitrant Rhymester

Mark Mower

In writing up the exploits of my dear friend Sherlock Holmes, I fear I may have given the reader the misleading impression that all of our adventures together were fascinating, colourful affairs, truly worthy of the consulting detective. In reality, many of the cases on which we were engaged proved to be far less interesting than he might have hoped for and barely worth recording for posterity. The narrative which follows might well have been one of those, had it not served as the last chapter in a long-running saga which had occupied Holmes for the better part of a year. For that reason alone, I believe it merits some attention.

Holmes and I had been asked to investigate a private matter at the end of September 1896. Thomas Jermyn, a West End theatre manager, had noticed for two weeks running that his takings had been significantly down on what he might have expected, given that his auditorium appeared to be filled most nights. Reluctant to turn to Scotland Yard—for fear that his somewhat seedy entertainment program might be exposed to the full scrutiny of the law—he had asked Holmes to undertake a discreet enquiry. Somewhat to my surprise, the great detective took up the case with apparent relish.

The chief suspects were a disparate group: a one-legged doorman who had worked at the theatre for over ten years, an aging showgirl who had previously worked the streets around Paddington Station, a ticket clerk who had only recently been employed, and a stage manager who had developed something of a gambling obsession. With little real effort, Holmes had easily determined that the latter had been pocketing a proportion of the theatre's takings each night to finance his poker habit. That man was Frederick Paget.

When Holmes put the matter to him that morning in the office of Thomas Jermyn, Paget did not deny that he was the thief, but began to plead with his employer to let him keep his job. He said he was desperate and owed a substantial sum of money to a major poker player who ran a popular card school in a country hotel some thirty miles northwest of London. If he could not pay off his debts, he feared for his life.

On hearing this, Holmes became strangely animated and silenced the theatre manager who had begun to say that Paget had no one to blame but himself and stood no chance of retaining his position. He addressed the thief very directly: "Is this country hotel the *King's Arms* coaching inn?"

Paget was visibly unnerved by the directness but responded clearly enough. "Yes, it's in the village of Amersham, in Buckinghamshire."

"And this poker player you owe money to…?"

"His name is Halvergate. Edwin Halvergate."

I realised immediately why Holmes had taken such an interest in what looked initially like a very trivial affair. For the past year, Halvergate had been a thorn in my colleague's side, teasing him with poetic conundrums alluding to real crimes but staying well out of reach of the law. Then, when Holmes had undermined his criminal operations by pitching him into an unwelcome turf war with the Italian families of the London underworld, Halvergate had been more explicit in his communiqués. Writing to the detective in early September, he said simply: "I will write up your obituary in sonnet form." Since that time, there had been one clumsy attempt on Holmes's life and a botched break-in at 221B.

Holmes said nothing of this to the two men, but did take Thomas Jermyn to one side, urging him to continue to retain the services of his stage manager for at least a week. Beyond that, he said the matter of the gambling debt would be resolved and the theatre manager could then decide for himself whether he still wished to dismiss Paget. With some reluctance, Jermyn consented, telling the stage manager that he was on his final warning and was not to do any more gambling.

In a cab travelling back to Baker Street, Holmes explained his reasons for looking into the theft at the theatre. "I have known for some time that Paget has been a regular at the gaming table of Halvergate. The Baker Street Irregulars have done a thorough job of watching all of the comings and goings at the coaching inn in recent months. What I could not be sure of, was whether the fellow was a trusted criminal associate or just another hoodwinked poker player. Our investigations at the theatre have proved him to be the latter, and the invitation to look into the matter could not have come at a better time."

"But I don't understand why Halvergate has suddenly placed himself at the centre of a gaming operation so far from town. It all seems a bit parochial. You told me earlier this year that he was the head of a powerful criminal gang operating out of Seven Dials, with aspirations to expand their activities to other cities across England."

"All true. But our little intervention in the Faccini murder case has created considerable problems for this one-time sidekick to Professor Moriarty. In placating the Italian families, he has had to relocate from London and pay over substantial sums of money. In short, they have bled him dry, and he is now attempting to replenish the gang's empty coffers before reasserting his authority within the capital's criminal fraternity. That I am the architect of his downfall has not gone unnoticed. My plan is to strike again while the man is temporarily weakened and to end his illicit activities once and for all."

I was not sure whether this was brave or foolhardy on Holmes's part but had to trust his judgement. As we pulled up to the pavement outside 221B, I asked, "What's the plan from here?"

"I have some immediate matters to attend to, but suggest we then dress for the evening and take the Metropolitan Railway out to Amersham. I favour a few hands of poker in a country inn. What say you, Watson?"

The *King's Arms* proved to be a sizeable hostelry in the centre of the old village of Amersham, just over a mile from the railway station. We arrived a little after seven-thirty to see an expensive private carriage draw up at the well-lit entrance. It was clear from the crest and monogram on the door of the four-wheeler that the establishment was attracting a few well-heeled patrons.

Holmes stepped forward as the coachman's assistant opened the door. A tall elegant man in a top hat stepped down from the carriage. He had a long angular face and deep-set hazel eyes framed beneath a dark brow. A large black overcoat with a thick astrakhan collar covered most of his body down to the ankles. And on his feet, he wore a pair of thin-soled elastic-sided boots. Seeing my colleague, his face lit up. "Mister Holmes! What a pleasure indeed. Are you to join us at the card table?"

"That is my intention, Lord Cranhurst. I am something of an infrequent gambler but cannot resist a hand or two every now and then." He turned and beckoned toward me. "I'm not sure whether you have met my close friend, Dr. Watson?"

Cranhurst moved toward me and extended a gloved hand. "I have not, but am delighted to make your acquaintance, Doctor. I have read so many of your excellent tales. Holmes and I go back some way—in fact, he once helped me to resolve a particularly sensitive criminal matter. So you might say we share an interest in sleuthing."

I exchanged some pleasantries so as not to appear discourteous but wondered at the wisdom of talking so openly given our mission. If Holmes had hoped to arrive incognito and to remain inconspicuous, his plans looked to be scuppered. Standing on either side of the entrance were two broad-shouldered doormen, each dressed in smartly tailored white tunics and neatly pressed black trousers. A look passed between them before the smaller of the two turned and headed off into the hostelry. The second greeted us with a polite, "Good evening, Gentlemen," while holding the door open to allow the three of us to enter. From there, we were ushered toward a small side room where we were able to deposit our coats, hats, gloves, and sticks.

What followed during the course of the next few minutes can only be described as farcical. It was quite clear from Halvergate's reaction that the would-be criminal mastermind was completely flummoxed by our appearance.

During our rail journey, Holmes had indicated that apart from a handful of bar staff employed purely to serve drinks, Halvergate had retained only six close associates as part of his criminal enterprise. We were shepherded into a large dining room at the rear of the inn, at the centre of which sat a sizeable oval table bedecked with all of the paraphernalia required for the poker game. Halvergate was already positioned at one end of the table, away to our left. He smiled uneasily as we entered and nodded for the broad-shouldered doorman—who had no doubt alerted him to our arrival—to return to his colleague outside. A quick reconnaissance showed that there were a further four well-dressed and extremely muscular men positioned around the room—the remainder of Halvergate's foot soldiers.

The man himself was somewhat shorter than I had expected, perhaps five feet, six inches in height, slender in build, and gaunt in the face. His grey eyes were darkly ringed, and his head topped with a heavily oiled crown of thin and silvering hair. I put his age at close to fifty years and observed that he had a slight tremor in his right hand, which seemed only to intensify the more he chose to glance across at Holmes.

Halvergate greeted Lord Cranhurst in an effusive tone and began to introduce him to the three other men who were already seated at the table. In summary, these were a merchant banker from Surrey, a stockbroker newly arrived from Chicago, and a self-made colliery owner who ordinarily resided in Nottinghamshire. Holmes and I received a less demonstrative welcome but were nevertheless addressed cordially and offered a seat at the gaming table. I declined the offer, preferring, instead, to be seated in a far corner of the room close to a serving hatch connected to the main bar. This meant that the poker school was now comprised of six men.

We were offered complimentary drinks, and I readily accepted a small glass of single malt whisky, more to steady my nerves than any genuine desire for refreshment. Holmes, I noted, asked only for an ashtray, so that he might smoke one of the small cheroots he pulled from a silver case in his side pocket. One of the well-tailored associates slid the desired item onto the table beside him. As he did so, I saw that his right forearm was exposed sufficiently so as to reveal a small tattoo—the wasp symbol under which Halvergate's men operated. The man then returned to a standing position against the wall opposite me.

With the introductions completed, Halvergate addressed the players around the table, outlining the house rules for the poker game. One or two queries were answered quickly, before another of the associates took his place at the end of the table opposite Halvergate and assumed the role of dealer. Each player then declared how much he would like to draw down in poker chips before the game commenced.

It is not my intention to provide you with a blow by blow account of the scrimmage which followed, but, after a period of some three hours, it was quite clear who the winners and losers were. For all of their supposed professional expertise, the banker and stockbroker had sustained the heaviest losses—by my crude reckoning, somewhere close to forty pounds apiece. The colliery owner was out of pocket by around half of that amount. Lord Cranhurst had played cautiously and opportunistically so as to minimise his losses, which I guessed to be about five pounds. For his part, Holmes looked to be up by some seven pounds, the neat piles of poker chips in front of him having grown steadily as hand after hand was played out.

By far, the clearest winner was Halvergate, whose composure had not changed throughout the game. There was no hint of conceit as he announced quietly that it had been an honourable and well-played game, which had, inevitably, left some "a little out of pocket."

I was surprised that the remark did not elicit any negative responses from the men now rising from the table, seemingly content to hide their disappointments and to disappear quietly into the night. In fact, it was Holmes who, while remaining seated, turned to Halvergate and announced curtly, "I cannot agree that this has been an 'honourable' game, Sir. 'Well-played' on your part, certainly, but not within the realms of any acceptable gaming conduct. I put it to you, that you are a cheat, and have deceived these good men as you have the many others who have passed through this illicit gaming establishment in recent months."

Even by Holmes's standards, this was a bold and provocative move. Halvergate's four associates looked primed and ready for action before their leader raised a hand, smiled enigmatically, and asked that all but my colleague and I be accompanied outside to the carriages awaiting their departure. This was achieved with no objections from the banker, stockbroker, and colliery owner. Only Lord Cranhurst opted to remain with us, stating that he wished to hear why Holmes believed the game to have been rigged.

It was a reflection of Halvergate's hubris that he now seemed prepared to act despite the obvious presence of Cranhurst. With two of his associates seeing to the departure of the other players, he directed the remaining men to search Holmes for any hidden weapons. Having roughed him up with no obvious result, they turned to me. My stubborn refusal to stand up and be patted down brought a sudden and painful punch to the head. Temporarily dazed, I was then held by the lapels of my jacket, with my head slumped forward, until my assailants were sure that I had nothing secreted about me. I was then flung back down into my chair.

Against his protestations, the two men then lurched toward Lord Cranhurst and removed him bodily from the room. For some moments afterwards, there was the sound of a considerable scuffle outside. I imagined that the peer had continued to resist their attempts to eject him from the premises. On his own, Halvergate then sought to gain the upper hand, deftly removing a small pistol from the inside of his tweed jacket and pointing it at Holmes's head.

"You've been a thorn in my side for some considerable time now, Mr. Holmes. How ironic that it should come to this. You couldn't have made it easier for me to be rid of you, along with your lap dog here..." He cast me a glance, his eyes now burning with hatred and his gun hand shaking almost uncontrollably. "I'll finally get to finish what my former mentor was unable to achieve!"

Holmes rounded on him without any apparent fear. "You're no match for Professor Moriarty. Not even a close second fiddle. Despite the animosity between us, I relished the mental stimulation I had in battling with the man. In comparison, you are nothing but a petty criminal and an obsessive narcissist." He shouted suddenly: "Go ahead, use that single shot in your pistol. Then take your chances with Dr. Watson!"

I realised then that the raised voice was but a signal. The door was flung open, and in raced a posse of uniformed police constables led by a red-faced inspector. Close behind them was a concerned-looking Lord Cranhurst. Halvergate was genuinely dumbfounded by the commotion. It was only when one of the constables grabbed his right forearm and began to wrestle the pistol from his grip that he seemed able to rationalise what had just occurred.

"I might have known that you'd bring your Scotland Yard chums with you, Holmes! Couldn't fight me on your own, eh?"

Holmes flashed him a mischievous grin. "I'd save the sarcasm, Halvergate. Inspector Hopkins here is indeed from the Metropolitan Force, but the other officers are from the Buckinghamshire Constabulary. Including Sergeant McClean, who was masquerading as Lord Cranhurst. I imagine that he has already arranged for your criminal associates to be hand-cuffed and taken into custody."

"I'm not interested in your charades," exclaimed Halvergate. "And I think you'll have trouble securing any sort of conviction for anything I've done here tonight. I'll argue that I drew that gun in self-defence. If you didn't already know, I have a very good solicitor that I keep on a particularly expensive retainer."

It was at this point that two more police constables entered the room, one carrying a stack of files and ledger books, the other in possession of some heavy looking cash boxes. Inspector Hopkins pointed for the items to be placed on the oval table.

Holmes seemed to be relishing the drama. "Oh, don't think for one moment that these officers are interested in your low-level poker scams. They have no intention of putting you before a jury to explain how you have been counting cards and using mirrors, a marked deck and coded signals from your henchmen, to dupe the hundreds of card players who have sat at this table. No, their interest is in something more fundamental. I think they will even be prepared to overlook the display with the pistol. Perhaps you could explain, Inspector Hopkins?"

Stanley Hopkins stepped forward keenly and looked Halvergate up and down. "Finally, we meet on my terms. Scotland Yard has spent months trying to find a way to reel you in. But I knew that if I planned any sort of official raid it would be destined to fail as you have some very highly placed informants within our ranks. And that costly solicitor of yours would intervene to scupper our investigations. But Mr. Holmes devised a very neat strategy. He suggested that we contact our colleagues in the Buckinghamshire Force who have responsibility for this part of the country. Sergeant McClean was most obliging and arranged for a dozen of his finest officers to accompany me here tonight. He even offered to go under cover, to ensure that no harm came to Mr. Holmes and Dr. Watson. They, of course, were placing themselves in the lion's den, given your recent threats. But Mr. Holmes reasoned that this bold approach would keep you and the bulk of your associates in this room while we went exploring…"

Halvergate snorted unexpectedly. "How very astute—and I'm touched that you've gone to so much trouble. But I fear that it will lead you nowhere. Search this building all you like. You'll find no stolen goods, no secret cache of weapons, nothing, in fact, which will point to any underworld activity. You've had a wasted journey."

"Not in the least," replied Hopkins. "Mr. Holmes made it quite clear that we would be unlikely to find anything that would point to your usual shady dealings. You were tutored by Professor Moriarty, after all. No, what we were looking for resides in the ledger books and cash boxes that now sit on that table. In your desperate quest to raise money to maintain some sort of toehold in the metropolis, Mr. Holmes reasoned that you were likely to be engaged in all sorts of fraud, tax evasion, and false accounting. And a quick look at those files and books earlier suggests that he was absolutely right."

It was Holmes who now spoke: "I suspect you have overlooked just how seriously Her Majesty's Treasury is likely to view your financial indiscretions. But I'm certain that a long prison sentence will be the most likely outcome—as well as the seizure of all your assets. You know what our marvellous London prisons are like, Mr. Halvergate, particularly when you have no money to protect yourself. Still, a cultured man like you can probably make a few friends. Perhaps you can read them a few of your published poems..."

Halvergate launched himself at Holmes, escaping the clutches of the constables on either side of him. He took a long and energetic swing at the head of my colleague, who reacted instinctively by parrying the blow with his right fist and following up with his left. The punch was enough to floor the card sharp, whose legs crumpled beneath him.

It took the best part of an hour for the police officers to finally clear the inn and ensure that they had not overlooked any evidence which might further incriminate Halvergate. The man himself was unceremoniously thrown to the floor of the police van which arrived to take the gang into custody.

With all of the constables gone, the four of us sat in the main tap room. Inspector Hopkins helped himself to a bottle of brandy and some glasses from the bar and passed them around to McClean, Holmes, and myself. He was fulsome in his praise for what we had all done in securing the gang's arrest.

"Do you think that will be the end of the gang?" asked McClean.

"Almost certainly," replied Holmes. "Halvergate will not come back from this and his men are all marked—those wasp tattoos will betray their allegiance. No rival gang will want to touch them given the ripples that Halvergate has created in the London underworld. The bigger question is who might now step forward to fill the void they will leave?"

Inspector Hopkins took a further nip from his brandy glass and smiled broadly. "All true, but that is a challenge for another day, Mr. Holmes. Let us just savour the moment. But I will say that you gave me something of a fright this evening. How did you know that Halvergate wouldn't pull that trigger at the first opportunity?"

A playful grin passed across my colleague's face. "In truth, I didn't. But as I said earlier to our bogus Lord Cranhurst, I am something of an infrequent gambler."

Sergeant McClean laughed heartily and offered his hand to me. I shook it and looked at him quizzically.

"Let's not forget Dr. Watson's part in all of this. He played a blinder himself. There aren't many men who'd take a beating for a comrade. Halvergate might easily have chosen to shoot him instead."

"Indeed," concurred Holmes. "Let's drink to Watson."

It was many months before Edwin Halvergate was finally to appear before a judge and jury charged with multiples counts of fraud and false accounting. Despite the expensive retainer, his legal adviser could do little but try to minimise the sentence which his client was likely to receive. In the event, his legal shenanigans proved unnecessary. On the evening before the judge was due to pronounce sentence, the recalcitrant rhymester was found dead in his prison cell. With a ripped sheet taken from the bed, he had hanged himself from one of the bars covering the small window of the cell.

There was one further postscript to the story. On the Wednesday following Halvergate's death, Holmes received an unexpected letter. It contained a single sheet of foolscap bearing the letterhead of Newgate Prison. On it was written in pencil a short haiku verse. It read:

> "Edwin hoped to win.
> Holmes—he was the better man.
> No more games to play."

What the Dickens!

Rhys Hughes

S herlock Holmes was engaged in silent contemplation of a clock on the mantelpiece when his door opened and the visitor he had been expecting entered. The new arrival was a gentleman in his late fifties, his eyes dull with sickness and perhaps regret, and Holmes nodded him toward a vacant chair. Slumping into it with gratitude, the man mopped his brow with a black handkerchief.

"Take your time, Mr. Boz," Holmes said affably, then he leaned closer to study the face of his visitor in detail. "I thought so," he added, then his conventional expression returned, and he was polite but rational again.

"I am not a well man, nor have I been for many months," said Mr. Boz. He shook with a sudden fit, yet the timbre of his voice was deep and compelling, as if he was a fellow familiar with the techniques of theatrical projection. "Overwork is to blame in part. But none of that is very important now."

There was a lengthy pause and the ticking of the mantelpiece clock seemed to be ten times louder than it ought to be. It was evident that the visitor felt uncomfortable to the point where he might not be forthcoming at all. Holmes made a rapid decision, turning to Watson with an airy wave of a hand.

"Be so good as to fetch Mr. Boz a stiff drink, would you?"

"Certainly Holmes. And for yourself?"

"Oh, I think I'll have an absinthe. But not mixed with water. Diluted with curaçao in the ratio of two to seven. And you, Mr. Boz?"

"Well, I don't know. Possibly just a glass of..."

"A Carnaby fudge for our guest."

Watson was baffled. He had been pacing the room while Holmes was sitting, both of them awaiting the arrival of the visitor who had earlier cabled his intention to visit the rooms on Baker Street as soon as darkness descended on the city. The tone of the message was urgent, but something in the prose style had given Holmes a strange idea and now he saw that his instincts had been right. But Watson had to be removed from the scene, in the most tactful manner.

"There's no absinthe or curaçao in the house, Holmes, and I don't even know what a Carnaby fudge is! This is most irregular."

"Quite so, Watson," concurred Holmes, "but it does one good to alter the habits of a lifetime once in a while. If there is no absinthe or curaçao on the premises, would it not be deemed an inestimable service if you could be so good as to go out and obtain them? Certainly, I would be very grateful."

Watson grumbled as he shrugged himself into his coat.

"I have no idea where to procure liquors of that sort. And I still don't know what a Carnaby fudge might be. I'm astonished."

"Good man. A Carnaby fudge is a cocktail that consists of vermouth, rum, brandy, tequila, grappa, pálinka, vodka, and port wine, with a piece of fudge floating in it. The tradition is to drink it while it is flaming, but I believe we can dispense with the quaint aspects of the beverage's consumption."

Watson huffed and puffed and said, "It may take me an hour or more to secure all the spirits on that list. I might have to go as far as Whitechapel or Limehouse, and it's a cold night tonight, even with a scarf."

"You are a noble friend indeed," and Holmes dismissed him with a brief salute. It was only when he heard the front door close, and he was certain Watson had left, that he turned his full attention on his visitor. His penetrating eyes bore deeply into sickly orbs and remained fixed there until his visitor could stand no more and looked away. Then Holmes lifted his pipe to his lips.

"You died eighteen, or was it nineteen, years ago. And yet here you are, not a day older than when you were buried. This is most curious, Mr. Boz. But allow me to drop that rather clumsy pseudonym and address you by your real name. My first instinct is to accuse you of being an impostor, but something is holding me back. There is much more to the story than meets the eye."

"I am at the end of my tether, Mr. Holmes."

"Indeed, you are. But how is that tether longer than it should be? This is the point I am making. Many peculiar people have come into my rooms, and some of them were unexpected in the extreme, but you!"

"I must offer my apologies if I am an inconvenience."

Holmes chuckled. "Oh, you are not that, not that at all. You are an enigma, and it's generally the case that enigmas are illusions, mere chimeras, shimmering mirages on the horizon of the stressed imagination."

"I wish I were a mirage, a fata morgana, I assure you."

"Charles Dickens," said Holmes.

"Yes," said the visitor.

"Your novels and other writings amused me when I was younger and might even amuse me now were I to permit myself to peruse them at my leisure. I recall that the Megalosaurus in the opening paragraph of *Bleak House* was incorrectly described, yet it remains the very first allusion to dinosaurs in literature, so I suppose we must make allowances. As for that Scrooge fellow..."

"Mr. Holmes, I have no wish to impose upon your time, but time itself in fact is an issue here, time and its nature, its vortex."

"Ah, yes. Time," said Holmes and he turned his gaze yet again at the clock on the mantelpiece. "What is it? Time is merely that which stops everything happening all at once. But we are drifting off the point. I can suppose several hypotheses for how you have managed to continue existing. Number one, that you froze yourself in ice or in some other preservative substance and have only just thawed out. Number two, that you are in fact a copy of the original and not the original itself, the product of some insane surgical experiment. Number three..."

"That's the correct one."

"But I haven't elucidated it yet."

"No matter. I am good at anticipating plots. Number three is time travel, isn't it? I thought so, and it's the truthful answer."

Holmes nodded. "I see. Remarkable! The theory has been described in terms of an advanced geometry, but no practical method has ever been devised or even suggested for traversing time as one does space."

"I stumbled on a method," replied Dickens.

"Tell me," said Holmes.

"You are doubtless aware of the bric-a-brac shop that forms the main locale of my novel *The Old Curiosity Shop*? Did you ever suspect that it was based on a real shop, one found at that time in Seven Dials near Covent Garden? I occasionally went inside and browsed. Most of the items on offer were frumps and fripperies, but once I found a very curious object and decided to purchase it. A dagger of unknown provenance, a black blade inscribed with mystic runes based on the Arabic script. It was something from the realms of oriental fairy tales."

"Are you in current possession of this weapon?"

Dickens reached down to his ankle. Strapped to his leg was a sheath containing a nightmarish knife. He drew it and passed it to Holmes, handle first. Holmes took the monstrosity and examined it. His nostrils quivered and then his eyebrows elevated. It was some long moments before he spoke.

"It must have something to do with Abdul Alhazred."

"I don't know the gentleman."

"A dread sorcerer of long ago. That is not so important. I can at least be certain that it was forged in order to perform occult rituals. The curve of the blade is very slight. When the hilt is aligned with true north, the tip of the blade points at the desert city of Zerzura, lost for millennia. The hilt is carved into the likeness of a cosmic ghoul. You know what ordinary ghouls are?"

"Yes, they wear dresses and arrange flowers."

"A ghoul, not a girl. An ordinary ghoul is a consumer of the dead. A cosmic ghoul is an eater of dead stars. It floats in the endless void, silently gibbering. It drools as it gibbers, and the drool is sticky and putrid in the void. Look at how the mystic runes of the knife catch the light. They catch it like a fat boy fielding in cricket. First a fumble and then they drop it. And it spills like weird ichor around the blade itself. I wouldn't like to meet this thing on a dark night."

And Holmes sat back in his chair with a superior smile.

Dickens became very agitated.

Holmes calmed him simply by raising his hand. "Do you know why he was called Abdul Alhazred? It's not his real name."

Dickens shook his head.

"Because," said Holmes, and he was plainly enjoying himself, "he had read all he needed to and all he could. He was Abdul *All-Has-Read* and no text, however arcane, ever remained outside his purview."

"I see." Dickens was confused, a little worried too, but he felt unable to challenge Holmes in any meaningful manner.

"One wonders," continued Holmes, "if he really had read everything. Had he read your *Pickwick Papers*, for example?"

"Well... I don't... I mean, if he was from the ancient days, how could he? My book was written in the 1830s... But he..."

Holmes nodded. "A discrepancy of more than a millennium. The reader came before the book. How is that possible? Time travel, my dear Dickens. Now tell me what you did with the dagger after you bought it?"

"For many years, I did nothing with it, or almost nothing. I might remove it from the drawer in my desk where I kept it to open a letter or to sharpen a pencil, but only when I was feeling a trifle whimsical."

"A trifle whimsical? Your phrasing reminds me of a case unknown to Watson, in which I was driven to the extremity of groping inside a big sherry trifle for a skeleton key that had been deposited there. But this is tangential to the present business before us. Pray continue with your revelations."

And Holmes licked the index finger of his right hand, as if traces of the felonious trifle still adhered to the joints of the digit. Dickens moped his brow again, cleared his throat and allowed another shudder to pass right through him. His teeth chattered; the hairs of his beard bristled. Then he said:

"Recently, as I have grown older and more dour, I began writing a new novel, one quite unlike any of my previous works. *The Mystery of Edwin Drood* was going to be about a murder and the solving of it."

"You finally decided to try your hand at crime fiction."

"Why not? I am flexible."

"Certainly, you are. As I have already stated, I was a devotee of your work. I know about *Edwin Drood* and how it was only half completed before your death. Even now, the speculation about how you intended to complete it is considerable. I am interested to learn the ending from your own lips."

Dickens folded his black handkerchief, sighed and said, "That's the real source of the trouble I'm currently in. The ending!"

"Carry on," prompted Holmes.

"I said earlier that I was good at anticipating plots. That was very true when I was a young man, and for most of my career, but these days the gift seems to be deserting me. Yes, I did know you were thinking about time travel before you mentioned it, but that's one of the rare exceptions to the general trend. I fear I am losing my talent, Mr. Holmes. I found the writing of *Edwin Drood* exceedingly difficult. I realised I had no idea of what was going to occur next."

"Some authors have used that to their advantage."

"But not me! For the first time in my life, I was making it all up as I went along. I became anxious. What if I couldn't complete the story properly? I had my readers to consider. I had already been paid an advance for the novel. Worry made matters even worse. I was sick. In the book, Edwin Drood goes missing. Has he been murdered? If so, how and by whom? The reader's suspicions are drawn to his uncle, John Jaspers, a dissolute opium addict. But the truth is..."

"That you didn't really know yourself," said Holmes.

"Exactly! I had *no idea* at all."

"And you became desperate. You became demented."

"A gibbering ruin of a man."

"What did you do?"

"One morning, in despair, I stood up from my desk and uttered aloud a wish. My eyes were shut tight. I wished that the book was already finished and that I could read the ending and steal it for my own use."

"Self-plagiarism taken to extremes," said Holmes.

"I was angry. I was miserable."

"And you expressed your feelings in what manner?"

"I opened my drawer and fumbled in it for the knife. My eyes were still closed. I felt I couldn't open them without destroying the spell. My fingers closed on the hilt of the blade and I lifted it up. Then I began waving it around, making weird patterns in the air with it. I slashed and lunged."

"You had a notion that Edwin Drood might have been knifed to death by Jaspers? It sometimes helps to act scenes out."

Dickens nodded. "But when I opened my eyes, I saw..."

Holmes leaned forward eagerly.

"...something odd," continued Dickens, in a very low voice.

"An unnatural phenomenon?"

"Yes! A rent in the fabric of reality. I saw I had cut a gash in space and that I was peering through it into another world. The dagger had magically cut open one plane of existence to reveal another. The landscape beyond the hole tempted me onwards. I climbed through the rip and stumbled into this new world. When I looked back, I saw the edges of the wound heal themselves up."

"You passed from your own age into the future," said Holmes.

"That's what I soon gathered."

"Into *my* present. Into the year 1888."

"Yes. And I was still holding the dagger. I concealed it by strapping it to my leg, because it came with a sheath for that purpose. Then I went exploring. London has changed in eighteen years, but I knew exactly where I was. I was fortunate enough to have a handful of gold sovereigns in my waistcoat pocket. I bought a newspaper and saw the date, and that's how I knew my wish had been granted. I went into the nearest bookshop and bought a copy of *The Mystery of Edwin Drood*. I hurried to the nearest park and sat on a bench to read it."

"You were disappointed to discover no ending?"

"I was shocked. It meant that..."

"You died before finishing the writing of the book."

"Indeed. The novel was only half done. This meant I was going to die soon. I was too ill to continue for much longer."

Holmes nodded. He sat back in his chair and crossed one leg over the other. For a moment, he wondered exactly how much of London Watson had traversed. Perhaps he was already buying bottles from a seedy proprietor in the East End. But Holmes kept his gaze on the man before him, the magisterial writer who was a national treasure in his own lifetime. "Continue," he said.

Dickens did so. "I wanted to get home, to put my business affairs in order before I expired. Time was running out. I no longer cared about finishing the novel. If it was fated to be left incomplete, why should I attempt to resist that? I just wanted to return to the year 1870 and my familiar environment. I was also scared that someone might recognise me, for that would cause all manner of problems. I would surely be called an impostor, or worse: a man who had faked his own death. My reputation might be compromised. I simply *had* to return."

"You discovered that time travel into the future is a lot easier than time travel into the past? Yes, of course. The paradoxes."

"I assumed that I merely had to repeat my actions with the knife but in reverse. If I made the same sequence of cuts and thrusts with my eyes closed, then it follows that another rent would open up in reality, one that led back to my own age. I would enter the gap and find myself back in my study."

"Tell me," said Holmes, very coolly, uncrossing his legs, "did you make your first attempt at returning on the last day of August?"

"Yes, yes I did. How do you know?"

"You closed your eyes and waved the mystic dagger about?"

"I waited until night to do so."

"Because there was less chance of being seen?"

"I didn't want to be mistaken for a lunatic. I found a quiet street and at about three thirty in the morning, I performed the ritual. There was a strange noise as I did so, but I kept my eyes shut tight. I was convinced that if I looked, the magic would fail. I stopped at last from exhaustion and opened my eyes. But no hole in reality had opened up. What confronted me instead was a dead woman."

"Mary Ann Nichols," said Holmes with a grim smile.

"You know her name!"

"An unlucky 'lady of the night' who happened to be in the area at the same time as you. She saw you, but you didn't see her. You had your eyes closed. She approached in order to enquire whether you were interested in 'business.' But at that very moment, you began slashing and thrusting with the blade. The strange noise you heard was the music of her death, two slashes across the throat, a jagged wound in the abdomen and other incisions, all inflicted *accidentally*."

Dickens was in a rush to pull out his folded handkerchief and wipe his brow again, and he was suddenly racked with sobs.

"I never had any intention to be a murderer, I swear! All I wanted to do was travel back in time. When I saw what had happened, I became even more eager to return to my rightful era. I waited a week because I was upset and the exertion had drained me, then I tried again. I chose not only a quiet street but the backyard of a random house where I was even less likely to be disturbed. I closed my eyes, drew my knife, and the thrusts and slashes I made were as forceful as I could manage. They went in reverse direction to those I had made in my study."

"But again, they failed."

Dickens nodded. "I opened my eyes and saw..."

"Annie Chapman," said Holmes.

"You know her name too? I swear that her killing was accidental. The same thing had happened again. She approached me at the wrong moment. The truth is that I am far too infirm to be interested in what she was offering. The strange noises I heard as I waved the knife about, I attributed to the tearing of the fabric of reality. But alas, the truth is that flesh was being ripped."

"Elizabeth Stride was next, at the end of September. Then Catherine Eddowes on the same night. You were becoming impatient. But when your second attempt failed that time, you didn't try again until November 9. You were demoralised, repelled by yourself. That is why your fifth and final attempt was so frenzied. Poor Mary Jane Kelly just happened to occupy the 'vacant' house you blundered your way into. After opening your eyes and beholding your appalling work on that occasion, you vowed never again to attempt the reverse ritual."

"Never," confirmed Dickens.

"You had to find another way. You were even tempted to discard the dagger in the Thames. But it came to your attention that there was a man by the name of Sherlock Holmes with rooms in Baker Street who had a mind of such reasoning power that he was able to solve very difficult conundrums. You decided to make an appointment with him and come clean. And here you are."

"I can see you merit your high reputation," said Dickens.

"One is obliged to do one's best."

"And as for myself..."

"You are Jack the Ripper," said Holmes.

Dickens lowered his head. He was devastated to hear the blunt accusation. "I read newspapers after the murders, of course. I was appalled as anyone else. Can you help me? Without involving the police, I mean."

"I believe that I can."

"You will return me to my own decade?"

"That is impossible, I fear. Time travel into the past is unfeasible. The dagger will cut a hole in reality in only one direction."

"What a terrible waste!"

"I know the ending of *Edwin Drood*," said Holmes.

"Really? But how..."

"There are enough clues in the existing text for me to deduce what will follow. It doesn't matter that you didn't know *consciously* where the plot was heading because your subconscious mind knew everything. When I read the opening chapters, I already had the answer to the method of the murder."

"What is that solution?"

"The uncle did it, of course. With the help of an orangutan he hired from a Maltese sailor fresh from Malaya who kept the beast as a pet. The uncle gave his razor to the orangutan. The great ape cut

Edwin's throat, egged on by the uncle, and then stuffed the corpse up a chimney, where it was eventually discovered by a chimney sweep many months later. The sailor was arrested for aiding and abetting a murderer. The orangutan was acquitted."

"Brilliant," snapped Dickens.

"Not as original as you might suppose. Nonetheless a diversion from your usual fare. But this is all theoretical only. You will never return to write that ending. It is too late now. The past can't be changed."

"What do you propose to do with me, Mr. Holmes?"

"You can't remain in this age. For one thing, less than two decades have passed since you died, and it is probable you will be recognised sooner or later. For another thing, you might be charged with the crimes of Jack the Ripper. It is essential to get you out of here. As you can't be sent back in time, my suggestion is that we send you further ahead, into the middle of the next century. You will be safer there. But I feel it might also be a good idea for you to atone for your crimes. You have killed women, Mr. Dickens, and that is a strain on your life."

"How can I possibly redeem myself now? I am damned."

"Become a policeman."

"Are you serious?"

"Deadly serious. In that future age, the century after this one, you will apply for a job as a policeman. If you get it, you must be a kindly example of the profession, and always helpful, polite, and considerate. You have a lot to atone for, Mr. Dickens and it isn't feasible for you to pay off all the moral debt. But you can surely make a start. It is the only way out of your predicament."

Dickens inclined his head.

They heard the front door open. Holmes said, "Watson is back already. Our words must be more guarded. I suggest that you shave before embarking on the next stage of your life. You may use my washstand."

Watson came in, his face red, his chest wheezing.

"I have the bottles, Holmes!"

"Well done, Watson. Did you acquire the fudge too?"

"Yes, in this paper bag."

Holmes nodded at Dickens. "Mr. Boz here is just about to shave. While he does so you may prepare the drinks."

Dickens said, "Where is your washstand?"

"Within that closet."

"May I borrow your razor too?"

Holmes shook his head. "No need, Mr. Boz. The blade you carry is sharp enough. I recommend broad strokes to remove your whiskers. Move the dagger in a particular pattern to achieve best results."

Dickens understood. He opened the door of the tall closet, stepped inside, closed it behind him. Watson arched his eyebrows. He was mixing the two drinks in glasses, but his attention was on the closet. Holmes was smiling to himself. The closet began to rock, as if the man inside it was lurching from side to side. Watson passed the glass containing absinthe and curaçao to Holmes.

He stood with the other drink, the Carnaby fudge, in his hand, waiting for the man in the closet to emerge. The beverage was a sickly and peculiar colour and the lump of fudge that floated in it rose and fell like a small drowned rodent. Holmes sipped from his own glass and pulled a face.

"Really, Watson, that is most disgusting."

"It's what you asked for!"

Holmes said nothing. A severe tranquillity radiated from him, but it wasn't enough to calm Watson, who was growing very impatient. The closet had stopped rocking, but its inhabitant hadn't yet come out.

"What is Mr. Boz doing in there, Holmes?"

"Why don't you check?"

Watson stepped smartly forward and opened the closet door with his free hand. It was such a shock to him to find nobody inside that he almost spilled the drink down his shirt front.

"What can this mean?"

"Has he left us, Watson?"

"Beard hairs in a basin, but no sign of the man!"

"Drink up, Watson."

"Ugh! This Carnaby fudge has an appalling flavour."

Holmes merely shrugged.

And far in the future, Dickens beamed as he remembered the time he had spent in the rooms of the renowned Sherlock Holmes. Life was better for him now than it had been for a long time. He stood outside the police station and the blue lamp above the entrance cast a radiance onto him that was like a nimbus. He was old, yes, but he was valued. His uniform was nicely pressed.

He bent his legs and said, "Evening all," to no one in particular. He found it more difficult to straighten up again, but that was to be expected. And now a figure loomed out of the shadows, another constable.

"You are the new fellow, are you? Dixon, isn't it?"

"Dickens," said Dickens.

His smile was kindly, helpful, polite, and considerate.

"Of Dock Green," he added.

He Who Howls

O'Neil De Noux

I am He who howls in the night;
I am He who moans in the snow;
I am He who hath never seen light;
I am He who mounts from below.

Psychopompos
H.P. Lovecraft (1918)

The young man wrapped in the blanket leaned back in the cushioned chair and closed his eyes. He wheezed as he breathed, and I stepped over and checked his pulse. His heartbeat was rapid. My friend Sherlock Holmes stoked the fire. I took a step back and studied the young man as did Holmes, moving next to me with pipe in hand. Behind us, incessant rain peppered the windowpanes. Tat. Tat. Tat. It had rained all day.

The young man appeared to be in his twenties, his dark brown hair matted on his head, a streak of mud on his chiseled jawline dotted with three day's growth of beard, his fine Burberry jacket also dotted with mud, a scrape on its left elbow nearly ripped the cloth. The knees of his navy-blue trousers, of the finest wool, were soiled, his Roxbury high-laced boots scuffed and covered with a film of mud.

A noise turned me as Mrs. Hudson carried in a tray with a coffee pot and three cups, sugar, cream, and spoons. She placed the tray on the nearest table, and I thanked her. Holmes continued studying the young man who had come to our rooms in such a state, the man collapsing in my arms but a half hour earlier. Mrs. Hudson quickly mixed cream and sugar into three cups of coffee before leaving us.

"We have coffee," I said to the man whose eyes blinked open.

"We find it more stimulating than tea," said Holmes. "A taste we acquired in our recent sojourn to America."

The young man looked from me to Holmes and back again.

His voice rasped. "Sherlock Holmes?"

I stepped back as my friend said, "I am Holmes."

The young man nodded, his eyes filling, and he took in a deep breath and said, "Fiend." His voice rasped again. "A...fiend...a fiend has stolen my bride."

The man coughed and reached two shaking hands to me and I presented him a cup of coffee, assisted him in his first sips, and he nodded slowly, sat up straighter, took another sip on his own.

"I am Dr. John Watson," I said, checking his pulse again. His heartbeat steadying, less rapid.

"Thank you, Dr. Watson." He turned to Holmes, the young man's voice stronger. "I am Reginald Portendon, second son of Albert, Lord Cleeth, and I come to you because you are my last chance to save my darling Violet."

Holmes and I sat as Reginald relayed his extraordinary story. My friend's eyes sharped with the telling of the tale and the malaise gripping Holmes these last three weeks seemed to fade. My friend's craving for mental exhalation sharpened his features as he watched Reginald speak.

"A dark stranger came into our lives shortly after we married and moved into lodgings four months ago on Swinton Street, King's Cross. We met him in Highgate Cemetery when we visited the grave of my darling Violet's father, Sir Thomas Harrow. The stranger claimed to have known Sir Thomas, had been a student of Sir Thomas at Queen's College.

"Obviously a man of wealth, the stranger always wore pristine suits of the finest cloth. He offered us a ride home in his brougham when we left the cemetery as rain threatened. He claimed he had been abroad, the Americas, both north and south. He invited us to dinner the following evening and then took us to theatres and dinners twice weekly where we discussed literature and history— his accounts of wars in the American colonies were so fascinating, Violet, who never expressed any interest in history, was spellbound. Learning Violet's birthday was August 1, the stranger took us to dinner at an exquisite, small restaurant just off Gray's Inn Road, not far from our lodgings. It was there he introduced Violet to his wine."

Reginald put his empty coffee cup down and I refilled it, adding cream and sugar. He thanked me and continued his story as he sat up.

"I cannot consume spirts of any sort, but Violet drank the dark red wine and that night when she came to our bed, she was a changed woman, no longer demure, shy. She insisted we not dim the light and came to me as a rapacious, lustful woman whose... enthusiasm...for love exhausted me. We had taken the bottle of wine home, and it did not take long to realise her consumption of the libation drove her into a nearly uncontrollable lust I had trouble quenching."

Reginald sipped more coffee as did I. Sherlock refilled his pipe and lit it, his sharp eyes focused on the young man who continued his story.

"She finished the bottle and I was relieved to throw it away. Some days later, I returned home to discover my wife waiting in our bedroom. Without clothes, she pounced on me and made love to me with the lights on again and kept me in the bedroom until I collapsed in fatigue. When I awoke in the middle of the night, I discovered another bottle of wine with a note written in neat copperplate: *Enjoy this. You are young but once.*

"I threw the bottle away and remained with my darling Violet for the next two days as she slowly came out of the fog. It was then she told about the dark stranger who called himself Monsieur Janvier. I shall describe him now. He stood six feet tall, a thin man who always wore black suits and a top hat. His colourless face was lean, his moustache thin and his lips narrow. His hair was black as pitch, blacker even than Violet's raven hair, his eyes the palest brown. Violet found him handsome. I found him cat-like, his movements purposeful, almost feline. He had a curious trait. Hair in the palms of hands. I have never seen such on a person.

"As Violet came out of her fog and she told me about this man, I knew he'd been to my house when I was not present, and it pained my heart so. In her fitful slumber, she had mumbled a word, over and over again: Gren. Gren. Gren."

Holmes let out a long breath, put his pipe down.

"Shock replaced my pain as my bride relayed the stories Monsieur Janvier told her. Tales of horrendous bloodlust, of hunting humans and devouring flesh."

Reginald shut his eyes, his voice deeper. "I can see her lovely face in the candlelight, a dispassionate face, expressionless as she spoke." His eyes snapped open. "The man described to Violet how he transforms into an animal, a wolf. The man threw back his head and let loose an horrendous howl. My bride relayed these stories to me without any feeling in her voice. It frightened me, but she seemed unfazed.

"I waited until the second day after her recovery, waited for her to nap in the afternoon and rushed to locate a physician. When we returned, Violet was gone."

The man's eyes filled, a tear rolling down his cheek.

"I have searched...everywhere. The police have been of no assistance and Scotland Yard apathetic." Reginald wiped his tears and focused on Holmes. My father has been of no assistance. He is hesitant of our marriage, believing such beauty in a woman can only bring heartache to a man.

"In my searching, a young copper gave me your name and address."

Holmes turned to me, his face paler than I have ever seen.

"The man you describe is Janvier Rabiem." My friend's voice came deep. "However, it cannot be Janvier Rabiem."

"Why not?" I asked after a few seconds had passed.

"Because I killed him."

Holmes walked to his desk and opened a bottom drawer, withdrew a mahogany box, and pulled out a Webley revolver I had never seen before. He opened the cylinder, reached back into the box, and loaded the revolver.

"I used six of these bullets to kill a man named Janvier Rabiem." He closed the cylinder and looked at me. "Silver bullets given to me, as was this revolver, by an elderly constable on the most harrowing night of my life." Holmes placed the revolver on his desk and came back to stand in front of Reginald Portendon, second son of Albert, Lord Cleeth.

Holmes declared, "We are off on the morning train to the Cambrian Mountains."

"Wales?" I asked in astonishment.

"Wales, my dear Watson. Let us pack."

The following morning found the three of us in a westbound coach riding the rails across Oxfordshire. Holmes settled next to me and told us the story of his most harrowing night—

"Before we met, Watson, I was called to consult on the Tolsack Affair in Aberystwyth along Cardigan Bay in Wales. I was young and had not perfected my methods yet."

I sat back. "I did not know you were involved in that affair."

"I shall relay that story one day, but we must remain focused on the case at hand.

"A chance happening had taken me off the train on my return to London. Mutton I ate aboard the train brought nausea, and I disembarked at the village of Gren at the edge of the Cambrian Mountains. I recovered quickly and prepared to board another train, only to discover the streets outside in turmoil. I went out and people rushed past me to their houses and locked the doors. The pub closed. A conductor at the train station warned me to return to the doctor's house where I'd been treated. I started that direction when Constable Andrew Colwyn intercepted me, warning me to go indoors. He rushed into the station, and I followed him.

"A host of men assembled, and the constable passed out firearms to all who did not have one, including me. Minister Angus Lyon gave us silver bullets as the constable told us about the demon who had killed four people there along the edge of the great undulating plateau Mynydd Mallaen. The incredulous statements seemed so foreign for a constable to utter, yet the pistol in my hand was real as were the bullets I loaded into it.

"I followed the group outside, and a noise froze us in our steps, a reverberating howl. Constable Colwyn said it was him, the object of our search. He had dragged off a young man and we were in pursuit before another hapless victim was slain. I stayed with the constable as the men split into groups."

Reginald watched Holmes as if spellbound.

"I followed the constable and he told me of finding the bodies of the men killed and ripped apart as if eaten by an animal. The afternoon waned and the constable said we must return to the station before dark. We moved through a small valley, past the ruins of Castle Gren when the howling froze us again. We raised our pistols and stepped into the castle, following the sounds of scraping and mewling until we turned into a large chamber. It took a moment to realise what I saw—a man bent over a prostrate body. We cocked our pistols and the man lifted his head and glared at us with a face covered in blood."

Reginald shuddered, closed his eyes.

"The man came at us at a run, growling, snarling. The constable and I took aim and fired in unison, again and again and I saw the bullets strike the fiend as he staggered and lunged for us. He moved too quickly for Constable Colwyn to avoid and crashed into the older man. They tumbled, the fiend snarling and sinking his teeth into the constable's neck. I raced over and shoved the muzzle of my pistol against the man's head and fired my final two rounds. His head exploded and he rolled off the constable. The air stood ripe with the scent of blood and gunpowder. I reached for Constable Colwyn whose throat was ripped open and he gargled, blood spurting into the air. He died before I could render any assistance."

"I dropped three bullets as I reloaded my pistol, jumped past the dead constable, and aimed at the fiend lying on his back. His chest rose and fell twice then lay still. The others found me still pointing my pistol at the dead man. I did not learn the man's name until they buried him just outside the castle ruins. Janvier Rabiem. And I've never returned to that dark place."

Holmes focused on Reginald. "Until now." He took in a breath, "Your wife is in grave danger."

"Holmes," I said. "Do you mean to tell us this fiend was a werewolf?"

My friend shook his head. "I believe he is a man insane enough to believe he is a werewolf and acting as if he were." Holmes stood and stretched. "Before we buried Rabiem, we examined his body and he is as Reginald described down to the hair in the palms of his hands. But bury him we did. This new man is someone else." Holmes turned to me. "And there lies the mystery."

We disembarked at Gren, found a rooming house, and left our luggage as Holmes led us to the police stationhouse where we discovered six constables loading pistols. A young constable with sandy hair stepped up to us.

"Mr. Holmes. How did you get here so quickly? I sent a telegram only two hours ago."

Holmes studied the man's excited face a moment, then recognised him.

"Ah, yes. Constable Aveenton. You telegraphed me?"

"Yes. Yes." Aveenton turned to the other constables. "This is Mr. Sherlock Holmes. He was with us when Constable Colwyn was murdered." He turned to me. "And Dr. Watson, I presume." He turned back to Holmes. "The howler has returned." The constable stiffened. "We found the body of Minister Angus Lyon last week. Chewed up as the ones were before. And this morning, I saw *him*. Rabiem. Walk away from the train with a young lady." Aveenton looked down. "I couldna move my legs. I shivered as I stood and when I was able to move, they were gone. We searched, but no one saw him. No one would go with me to where we buried him, but I went and found an empty hole. Grass grown within. It has been empty a while."

Reginald pushed past me. "What did the young lady look like?"

"Lovely. Young. Maybe not yet twenty years old. She wore no hat and her hair was black as coal."

"Violet!" Reginald grabbed my arm.

"We have silver bullets as before," said Aveenton. "Do you need pistols?"

Holmes explained we had pistols and silver bullets.

"Then we are off. We have six hours until sunset."

Aveenton split us into two groups. The first with four constables, the other with Aveenton, a younger constable, Holmes, Reginald, and myself. We stopped by our boarding house for Holmes to retrieve the mysterious item he'd brought in his portmanteau.

"A walking stick?" I asked.

Holmes showed me the heavy round handle. "Solid silver. I had it made after my investigations into lycanthropy and reading Sabine Baring-Gould's *The Book of Werewolves*. The cane has been blessed by the Archbishop of Westminster."

"Catholic?"

"Of course. The only church still believing in demons and exorcism."

I was astonished. My friend's uncanny ability to become expert on so many subjects intrigued me, but research into superstition surprised me.

"Come, Watson. We are off."

Constable Aveenton led us through the village, knocking on doors, inquiring again about the mysterious man and beautiful lady and receiving frightened looks and shaking heads. Holmes, per his modus operandi, questioned every youngster old enough to communicate and found none had seen the two. We returned to the stationhouse an hour after dark, the nervous constables letting out sighs of relief once rejoined. Aveenton assembled what little information had been gleaned in the canvass, which amounted to nothing. When the clamoured relief subsided, Holmes asked if anyone had noticed anything out of the ordinary. No. Nothing.

After an indifferent dinner at the rooming house, we retired to a sitting room to smoke our pipes. Reginald collapsed in a thick chair and was dragged into much needed slumber. The warmth of the room's fire made me drowsy until Holmes whispered, "Watson."

He raised his hand and I heard low voices outside the open window on the side of the room. We both inched over and heard boys talking. I could not make out sentences, but I heard the words *lady*, *beautiful*, *naked*, and *scary man*.

Holmes went out the front door and I went out the back door, and the three boys sitting on wooden boxes between the house and tall fence were trapped by us. One tried to reach the top of the fence to pull himself over, but he was too short.

"You boys are in no trouble," said Holmes, pulling coins from his pocket. He stepped to the boys and handed each a copper.

He held up another and asked where the boys had seen the beautiful lady and the scary man.

The youngest reached for the second copper and said, "The haunted house."

"Heston House." The oldest boy said, "We saw a light and went to the back. Saw a beautiful lady coming down the hall."

The youngest lad added, "She were naked sir, and the tall man took her hand and led her back up the hall."

"Tall man."

"Scary face."

"He were a monster."

"Had big teeth."

"Red eyes."

"We run, sir. We didna take anything."

Holmes gave them each a second copper and allowed them to depart. We woke Reginald, and Holmes brought his cane, and we rechecked our pistols with their silver bullets although they needed no rechecking. We found Constable Aveenton and another constable finishing their dinner at the stationhouse.

"Where is the Heston House?" Holmes asked before hurriedly relaying what the boys had said.

"It is at the far end of the village. Abandoned. The widow Heston died two years ago." Aveenton lit three lanterns for us as he and his constable picked up their lamps. Aveenton led us out, sending the other constable to fetch the remainder of the constables from their houses. We raced off, rushing along the dark street, Holmes holding back to allow Aveenton to lead us to Heston House, our footfalls echoing along the empty street. The village darkened as the streetlights became sparse. Moonlight peeked from behind the clouds, and I saw a full moon beaming above. A grey cat hissed as we passed. A moment later, a piercing howl stopped us.

"As before," Aveenton said as another howl reverberated. I tried to ascertain the direction from whence it came but was unable. The moonlight dimmed as clouds moved above.

A third, longer howl drove us onward until we were beyond the streetlights and I realised a gothic building of four stories stood to our left. It loomed like a black sphinx in the gloom. We four stopped and raised our lamps and the light danced on the façade of a grey house with tall windows, dormers above, and a towering spire. We stepped through a wrought iron gate, dangling on one hinge from the small brick wall surrounded the property, and moved to eight steps leading to the front door. Aveenton reached a shaky hand to the knob, turned it, and the door opened. He let go, took a step back, and pulled out his revolver. We raised our lamps and Reginald made a high-pitched sound.

Aveenton raised a boot to the door and pushed it. The squeak sounded like the squeal of a mouse and the door swung open. The odor of mildew filled my nostrils as we stepped into a dark foyer, our lights dancing on a tall staircase. A faint scratching of small animals scurrying away drew my lamp toward the right where the light showed a wide doorway and another room with a dark wood dining table and chairs. A gasp turned me back as Reginald bumped my shoulder and he went forward and stopped at the bottom of the stairs. We all raised our lights to a pair of pale feet coming out of the blackness, feet moving down the stairs.

Slender, lovely legs came slowly into the light, the naked woman moving languidly, the light on the dark bush between her legs, her round hips, narrow waist, and full breasts. I held my breath as her face came to light, a face so beautiful it seemed unreal, and her bright eyes such a pale blue, wide eyes, shining eyes, long luxurious black hair hanging nearly to her breasts. The woman was an exquisite vision. I felt my heart stammering. She opened her arms. Reginald stumbled on the first step and Aveenton let out a choking gasp.

"What?" Holmes swung his lamp around, which drew me to see Aveenton was no longer next to us.

A shuffling in the room to our left drew Holmes and I, him holding his cane high, me pointing my pistol. Aveenton's pistol lay on the dirty floor and a gurgling sound stopped us for a moment, followed by a weight falling to the floor. We moved into the room from either side of the wide entrance, Holmes on the left, me on the right. A figure stood just beyond the reach of our lamps. We inched closer and saw the constable on his knees with both hands to his throat and blood spurting. His wide eyes fluttered, and he fell over. I rushed to him, reached to stem the blood. Aveenton convulsed and my blood-slick hands failed to stem the gushing as the man's lifeblood slid through my fingers. He stopped moving and I attempted to locate a pulse, but the young man was gone. I leaned back and Holmes brought his lamp forward which revealed the man's throat had been ripped, shredded.

A snarl turned us to a figure emerging from the blackness—tall, thin, black hair standing out, deep-set eyes, mouth half-open. He crouched and snarled louder. I sat back, levelled my pistol, and fired as the man came forward on tiptoes. The bullets struck him in the stomach, chest, throat, and forehead, all six rounds, and he shook the shots away. He reached for me and Holmes dropped his lamp and swung his cane, its silver crown striking the side of the man's head. The head snapped and blood squirted from the bullet hole I'd put there. The man turned to Holmes who struck him atop the head. The man's knees buckled, and Holmes struck again and again, the man growling.

Thump. Thump. Thump. Holmes slammed the silver crown atop the man's head. With each thump, the man snarled until the cane shattered the man's head. Blood splattered, brain matter splayed, cranial bone splintered, and Holmes continued to pummel the man after he was prostrate.

Smoke rose around us and a stream of fire from Holmes's lamp rushed across the floor. Holmes reached down to help me up and I slipped on the gore at my feet. Holmes also slipped. We both regained our balance and staggered through thickening smoke. Holmes tried to go back.

"I need...to make sure...he is destroyed," Holmes gasped.

I yanked Holmes away. "His head is gone."

"We shot him to death before."

Smoke filled our lungs and we coughed as we stumbled back the way we came and made it to the front door.

"Reginald," I managed to say, and Holmes pointed to the street where Reginald stood hugging the still-naked woman. I was able to regain my breath and removed my coat to drape over the woman's shoulders. She stared into the inferno. Reginald helped her into the coat, and we all backed away as the Heston place burned to the ground.

❦

Holmes and I left Reginald Portendon, second son of Albert, Lord Cleeth, and his lovely wife in the hands of the good doctors at Cannock Hospital in Birmingham. We rode the train home. She had said nothing to us on the journey from Gren, just clung to her husband. Sherlock Holmes, who rarely spoke of carnal matters, declared to me as we left Birmingham, "Violet Portendon is the most beautiful naked woman I have ever seen."

I agreed but did not say so.

The inferno at Heston House had been so intense, only fragments of charred bones were found of the two bodies. We gathered the fragments and crushed them with a hammer. Holmes scattered the dust from the train as we rode from Birmingham to London. The dust of poor Aveenton floated away with the dust of his murderer.

Not until we were sequestered in our cabin rolling back to London did Holmes return to the subject.

He spoke in a hushed voice. "I have slain the demon twice. Janvier Rabiem. Will he return? Is this malady a repeated affliction? How many must we slay? Is it a form of mass hysteria?" He looked me in the eyes. "Or truly a demon." He let out a long breath. "I fear there are evils in this world we cannot fathom."

The click-clack of the train closed both our eyes and I felt jittery.
I heard myself say, "This is a story I can never put on paper."

"I know, my dear Watson. I know."

The Adventure of the Missing Fiancé

Catherine Lundoff

Mrs. Hudson looked both annoyed and concerned as she knocked on the door of the upstairs apartment at 221 Baker Street. After what seemed like a lengthy interlude, the door opened slowly to reveal a cloud of chemicals and a smoking apparatus on the table behind a tall, thin figure in a terrifying mask. Mrs. Hudson's companion staggered backward, a startled small shriek cut off by the knuckle pressed between her teeth.

Mrs. Hudson, in contrast, simply eyed the figure with annoyance. "Mr. Holmes, can you not find somewhere besides my house to play your terrifying games? It frightens the other tenants and now you've put a shock into your visitor." Mrs. Hudson scowled, then addressed the young woman at her side, "He don't mean no harm by it, Miss."

After a moment, Sherlock Holmes, for it was he, pulled the mask up and turned away to open a window, waving the cloud out into the fetid London air, before returning to the door. Both women eyed him warily, though the younger one had recovered quickly and was no longer in an obvious state of dismay. He studied her briefly, then stepped aside and waved her in, "Miss Violet Hunter, please come in."

"You'll not be seeing a respectable young lady in your rooms all on your own, Mr. Holmes. Dr. Watson is still on shooting holiday, so I'll be coming in as well." Mrs. Hudson drew herself up to the top of her not very substantial height and glared up at Holmes. One foot tapped impatiently on the rug.

"Indeed. Very well. But you will need to be silent while Miss Hunter and I converse." He turned away, his landlady clearly no longer of consequence to him, and led the way into the room.

"Don't mind the rudeness, Miss," Mrs. Hudson remarked to their guest. "It's just his way." Her gaze shot daggers at the detective before she retreated to a chair that she had to first clear of papers. She pulled a bit of darning from her pocket and went to work, occasionally looking up to watch them both.

Miss Hunter looked flustered but swept around a small table and sundry bits of equipment to perch on the settee. "Mr. Holmes, you must be surprised to see me again, after so long."

"I observe, Miss Hunter, that your fortunes have improved since last we saw each other at the Copper Beaches four years ago. Dr. Watson informed me that you went on to administer a school for young ladies at Walsall, and I see that at some point since you have become engaged. To what end do you seek my services again?" He sat in the chair opposite, steepling his fingers below his chin and waiting.

"I could never hide anything from you, Mr. Holmes, even had I wanted to. Yes, I am engaged and that is what brings me to you today. I am set to marry my fiancé, Mr. James Longrin, next month, after the school term is done. But he had to travel to London on business some weeks past and that is what brings me to you today." She reached into a bag at her side and pulled out a small bundle of letters, tied in a pale green ribbon. "Jimmy has always written me every week, like clockwork, ever since we became close. He wrote me one letter after he arrived in London, but then there's been nothing since."

Miss Hunter wore a worried frown where a more highly-strung young lady might have wept, Mrs. Hudson noted with approval. She continued with her tale, her voice low and controlled, "I know it doesn't sound like much and he might just have business to occupy him and no time to write, but this last letter suggested something more sinister, and frankly, Mr. Holmes, I am becoming terrified that something may have befallen him. I came here on a short holiday to visit friends and to look for him in order to sooth my fears, but I have looked for him at his hotel and they say that they have no word of him. I have twice attempted to visit his employer, an engineering and manufacturing firm, much respected as I am told, but have been unable to get past the head clerk, who will tell me nothing." Here, she did break off to apply her handkerchief to her eyes before going on. "Can you help me, Mr. Holmes?"

"Is there a possibility that Mr. Longrin has found other concerns to occupy him?" Holmes looked politely disinterested.

Miss Hunter put her handkerchief down and folded her hands in her lap. She took a deep breath before speaking again in quiet and dignified tones. "I had thought of that. You are familiar with my history, Mr. Holmes, and you know me to be a careful studier of character, one who does not trust easily. Could I be deceived in him? Possibly. But I do not believe that I am and even if that turns out to be true, I think I would prefer to know that he is safe and well, even if he no longer loves me."

Mrs. Hudson gave her a look of great sympathy from her corner and she began to say something, but Holmes sent one sharp glance her way and she closed her lips with a small grimace. He turned back to the lady. "I understand, Miss Hunter. If you provide me with his hotel and the direction of his employer, I will look into the matter. Will you be staying in London for a few more days?"

She stood up and held out two cards. "Here are both addresses and almost all of his letters. Yes, I will be here for the next sennight. You can find me at—" Here, she named a prominent school for young ladies, still in existence, before continuing, "—where I am staying with my friend, the director. Thank you, Mr. Holmes. I know this is a smaller matter than those you generally concern yourself with. I greatly appreciate your interest in my troubles." She bowed slightly and placed the packet of letters on the table before letting him guide her to the door.

Mrs. Hudson rose with a much put upon sigh, her darning vanishing into her pocket as she rose. "Come along, Miss. Come downstairs with me and I'll make up a pot of tea. You've had a hard time and shouldn't be out on the streets until you've recovered." She herded Miss Hunter downstairs, over the lady's mild protests, leaving Holmes to look at the cards and the letters.

Holmes had just finished putting aside his experiment and changing his clothes when a familiar knock on the door interrupted him. He opened it to admit Mrs. Hudson with a tea tray. The difference between her previous expression and her current one was marked by its improvement. "Well then, Mr. Holmes, you'll be wanting to go out to see what's become of the young man, but I thought you might want your tea first." She placed the tray on a table and eyed his costume critically. "You'll be needing an ink splash on the collar if you want to look like an elderly clerk, with all that powder in your hair. And you might want to be hearing something Miss Hunter mentioned when we sat down to tea."

She sat across from him and watched as he drank his tea. When he finished, she remarked, "She said that her young man had not spoken to his father in many years, but a lady and gentleman claiming to be his parents suddenly called upon her at her school last week, inquiring as to their son's whereabouts. Miss Hunter mentioned that this was when she became concerned about Mr. Longrin since it struck her that things did not seem right."

Holmes frowned for an instant before rising to add a splash of ink on the lapel of his slightly ragged coat. "Fit enough for a country lawyer's clerk, come to London making inquiries after a client regarding a small inheritance? Good. Now, then, Mrs. Hudson, in Dr. Watson's absence, I will ask you to examine the letters that Miss Hunter left with me to see if you notice anything else amiss."

Mrs. Hudson gave him an amused look. "I know your methods, Mr. Holmes, or some of them, at least. It would be my pleasure to help Miss Hunter however I can."

<hr>

When Sherlock Holmes returned several hours later, there was another unexpected visitor waiting for him in the downstairs drawing room. Once he had time to change, Mrs. Hudson brought him up and announced him as "Mr. Peter Longrin come to see you, Mr. Holmes," but apart from leaving a new pot of tea and two clean cups on the table, showed no inclination to stay. Holmes noted that Miss Hunter's bundle of letters, present a moment before, had vanished from the table, presumably into Mrs. Hudson's capacious apron pockets, and sat down to pour his tea.

The older man stood, uneasily shifting from foot to foot and twisting his cap until Holmes gestured at him to sit. He crumbled his cap in his hands and his gaze shifted away from Holmes's face when he cleared his throat and finally began to speak. "Mr. Holmes, I come to you on behalf of my son, James Longrin. The young lady he's engaged to, Miss Hunter as she is known at the moment, says that he is missing." His voice trailed off, as though he had lost his train of thought.

"Indeed. Do you also believe him to be missing?"

"I don't know what to think, sir. My son and I, we have not spoken in some years, but my own father died this last year and there's a matter of an inheritance, so I went to find him to tell him of it." He stopped again, as if searching for the words to describe what had happened. "I thought we might reconcile, if I did that, you see, sir."

"But you were unable to locate him? How did you know where to make your inquiries?"

"His sister kept writing to him after she married and left us. I asked her for his direction." Mr. Longrin's hands trembled slightly on his cap before he went on. "We, his mother and I, went to his home and learned that he was away. But his landlady had his young lady's school address and we went there to ask. She, Miss Hunter, that is, allowed as she had heard nothing of him for a fortnight, but that we might seek him here in town. So far, though, Mr. Holmes, I have not been able to find hide nor hair of him."

"Where have you searched, Mr. Longrin?"

There followed a catalogue of places that resembled Miss Hunter's to the letter, followed by entreaties that his son be found, before he finally ran out of words and departed. Holmes watched him walk down the stairs, then went to the window and opened the chord that held the curtain open so that the window was covered. He stood there for a few minutes, then opened the curtain again.

Mrs. Hudson appeared a short time after Longrin departed to retrieve the tea tray. Holmes was sitting in his chair, chin resting on one hand and gaze distant. She cleared her throat quietly and waited for him to indicate that he was paying attention.

"What did you think of your caller, Mr. Holmes?"

"That he was a remarkably bad liar. What, if anything, did you find in the letters, Mrs. Hudson?" His tone suggested that this was the more important question.

"Most of them are the sort of letters that any courting couple would exchange, but for the part where she told him a little of what happened at the Copper Beeches. And yes, I read Dr. Watson's tale of it, too, and I know there must have been things that didn't appear in *The Strand*. Mr. Longrin was very interested and asked a number of questions about how you solved the case and what happened to her right afterwards, as a young man in love might. He also asked if she knew what had happened to the Rucastles after she left and seemed rather persistent about that until she told him that she thought they were still at the house but knew no more than that."

"As if he thought that she was concealing something? Or because it looked as if he wanted to know more for his own ends?"

Mrs. Hudson frowned in thought. "The latter, I think. It's hard to be sure, but it seemed as if he might have known something of the Rucastles, or the house, mayhap."

"Hmmm. That may be unfortunate. As to the Mr. Longrin who just left, he is nothing more than a drunken actor, sent in to see what I already know. He has little or no connection to the man he claims is his son. Clearly, more than one party is looking for Mr. James Longrin, which makes this case more interesting than it appeared at first. Miss Hunter may be quite deceived in the nature of her fiancé."

"Oh, I do hope not, Mr. Holmes! She's a clever lass, one who misses little. And after what she's been through, it would be so hard not to always see the darker side of other people."

"You seem to manage well enough, Mrs. Hudson."

"I've always had a sunny nature, Mr. Holmes. Mr. Hudson, bless his soul, often remarked upon it."

Holmes's expression did not change, but the corner of his mouth quirked up in what might have been a slight smile. She gave a toss of her head in response. "Laugh at me all you like, Mr. Holmes, but I knew you'd get little from that man as soon as I laid eyes on him. Here's the letter where her fiancé asks all those questions." She handed him one of the letters and put the rest of the bundle, wrapped once again in its ribbon, on the table. "Did you found out aught about him when you went searching for him today?"

Holmes said nothing but waved his hand in a brusque gesture of dismissal and she left him sitting there, reading the letter and eating one of the sandwiches she had brought with her. Some hours passed before she heard him first play, then put away his violin. Shortly afterwards, there came a knock on her sitting room door, and she opened to admit him to its cosy comforts.

Several slices of beef, a bit of hard cheese and some bread and carrots appeared as if by magic at his elbow, along with a pot of tea. He propped up his feet near the crackling fire and favoured her with a rare smile. "It's as well that we don't let Dr. Watson into our little secrets. I doubt that his readership would find this version of myself as entertaining."

He dug in and ate his meal as Mrs. Hudson murmured, "He's a good man and tries to keep you out of trouble." She had returned to her darning, which as she had occasionally told Holmes, helped her think. At the moment, it was obvious that her mind was elsewhere though her fingers on the yarn and needle were still sure. "Just so's it's all clear in my head, Mr. Holmes, we have a missing young man, who may be involved in Miss Hunter's former troubles. Miss Hunter and another party, represented by the man claiming to be Mr. Longrin's father, are both searching for him. Did you find aught from his employer or at the hotel?"

Holmes sat back in his chair, fingers warming around his hot cup of tea. "Less than I would have liked, Mrs. Hudson. The hotel acknowledged that he had been a guest but thought he had left for another establishment. They claimed that they had no knowledge of where he went next. It may be that he was indeed somehow involved with the Beeches and the Rucastles and wished to disappear from his engagement. It is also possible is that he is aware that the other party is looking for him and wishes to avoid them."

Mrs. Hudson tilted her head. "In that case, he might be trying to attempt to protect Miss Hunter."

"Or his own interests. As for his ostensible employer, the chief clerk declined to speak to me or to provide me with any information about Mr. Longrin's whereabouts. I think we may be sure that he knows something of this matter. I shall return there tonight to see if there is anything of interest to be observed. Thank you for my supper, Mrs. Hudson." With that, he slipped away upstairs to change once more.

She watched him disappear and went on darning for some time after she heard him leave, but he did not return before she went to bed.

❦

Mrs. Hudson was returning from the market with her maid when she heard an odd noise upstairs. She stood in the hallway, listening for a moment, and wishing that Dr. Watson still resided here. He was a soothing presence at times like these. She could never tell if Mr. Holmes was up to something or had brought a visitor home with him or if there was a burglar on the premises. All of these possibilities flashed through her mind as she listened and wondered if she should call the gardener in for assistance.

After a few minutes, the noises settled into a more familiar pattern and she relaxed her vigilance a trifle. She told the maid that she was going upstairs and filled her ever present tray with tea and a couple of scones. As she paused outside the door, it occurred to her that she wasn't sure who needed the pretense of the tray more, her or Holmes. Certainly, she had no idea what or when he ate if she didn't bring it to him.

At first, there was no response to her knock and her earlier fears returned in a rush. But then, the door opened slowly to reveal a haggard looking Holmes, his left arm bleeding and half-bandaged. She bustled inside and fussed over him until she got him to sit down and drink his tea while she cleaned the wound and wrapped it up in a clean bandage.

Once he was attended to and had eaten, she asked the question that been bursting at her lips since she had arrived, "What happened, Mr. Holmes? Was it Miss Hunter's case or something else?"

"The evidence suggests that Miss Hunter's fiancé is caught up in something that does not bode well for her future happiness. This—" Here, he waved his bandaged arm, "—is the result of a knife attack by a young man fleeing from the office of Mr. Longrin's employer, under cover of darkness, leaving behind a broken door and a wounded detective, to borrow from some of Dr. Watson's more exciting tales. I do not believe that he intended to do more than escape me, nor did he have reason to know who I was and yet, such a panic does not suggest a man free of the burden of guilt for more nefarious deeds."

"Oh no!" Mrs. Hudson pressed her hands to her face. "Were you able to follow him or see what he might have taken? Are you sure that he was Miss Hunter's young man?"

"I arrived as he was fleeing the scene and I did follow him some distance before it became necessary to tend to my wound. He went to ground in a part of Whitechapel that I shall have to revisit today. I also returned to see what, if anything, had been found at the office and arrived as they gave out Mr. James Longrin's name to the police as a former employee, one who had been dismissed, but who had returned to the office from, perhaps, a misplaced desire for revenge."

"Will you tell Miss Hunter?"

"I believe I must."

Mrs. Hudson looked at him critically and shook her head. "I will go to her. You rest and then go find the young man. I think she would prefer to hear whatever explanation he's got from his own lips, if he can be compelled to honour her that much."

Holmes didn't answer for a moment, but eventually responded with a nod. It was, after all, the kind of errand that he had often sent Dr. Watson on. "I think that before I go to Whitechapel, I will go in search of our caller and determine who might have sent Mr. Peter Longrin to us and what became of him after he left. I signalled the Irregulars to keep an eye on him."

"I will see what Miss Hunter has to say about it. Perhaps he left her with their direction or other useful information, or she noticed something about them that might be of use."

Holmes held up his hand, keen eyes distant, as if lost in thought. "Mrs. Hudson, ask Miss Hunter to come here tomorrow, precisely at eleven, please. I will have news for her by then."

⁂

It was several hours later when a Hansom cab deposited Mrs. Hudson back at Baker Street. As she walked wearily up the front steps, she noticed a dishevelled urchin loitering near the lamppost out front. Her eyes narrowed as she glanced his way, trying to remember which one he was. She waited until she caught his reluctant eye and jerked her head toward the alley to indicate that he should come to the kitchen door.

Then she let herself in, put up her hat, and told the maid to put on some tea. "The greengrocer's lad is coming to the back for a special order for Mr. Holmes. I will attend to it." She walked wearily back to the kitchen, dug a coin out of her purse, then opened the door and stepped outside. Eventually, the boy appeared at a reluctant pace, sauntering as if he had no message to convey or as if she was of no importance.

"If you want your shilling, you'd best tell me what you know and smartish, my lad. Himself's not here and I'll not have you lingering about. This is a respectable house."

He snorted with laughter and wiped his nose on his sleeve, which was enough to remind her that his name was Ezra and his nose was always running. He made a crude remark in the language that the Irregulars used amongst themselves and gave her a gapped tooth grin of pure contempt. Mrs. Hudson met his grin with one of her own and replied back in the same tongue. Ezra's jaw fell and his brown eyes bulged.

Cowed now, he delivered his message, took his coin, and vanished, though not without a lingering startled glance over his shoulder at the grandmotherly woman standing behind him. She chuckled as she went back into the house to put her weary feet up and wait for Holmes.

❧

A sharp knock on the door the next morning woke her from a sound sleep on the settee in her front room. She got up slowly and awkwardly, her years making it harder than it had once been to sit up late and ignore her comfy bed. But she was needed and there was a case to be solved. Holmes barrelled inside the moment she opened the door.

"Quick, Mrs. Hudson, any message on the whereabouts of our guest?"

She passed along Ezra's message and a rare expression of enthusiasm crossed his face. "I'll have Lestrade and his men pick him up and bring him here. I'm off to go find James Longrin. I need you to wait here and prepare my sitting room for our visitors." And with that, he vanished upstairs and emerged in a new disguise. Mrs. Hudson watched him disappear out the door and around the corner before she went to go begin her preparations.

The morning dragged on despite her best efforts to remain alert. In the end, it was the arrival of two study policemen with the erstwhile Mr. Longrin dangling between them that woke her from a lengthy nap. She had all in readiness, however, and showed them up to Holmes's sitting room. Miss Hunter arrived a few minutes later. She seemed shocked into silence at the sight of the policemen and the man who claimed to be her future father-in-law.

It felt interminable, and Miss Hunter had begun to ask awkward questions when he finally appeared, a somewhat battered-looking young man in tow. He nodded his thanks at Mrs. Hudson and ushered the man into a seat. The policemen took up their stations at the door, their expressions expectant. Miss Hunter was rigid in her chair, her gaze fixed on the young man sitting next to Holmes while he gazed down as his feet, a sizeable bruise turning purple along his cheek.

"Very well. Let us begin with you, sir." Holmes gestured at the man who had claimed to be Peter Longrin. It was clear to all that the young man was a stranger to him and equally clear that he was no stranger to strong liquor. He smiled blearily at all of them as Holmes continued, "Someone came to you and your wife and paid you to tell this young woman that you were Mr. James Longrin's parents. I have confirmed as much from your wife as well as some of my informants. Are you sober enough to tell us why?"

A longwinded explanation followed, little of it comprehensible, even to Mrs. Hudson, thought she had begun to have her suspicions about who had hired him and why. At last, Holmes held his hand up. "The point was to lure Miss Hunter to London, was it not?"

The erstwhile Peter Longrin sat with his mouth open for a few minutes. He nodded reluctantly when it became clear that Holmes would not let him remain silent. It was Miss Hunter who interrupted, "But why?" Her face was pale and growing paler, and Mrs. Hudson wondered if she should look for the smelling salts, but the lady seemed determined not to faint.

"I think that explanation should come from you." Holmes nodded at the young man.

The latter closed his eyes, sighed, then sat up and looked straight at Miss Hunter. "I...I am so very sorry. Before we met, I was summoned to a house in the country called "The Copper Beeches." The lady of the house, Mrs. Rucastle, met with me and told me that her cousin worked for my employer and he had told her something about me, something from my past. She said that she would tell my employer about it unless I did what she wanted. She told me that I should court you and get you to fall in love with me because seeing you jilted would give her some measure of revenge for the harm you did her family." He paused as Miss Hunter jumped to her feet and began to pace. Her cheeks flushed and her eyes filled with anger and James fell silent.

At Holmes's gesture, he continued, "Then, when I came to London, someone let slip that I was to be dismissed for embezzlement. You see, I was once in dire straits and I stole some funds once from my firm, and though I intended to repay them before we married, it was too late. My misdeed had already been discovered. As for the rest, Mrs. Rucastle, she hates you very much, Violet. I realised then that they were going to use me to expose and ruin you by creating a scandal that would cost you your position. That was why I tried to break into the office, you see. I wanted to steal the evidence, the letter that she had sent them." He leaned forward and buried his head in his hands.

Miss Hunter stopped and turned to look at him. "Was it all a lie?"

He looked up. "It was at first, but then, no. It became the greatest truth of my life, and I love you more than anything. But I could not tarnish your good name by giving you mine or dragging you down with me. I planned to take the letter, destroy it, and leave England before you fell with me. Mr. Holmes found me, made me tell him all, then said that I had to confess all to you, that you deserved that and more." He paused and drew in a loud choked breath.

Miss Hunter walked over to him and knelt down, studying his face. What she saw there convinced her, and she reached out and held his hand. They spoke together in low tones.

"Do we take them in, Mr. Holmes?" one of the policemen asked, clearly wondering what their role was to be.

"Take this man into custody, if you will." Mrs. Hudson gasped, then realised that he had gestured at the man who had pretended to be James's father. "His testimony will be needed to bring up Mrs. Rucastle on charges." He looked at Miss Hunter and James Longrin, as if seeking assent.

She rose to her feet and walked to his side to whisper something too softly for the others to hear. Holmes looked at her in something as close to astonishment as Mrs. Hudson had ever seen. "Are you certain, Miss Hunter?" She nodded and after a moment, he gestured to the policemen to leave with their charge. "He may yet prove useful to you."

Miss Hunter and Mr. Longrin stood gazing into each other's eyes for a long moment, then Miss Hunter looked at Holmes. "You will speak to his former employer, won't you, Mr. Holmes? We can repay them and make this good." At his nod, she placed a handful of pound notes in his hand and thanked him. She squeezed Mrs. Hudson's hand in thanks before exiting slowly with her fiancé.

"Where are they going?" Mrs. Hudson asked.

"Copper Beeches to confront Mrs. Rucastle. Miss Hunter assured me that she has some means of resolving the situation that does not require my aid." Holmes sat back down. "And now, Mrs. Hudson, I could really use some of your excellent tea. And discretion. Dr. Watson must never hear of this. I cannot imagine what he would make of it."

She laughed as she went downstairs.

The Tell-Tale Tea Leaves

Keith Moray

In my long association with Mr. Sherlock Holmes, the world's first private consulting detective, whose many cases it has been my privilege to occasionally assist him with and chronicle in the pages of *The Strand* and *Collier's Weekly*, I never anticipated that his career would end so tragically and ignominiously.

That was my reason for packing away those few personal items and artifacts of the case in this old shoebox until such time as the world was ready to hear the true account of the whole sad business. I believe that I have now left sufficient years after his death to bring the truth of the case before the public eye.

So here, with a couple of my friend's old test tubes on my writing desk and his Wedgewood teacup in front of me, still with its sepia-coloured stain and the dried tea leaves that have long since fallen from the bone china surface, I am tempted to once again put on the muddied and torn black armband that I had worn afterwards amid all of the opprobrium and rancor that was stirred up when news of his death burst upon the public. Yet memories of being spat upon as I walked along Baker Street and of myself furiously ripping it off and grinding it under my boot in the gutter proved too painful and I desist, choosing instead to merely drape it across the teacup rim as I pick up my pen and dip it in the inkpot.

The expression, how are the mighty fallen, comes to mind. And how quickly do the carrion land to feed on the flesh.

London had been seized by an influenza outbreak in that gloomy, foggy October of 1895. My dear wife had suffered from it for a whole week, and I had found it difficult to find adequate time to care for her as my practice had been exceedingly busy. It was only as the epidemic began to subside that I realised how exhausted I had become and how low my own resistance had fallen. As soon as she was fit enough, I arranged for Mary to stay with her sister in Bournemouth to convalesce in the sea air.

I spent the first day as usual, with a long morning surgery, before pounding the streets on a gruelling round of my recovering patients. By the end of my evening surgery, I was almost on my knees and ready to tell Miss Templeton my secretary to lock the door so that she could go off to her regular weekly spiritualist meeting, while I could head for home, a stiff hot toddy, and a cold collation.

She tapped on the door and came in. "One last patient, Dr. Watson, I am afraid," she announced. "It's a Mrs. Hudson, who says she is desperate to see you." She leaned forward and in a low voice added. "She seems very anxious, Doctor."

Of course, although Miss Templeton knew of my association with Sherlock Holmes, she had never met my old landlady. For her to describe the doughty old Scottish housekeeper as anxious immediately piqued my professional interest.

"It's Mr. Holmes, Doctor Watson," Mrs. Hudson told me some minutes later. "I'm so worried about him. I fear he's been working himself to death. Out at all hours, smoking his pipe so that the whole house reeks, shooting at my walls again, and playing his violin in the middle of the night."

I tied to assuage her obvious concern with a smile. "Not so very different from when I too was lodging with him, Mrs. Hudson. But has he been ill? I have heard nothing from him for some weeks, as my practice has been so busy with this influenza outbreak."

"It is not his physical health, Doctor, but his mental state that I worry about. His behaviour has been odder than usual. He seems to have become exceedingly superstitious. He is obsessed with the future and omens and seems much addicted to tea, sir." She hesitated and then added. "He is forever boiling a kettle on a grille he has set up in the fireplace to make fresh pots of tea. Perhaps he is drinking too much of it. He has all sorts of teas delivered by some of those urchins he has coming and going all the time. Raving a lot, he is, too. Doctor. During these angry rants, he throws things and I have had several smashed teacups where he has thrown them and their contents at the wall."

She shook her head and sucked her lips inwards, replacing them with a thin line of exasperation. "And as for the letters to the press! He is inundating them and sending telegrams to all sorts of people."

"Is he smoking excessively? Or…using other habits?"

Mrs. Hudson eyed me shrewdly for a moment, for she was well aware that he kept a case containing a seven per cent solution of cocaine and a glass syringe in a drawer of his dressing table. She bit her lower lip and shrugged her shoulders. "I'm not sure, Doctor. There is a Chinese man that comes every now and then to deliver something, but I never see paper or bags."

"Do his rooms smell—different, Mrs. Hudson?" I was starting to be concerned that he might have moved on from cocaine to opium.

"It always smells odd, sir. What with his chemical experiments and that beastly strong tobacco of his. I'm afraid that I've been called away to see my niece in Margate and I'm worried about leaving him, Doctor. But I told him straight that I was going to have a word with you. Could you call on him, Doctor Watson?"

I put a hand on hers. Tired though I was, I had faith in Mrs. Hudson's intuitive sense. "I'll call round this evening."

Sherlock Holmes had never been predictable. Sometimes between cases he would not leave his rooms in 221b Baker Street for weeks on end, devoting his energies to his chemical experiments or to the solving of abstruse cryptograms or spending inordinate amounts of time writing monographs on obscure subjects, most of which he felt had some application to the detection of crime.

On this foggy October evening, the front door was unlocked as Mrs. Hudson said it would be, so I mounted the steps to the first-floor landing and raised my hand to knock, when Holmes's familiar staccato voice called out.

"Come in out of the cold, Watson. The chair by the fire awaits you."

I entered and found him dressed in his old purple dressing gown, deep in study at his chemical table, with the fire stoked up and his long-blackened churchwarden's pipe belching smoke. Had I been unfamiliar with his ways, I might have expected a warmer greeting, but instead, after a cursory glance in my direction, he returned his attention to the test tube he held in one hand and the reagent bottle in the other.

"You saw me arrive from the window, I take it?" I asked.

"Ha! In the dark and with the fog as thick as pea soup, of course not," came the taciturn reply. "I have not moved from my chair this half hour. My ears have not yet begun to fail me and your tread upon those stairs is distinctive, thanks to that Jezail bullet you took in the leg at the Battle of Maiwand. This weather always causes you a slight limp that produces a characteristic cadence as you mount the middle nine steps. When you carry your medical bag, it is exaggerated somewhat. Now pray sit and take a cup of this excellent oolong tea. The pot is freshly brewed. I will be but a moment in finishing this experiment."

"What is it now, Holmes? Anything to do with the guaiacum test for haemoglobin you were trying to improve on?"

There was the sound of effervescence as the liquid in the test tube threw off a white precipitate and suddenly frothed over. A garlic scent suddenly started to pervade the room and Holmes gave an exultant laugh as he replaced the still fuming test tube in the rack and the reagent bottle in a row of similar chemicals.

"Ah, nothing quite like the aroma of arsine gas!" he exclaimed, turning and rubbing his hands. "No, Watson, that work was completed six months ago and has been published in the *Annals of the Royal Society of Chemistry*." He pointed to the chemistry table with its retorts and assorted paraphernalia. "I have these past few weeks turned my attention to tea and its multitude of attributes. An amazing plant well worthy of scientific study. As I am sure you know, it is a natural chemical indicator, turning pale in the presence of acid, as in lemon tea, and very dark brown with a strong alkali. Milk, of course, is alkaline, yet you do not see the transition because of the whiteness of the milk emulsion, and, like everyone, you are simply satisfied to have some sort of muddy liquid in your teacup. You are probably not aware that it is also a great concentrator of chemicals, including arsenic. Mrs. Mulligan the Stepney Poisoner was aware of this and went on to poison at least three husbands before I was called in. Had they used my modified Scheele-Marsh-Holmes test here to test infusions from her teapot, she would have gone to the gallows three years sooner."

I laid down my bag and reached for a teacup.

"Not the upturned one, I pray you," he said quickly. "I am expecting someone in the next ten minutes, and it is laid for him."

"A client?"

"Hmm, more a lead in a case I am working on already. I have invited him by way of a piece I posted in the agony column of several newspapers." He tapped out his pipe on the palm of his hand and tossed the dottle into the fire before reaching for his Persian slipper to recharge it.

"But that is not all that you are working on, I see," I remarked, noticing the two blackboards in the corner which were covered in chalked circles with all sorts of lines and dots inside them. On an old aspidistra table was a strange antique piece that I recognised as an astrolabe.

"What are the drawings?"

"Horoscopes, Watson. A fascinating study. To think that I once said it mattered not a whit to me whether the sun went round the earth or the other way round. I couldn't have been more wrong, my good fellow. Everything that happens on earth is influenced by the movement of the planets against the zodiac belt. What a fool I was not to realise that impulsive crime is as capricious as the phase of the moon and that Uranus governs the mind of the murderer."

I stared at him in amazement for a moment then reverted my attention to the tea tray in an attempt to bring the conversation back to the mundane. "Any milk, Holmes?"

He laughed. "No, but not because of the chemical reason I just mentioned. I have dispensed with it so that I can follow and see the movements of the tea leaves. Oolong is the best, in my opinion, for tasseographic readings, since the leaves can weave themselves into any shape."

"For what?"

"Tasseography, teacup fortune telling." He struck a light to his pipe and began puffing furiously.

I suppressed the urge to laugh, for there was something about Holmes's demeanour that concerned me. As Mrs. Hudson had said, he did seem to be obsessed with what he would ordinarily have called superstitious claptrap. I humoured him. "Tell me about the horoscopes."

He bounded across the room and tapped the first board with the stem of his pipe. "I am preparing a monograph on the Astrological Analysis of the Natal Charts of Notable Criminals. These are the birth charts of six convicted murderers and of six petty thieves. You can see the similarities between all the murderers and between all the thieves. Yet they are quite different as groups."

I had to admit that I could see the patterns.

He tapped the other blackboard. "And these are horary charts, Watson. This is the astrology of the ancient Chaldeans and of the enlightened genius of the Renaissance, the astrologer William Lilly. A horary chart is set up for the exact moment that the astrologer understands and asks a question." He beamed at me, his eyes fervent with enthusiasm.

I also noted that his eyes were slightly bloodshot, and his pupils were large and dilated, indicative to me that he had very recently imbibed a drug like cocaine.

"This rediscovery of horary astrology can be of inestimable value to me as a detective," he went on. "As indeed can tasseography or teacup reading. Why, I am proving myself to be a gifted reader of both stars and tea leaves."

He bounded across the room again and picked up a book. "The author of this book *The Cyclopedia of Tasseography* is the guest I await, Watson. He goes under the name of *Denarius*. Mister Roland Deauville, his actual name is the foremost exponent of the teacup in the country. He is also the author of *The Stars for You*, a popular daily horoscope column in *The Lone Star.*"

I could scarcely believe what I was hearing, but I was wary of challenging my old friend.

"Deauville isn't his real name either, of course, merely a professional sobriquet designed to make him sound both mysterious and cultured. In fact, in his youth Albert Wilson, his real name, used to be a proficient cat burglar and canary trainer, plying his trade from Jacob's Island in Bermondsey. He still keeps his most precious canaries caged close. But apart from that, he is one of the most dangerous men in London." Holmes's expression suddenly hardened, and his jaw muscles twitched, a sure sign of anger within. "He is a wheedler, Watson. He is the conduit for an even more dangerous blackmailer that he works for whom I have been after for many months, a rogue with the blood of several people on his hands. Several of the victims took their own lives rather than submit to blackmail. But I fear he has darker plans in mind and yet still, he evades me."

"This blackmailer—are you talking of a person of the ilk of Charles Augustus Milverton?" I said, once more humouring him.

"Worse, Watson. This monster is like a large black spider who sits upon his web. Denarius is a minion, a brightly coloured insect that hovers close to the web and lures victims close to their destruction without being devoured himself. With his teacup fortune telling and his horoscope column, he is immensely popular among the working and servant classes. Ladies-maids, housemaids, companions, and governesses; women in particular are beguiled by him, yet so too are some butlers, footmen, and gardeners. People who want to know the future invite him for high tea, soirees, fetes, and luncheon clubs. He tells their fortunes from their teacups and gains their trust. He tells them that people close to them are betraying their trust, taking advantage of them. Then he offers a means of getting their own back by making some money in the process. He buys information, letters, anything incriminating about their employers, and then hands it on to his blackmailer boss who reels them in to squeeze money out of them in return for silence about their indiscretions and peccadilloes."

He laid his pipe down on the mantelpiece and took down a folded copy of *The Daily Telegraph & Courier*, which lay there. "He replied to my piece in the agony column, which simply read: Silver-tongued Roman soothsayer invited to tea with a sympathetic listener. It may be to your advantage to know that the leaves keep showing a tight net, twisting and falling upon you. Sherlock Holmes, 221b Baker Street."

"A denarius was a Roman coin," I said. "So the silver-tongued soothsayer is the said Denarius?"

"Exactly, Watson." He replaced the newspaper and took down a handwritten note. "This letter came in the evening post. 'Mr. Sherlock Holmes, I perceive you are in need of a reading, so I will call at nine o'clock this evening. Cordially, R.D. (Denarius).' "

I finished my tea and placed it on the tray. "But what about the police? Surely if he and his boss are blackmailing people, they should be reported to the authorities."

"And risk having all of their current victims face ruin or suicide? No, Watson. That would never do."

He laughed and, turning, pointed to one of the chalk-drawn charts on the second blackboard. "I knew he would come, the horary chart I cast said he would." Putting the letter on the mantelshelf, he picked up the jack-knife that he kept there for the purpose and, with some force, skewered the message into the wood. "I'm going to challenge him, Watson, and give him a teacup reading myself. Then I will make him see what he needs to do. I cannot fail, as my charts have shown me the outcome."

He sprang across the room and darted into his dressing room, returning after a few moments dressed in a frock coat.

"And now my good fellow," he said, consulting his Hunter watch. "It is almost nine and he will here shortly."

"Would you like me to stay, Holmes?"

"I fear your presence might incommode me, Watson."

I was in two minds about leaving him, for I was sure that he had been abusing his cocaine again. I wondered if his fixation with teacups and horoscopes was all part of a delusion. Certainly his fervour and energy were characteristic of the drug.

But before I knew it, he had picked up my bag, thrust it into my arms, and started to shepherd me toward the door.

A few moments later, I was walking away from the entrance to 221b Baker Street. There were a few people about, all walking carefully in the thick vapors. The sound of hooves on cobbles was followed by the emergence of a Hansom cab from the thick fogbound street, and in its dim interior, lit by a bulldog lantern, I saw a flamboyantly dressed man with a neat pencil moustache, his face half shadowed under a floppy, wide brimmed hat. I did not know it at the time, but it was my first sight of Denarius. I thought he looked almost comedic, not at all as I imagined from Holmes' description of one of the most dangerous men in London.

<hr />

I barely slept and was woken in the small hours by an urgent rapping on my front door. Being used to such emergency calls, I quickly pulled on a dressing gown and descended the stairs. I was not expecting to see a police constable and a waiting carriage. Other than the fact that I was wanted urgently and they had been sent by Inspector Lestrade of Scotland Yard, he had little information to give me.

It was a shortish journey and a clock somewhere alerted us that it was three in the morning as we reached our destination through the fogbound London Streets.

I descended to the pavement to find several more burly police constables guarding the doors of 221b Baker Street. A police hearse was waiting directly outside, and I started to feel my heart race as anxiety crept upon me.

"A sad business, Doctor," said a tall PC with a thick moustache. "The inspector is waiting upstairs for you?"

He saw the mystified look on my face, and with a nod to his fellow, the door was opened. "You'd best go up, sir. You know the—" He hesitated and looked embarrassed. "Of course you know the way, sir."

A younger detective constable called out my name through the open door of our old rooms, and I heard Inspector Lestrade's familiar voice call out to let me through.

The sight that greeted me took me totally by surprise. A middle-aged man was sprawled in the chair by the dying embers of the fire, an empty teacup clutched in his hands. It was the man I saw in the Hansom cab a few hours before. His eyes were open and staring sightlessly at the bullet pocked wall where Holmes had shot the initials VR. His mouth had fallen open and his pencil moustache was pulled down into an inverted V shape that gave his visage an expression of total shock. A bottle green waistcoat was soaked with blood from a chest wound where Sherlock Holmes's jack-knife was protruding.

I could tell that he was dead without further examination, stabbed through the heart.

"Where... Where is Holmes?" I gasped, seeing Lestrade, dressed in his usual brown dustcoat and bowler hat, standing and staring at the blackboards.

He turned and eyed me keenly. "That's just what we want to know, Doctor Watson. When Constable Derby responded to the police whistle just after two this morning, the only witness, a young woman on her way home, saw him dash out into the street like a crazed lunatic and head straight into the fog."

"Have you talked to her yourself?" I asked.

He snorted. "What do you think? As soon as Derby went off, so did she. You can guess why she was out at that time of night." The inspector stared me straight in the eye. "There is a warrant out for the immediate arrest of Sherlock Holmes."

The next two days were a complete blur to me. I asked Mathieson in the neighbouring practice to look after my list for a few days, which he was happy to do as I had done the same for him when his sister died. I divided my time between going over the notes and drawings that I had made with Inspector Lestrade's permission at our old rooms and immersing myself in the extensive newspaper coverage of the story the press was referring to as "The Search for the Slaying Sleuth."

Roland Deauville, as known as Denarius, but yet not referred to by his real name of Albert Wilson, was being portrayed as a benevolent practitioner of astrology and teacup fortune telling who had been lured to the rooms of Sherlock Holmes and brutally murdered. No obvious motive was given, but the facts were stark. He had been discovered with Holmes's jack-knife buried in his chest and the room bedecked with what the press described as chalked drawings of the Black Arts on blackboards, signs of fortune telling, and a table devoted to alchemy. The testimony of PC Derby and the unknown woman's description of Holmes fleeing into the fog in the middle of the night was taken as evidence of a murderous lunatic fleeing the scene.

Various articles in the gutter press commented on his mental health and his recent strange behaviour as evidenced by the deluge of bizarre letters and telegrams that various editors had received, some of which were quoted. Then they reported interviews with Mrs. Hudson and several obviously disgruntled people that reporters had encouraged out of the shadows to assassinate Holmes's character. I realised that our old housekeeper would have been reported out of context, but I was particularly angered to read quotes from Lestrade inferring that Holmes was well known to Scotland Yard as a bungling meddler in criminal cases.

Our chimney sweep and our plumber both informed me of rumours of vigilantism. The local PC broke off his beat to inform me that a brick had been thrown through a window at 221b Baker Street, with a newspaper page with Denarius's horoscope column wrapped round it, together with the written message, "Vengeance is in the stars!"

There were numerous attempts to contact me for interviews, but I had left instructions with Miss Templeton and with the concierge at my club that I was unavailable for comment.

In retrospect, I realise that may have made matters all the worse.

At last realising that my mood was becoming both melancholic and irritable, I sent a note round to the Diogenes Club and made an appointment to see Sherlock Holmes's elder brother, Mycroft.

He was not overjoyed to see me.

"I am afraid that my brother's drug addiction has finally turned his mind and he has sunk into the depths of paranoid madness, obsessed with murders, crime, and the occult."

"But surely you don't believe he could have committed murder?" I implored him. "Can you not come to 221b Baker Street and cast an eye at his rooms?"

"Futile, I am afraid, Doctor."

"Or give me your opinion and the benefit of your deductive powers by looking at my drawings and notes."

"I fear that I must leave this to the correct police channels." He pulled out his watch and consulted the minute hand. "Now I really must ask you to excuse me. I have several important appointments involving people of the very highest authority of both national and international importance."

Diplomacy was never the elder Holmes brother's strongest suit, and I left determined to find Holmes before the vigilantes did.

How the denizen of the press knew that I had visited the Diogenes, I had no idea, but several reporters were waiting to accost me outside. I was polite, but firm and used the fog and my knowledge of the back streets to escape. I had formulated five places spread across London that I needed to visit, all places that Holmes had confessed to me when I was writing up his cases, that he used as safe houses or lodgings where he kept disguises. I had out of curiosity visited them all before and I did so again, without finding signs of recent use by the detective. I did, however, drop in on a couple of teashops, an opium den, and two public houses in the vicinities, where I was able to make subtle enquiries.

At *The Ship Aground* public house in Jacob's Island, I had my first lead. There I discovered from Ebenezer Garside, the landlord and a contact of Holmes, that a canary was not a yellow bird as I had thought, but a woman lookout for a cat burglar. I remembered Holmes giving me a brief rundown on Denarius's previous history and I immediately thought of the mysterious woman, whom Lestrade had assumed to be a prostitute. He also admitted to knowing Alfred Wilson before he reinvented himself as Denarius.

"He married his best canary, Polly Washburn, as pretty a pickpocket as ever you saw, before he turned her into a songbird. She had a temper, did Polly, but Albert tamed her all right."

I drank my half pint of warm beer and quickly headed for home. There, I resumed my study of my notes, trying to find some connection. I looked at the drawings I made of Holmes's horoscopes, but could make nothing of them and wondered whether they were indeed just the incoherent daubs of an irrational, cocaine-intoxicated mind. Then I looked at the drawing I had made of the teacup in Denarius's hand and the pattern of tea leaves. With a copy of the deceased's book I had purchased on my way home, I began to study. I read that the Denarius method involved using both hands to hold the teacup rim in both hands, imposing a series of imaginary divisions according to the positions of the finger and thumb joints, using the teacup handle as a reference point. Then the depth of the cup could be divided into past, present, and future.

The teacup the dead man had held showed three distinct shapes. A net, a crocodile, and a sword or a dagger. I looked up their meanings and pieced them together.

"The net means a trap. The crocodile is betrayal and the dagger is danger or death!" I said out loud to myself. Was this the reading that Holmes gave Denarius—before he stabbed him through the heart?

My God, I thought. Holmes badly needed help. But where was he?

I determined that I needed to see Lestrade as soon as possible.

⁕

Sherlock Holmes prided himself on being able to do without food. He could get by on a minimum amount to drink but being deprived of his pipe was proving to be hell.

His mouth ached from the gag, as did his muscles from the cramped position he was forced into by the manacles and chains that held him fettered to the wall of the dank, pitch-dark cellar. The pain from the head wound where he had been poleaxed while he leaned over Denarius's teacup had long ceased to hurt, although he was aware of the bump whenever he leaned his head back against the wall.

As he expected, he heard the rattle of the key in the lock, the creak of the door, and the sudden flooding with light from an oil lamp. Then, he followed the sound of a man's leather shoes descending the stone steps a few paces ahead of the more delicate tread of a woman.

"Still alive, Holmes?" the man's voice asked a moment before he became visible as he turned the corner in the light thrown out by the lamp.

"But not for long, my love," a woman's voice added with a laugh. The cockney lilt in the voice was unmistakable.

The man was dressed in a black great coat with a fur collar and a top hat. He was tall and well-built with a military bearing and a brisling, well-tended moustache. He set down the lamp and held up some lengths of rope. "You are lucky, Holmes. Your last hours will be more comfortable with ropes instead of chains. When they discover your body, the rope fibres will be as incinerated as your flesh, but there will be no sign of your incarceration. It will look entirely as if you set the bomb off yourself at exactly the right moment to dispatch everyone meeting upstairs. Exactly as the confession and suicide note that will arrive in the hands of Scotland Yard's finest."

And while the woman, well-dressed and pretty, despite over-much make-up, watched with a look of unpleasant enjoyment, he tightly bound Holmes hand and foot before unlocking and removing the chains.

"You don't know how fortuitous your madness has been, Mister Sherlock Holmes. You have given me the means of avenging my brother officer by killing the imbecile that the world and the despicable old woman fawns over, who ruined his reputation." He put a hand round the waist of the woman and drew her closer to him so that she could kiss his cheek. "It also gave us the opportunity to get rid of the deluded clown, Denarius, who had passed his usefulness to us and was standing in our way. And most importantly, it will provide us with the means to bring the whole of Europe tumbling to its knees." He crouched in front of Holmes and pulled down the gag. "So what do you say to that, Mister detective?"

Holmes worked his jaw muscles. "I say what I said to Denarius before you crept behind me and knocked me out before you murdered him. I saw it all in the teacup."

"And did you see this?" the man asked with a laugh, straightening and turning to a large object covered with jute sacking. He pulled the sack free to reveal a large wooden chest with wires protruding from it, leading to a clockwork mechanism.

He drew out a gold watch and checked the time, then adjusted the hands of a clock on top of the chest.

"Not that you would be able to reach it, but it is as you imagine—a bomb. It is set to explode if anyone tampers with the mechanism. Left to its own devices, it will do its duty at the appointed hour!"

He nodded to the woman, who replaced the gag, and, with a smug smile and a coquettish kiss on his nose, she tied it tightly.

A quarter of an hour later, left in the dark with the tick of the clock sounding sonorously in his ear, Holmes waited. And then he heard another sound high up in the cellar air vent where he could see three pinpoints of light from outside. Three small fingers appeared and waggled.

I left Lestrade's office in Scotland Yard convinced more than ever that Holmes's impression of the inspector as a simple plodder was more than generous. In my opinion, he was a bumpkin. I had asked him to let me see the teacup that was found in the fortune-teller's dead hands. How he failed to see the significance of the signs after I showed him that they had been stuck on with some sort of glue was beyond me.

As I disconsolately ambled back in the fog, I felt the urchins jostle past me before disappearing into the vapors. A laugh and a whistle made me check my pockets, expecting to find my pocketbook gone. I did not expect to find a note with "For Mycroft" written on it.

It was written in pencil—clearly in Sherlock Holmes's handwriting.

The explosion under the Colonial Office's special board room in Whitehall had repercussions across the country and Europe. Although the deaths of the heir to the throne, His Royal Highness Prince Edward, the Secretary of State for the Colonies, Joseph Chamberlain and the German Chancellor Chlodwig, Prince of Hohenlohe-Schillingsfürst and three other high ranking civil servants were not confirmed, yet the press were sufficiently tenacious to extract the fact that a bomb had been planted and detonated by Sherlock Holmes, who had already been on the wanted list for drug-fueled murder of the fortune-teller known as Denarius.

The press had a field day and patriotic fervour was unbridled. My name was bandied around the press and I was badgered by reporters and hounded in public when seen wearing a black armband in memory of my friend. I was, as I said as I began this missive, spat upon in public until in a fit of anger in front of a group of reporters I tore it off myself and tossed it into the gutter where I ground it under my foot.

It was three days later, and the newspapers were full of the diplomatic efforts to prevent the plunge into European War when I was invited by Mycroft Holmes to attend a private dinner at an unnamed private club in Mayfair. He arranged to have me collected and taken to the place, only to be taken aside and dressed as a waiter.

"Did you bring your service revolver as I suggested?" the elder Holmes asked me as I and several other waiters were prepared before the dinner.

Having done as instructed and served at table as instructed, I took my place, standing at attention at the side of the dining room.

There were eight diners, seven men and a woman. They chatted through the dinner and politely clapped when an elderly Prussian gentleman was introduced and stood to make a speech.

"My friends and fellow anarchists," he began, his voice slightly slurred from an abundance of wine. "Let us drink to our successful assassination of—"

A tall military man sitting beside the woman shot to his feet. "Count Leo, have a care!" He looked meaningfully at myself and the other waiters.

"But why, Colonel Maltravers?" replied the speaker, suddenly growing tall. The voice was that of Sherlock Holmes. "After all, you and your fellow anarchists are here to celebrate your botched attempt to drop the world into war. Your plot failed and Prince Edward, Joseph Chamberlain, and the German Chancellor are alive and well."

A revolver suddenly appeared in the diner's hand and the hammer was ratcheted back.

My reaction was cool and professional. My service revolver spat flame and the man Holmes had identified as Colonel Maltravers, and whom I knew to be the Member of Parliament for Holborn was hurled back, clutching his shoulder.

Panic seized the other guests and they attempted to leave but were immediately detained and arrested by Inspector Lestrade and his officers, the other waiters.

⁂

"I am so sorry to have had to subject you to this prolonged charade, my good fellow," said Holmes as he, Mycroft, Inspector Lestrade, and I sat drinking whisky and sodas late that night in the familiar rooms at 221b Baker Street. "It was necessary to have you believe that I had lost my sanity."

He looked grim. "Although I will chide myself for Albert Wilson, the notorious canary trainer's murder. I had not expected Maltravers to be so stealthy as to have avoided the creak in the stairs."

"He and his fellow anarchists had plotted to sabotage Her Majesty, Queen Victoria's Diamond Jubilee," said Mycroft. "When Joseph Chamberlain suggested having a Festival of Empire, which is to be attended by the prime ministers of the Dominions rather than the crowned heads of state, they saw their opportunity. The queen seized on it, as she did not want to invite her nephew Kaiser Wilhemm II of Germany. Prince Edward was tasked with discussing the situation and help with the planning, hence this preliminary meeting with the German Chancellor Chlodwick, Prince of Hohenlohe-Schillingsfürst. We knew that there would be an attempt at assassination, but we did not know where or when."

Sherlock Holmes took over. "I had been acting for several clients who had been snared by the character known as Denarius and I knew something of his blackmailing boss, but I did not know who he was masquerading as in his new identity. He is actually Colonel Peregrin Maltravers, cashiered out of the Royal Artillery for embezzling regimental funds. Ironically, his brother officer and a distant cousin, Sir William Gordon-Cumming, was also cashiered out of the Scots Guards after having been found guilty of cheating in the Royal Baccarat Scandal of 1890. Prince Edward, the Prince of Wales, was called as a prosecution witness and there was bad blood ever after. Maltravers wanted to avenge his cousin by assassinating the prince."

Holmes sipped his whisky. "I devised this elaborate scheme with Mycroft and Lestrade, in order to flush out Maltravers. I had not anticipated that the colonel would have fallen in love with the fortune-teller's wife, his precious canary Polly Washburn and that the pernicious pair had taken the opportunity to murder him and pin the blame on myself. Then that night, I was so intent upon selling Denarius my pre-arranged tea leaf message that I did not hear Maltravers sneak upon myself with whatever he used to knock me out. What happened then I can only speculate about, but it is clear that he slipped my jack-knife into Denarius's heart. For that alone, he will hang, and Polly Washburn will stand trial as an accessory."

"I am sorry that I gave you a rough time, Doctor," said Lestrade apologetically.

I harrumphed. "I take it Wiggins was the urchin who planted the message to Mycroft in my pocket?"

Holmes nodded. "My Baker Street Irregulars will each of them make fine policemen one day, I have no doubt. They are like wraiths and can follow anyone about London without being seen themselves. I had instructed Wiggins to follow anyone who came out of my rooms that night. When I was carried out by Maltravers and bundled into the Hansom cab, he and his fellows were able to trail it without any difficulty. They also tailed Maltravers to his home. It was easy work for Mycroft to discover the plans for this celebration of the anarchist group."

"So it was known where you were all the time?" I gasped in disbelief.

"We knew," acknowledged Mycroft. "But we did not know when the deed was going to be done. We think that as an MP Maltravers somehow got news of the meeting and arranged the planting of the bomb. He was a bomb expert when he served in the Royal Artillery, you see."

Holmes nodded. "It was fortunate that I had personally studied under Sir Vivien Dering Majendie, the bomb disposal expert for just such an eventuality. Thus, I was able to disable the device and yet cause an impressive light, noise, and dust pseudo-explosion at the arranged time. And since locks, chains, and ropes present little difficulty for me, between their visits, I was as free as I wanted to be. I kept in communication with Mycroft and Lestrade through Wiggins and the Irregulars."

"And so, war with Europe was averted," I said.

"For now, at any rate," said Holmes, reaching for the decanter and the gasogene to replenish our drinks. "But who can say what the tea leaves might say tomorrow?"

The Adventure of
the Black Key

Naching T. Kassa

"The evils of the countryside never cease to amaze, Watson," Sherlock Holmes said, one dreary February morning. "The great houses stand as communities to themselves, isolated from the others by fields of green and gold. Many a scream has gone unheard in such places. Many a victim has gone unaided." He tossed an envelope upon the table before me. "Our new client fears for her sanity."

I picked up the plain and inexpensive envelope which bore Holmes's name and studied the Surrey postmark. The faint scent of lavender wafted toward me as I opened it. The note, written on foolscap and in a neat and feminine hand, read thus:

> Mr. Sherlock Holmes,
>
> I am in need of your services. I will call upon you the morning of the 27th at nine.
>
> Yours,
>
> P.B.

"She does not seem fearful to me," I said, looking up from the missive.

"Then you have not read it as I have. Look closer. Perhaps, you will deduce her identity as well."

"You know who she is?"

"The moment I opened the envelope, I knew. The author of the note is Lady Penelope Bramstead."

"Lady Bramstead!" I cried, staring at Holmes with wide eyes. "The renowned recluse? What has brought you to such a conclusion?"

Holmes chuckled. "The solution is not as complicated as it may seem. Taken separately, the clues mean little. Together, they mean the world. Though the envelope and paper seem cheap, the traces of perfume which permeate them are not. The perfume costs three pounds per ounce. Only a woman of means could afford such a scent. There is no return address; however, the postmark from Surrey identifies the lady's place of origin. And the initials, of course, hint at a name. Also, I find a certain air of imperiousness in the wording of the note. There is no request; there is only command. It says, 'I *will* call upon you,' not '*May* I call upon you.' She is accustomed to being obeyed."

"But...her fear...how did you deduce that?"

"Her efforts in hiding her identity have been painstaking ones. In case the letter was discovered, she did not wish anyone to know she was on her way to see me. She is reclusive and yet, she would leave her home in order to come to Baker Street. Only a fear greater than she has ever known could induce her to come here. She has composed this letter several times before sending it. It is all there, if you know where to look."

Holmes plucked a pencil off the table and gently rubbed the lead over the page. Unseen words suddenly appeared.

"My sanity is at stake," I read.

"Impressions from the pages which came before," Holmes explained. "And, here, where she has pressed hard upon the pen. Read here."

"I am at my wit's end."

"And the last, here."

"Lady Bramstead." I shook my head. "Amazing, Holmes."

My companion grinned. "It is elementary. But, come. The clock has just struck nine, and I hear the lady's foot upon the stair."

The door opened then, and Mrs. Hudson entered. A woman, dressed in black and wearing a heavy veil, followed.

"Would you be good enough to bring us tea, Mrs. Hudson," Holmes said, before our landlady could say a word. "I believe the lady will need it after such a trying morning."

Mrs. Hudson took her leave as Holmes motioned our visitor to the settee.

"Dr. Watson has my complete confidence," Holmes said, as she took her seat. "You may trust him as I do, Lady Bramstead."

The woman froze, then lifted the veil, revealing a pale face. I nearly gasped in surprise. Hers was not the countenance of an old and frightened ascetic, but one graced with wisdom and beauty. She stared at Holmes with melancholy eyes. "How ever did you know?"

"Your note revealed much to me. However, time grows short and it seems things have grown worse since last you wrote. Pray, tell us what has occurred."

"You must be a magician, Mr. Holmes," Lady Bramstead replied. "Indeed, events have transpired which have sharpened my terror. My housekeeper, Mrs. Thomas, was murdered last night."

Having uttered these words, the lady began to tremble and sway. I hurried from my chair and to her side, clasping her cold hand in my own. She rallied and favoured me with a weak smile.

"When did this unfortunate event take place," Holmes pressed gently.

"Her body was discovered in the kitchen, a little after midnight."

"Who found her?"

"My brother, Harrison Lettridge. It is his habit to check the locks when the staff has gone for the night."

"They do not stay at the house?"

"Most leave in the evening and return in the morning. Mrs. Thomas was the only one who remained all night." She pulled her left hand from mine and clasped it with her right. "Oh, Mr. Holmes! I feel I am to blame for her dark fate."

Holmes settled into the chair facing her and closed his eyes. "What makes you say so?"

Lady Bramstead lowered her eyes and, for the first time, a hint of colour touched her cheek. "It is difficult to speak of this. I fear you will not believe me. I scarce believe it myself."

"Fear not," I said. "You are among friends here."

She smiled again and continued. "Perhaps it is best if I begin at the beginning, then. You have, no doubt, heard of my husband, Lord Richard Bramstead."

"The famous adventurer and linguist?" Holmes said, lifting an eyelid.

"The same. He was a handsome man with the strength of Samson. Most thought him a quick-tempered brute, but he was always as gentle as a lamb with me. We had been married but a year when he took his last journey to Africa. He met his death there, felled by a spear which pierced his dear heart.

"I was inconsolable for the first year and, I am ashamed to say, became a danger to myself. It was my brother who saved me. He came to live with me during this terrible time, and I don't know what I should have done without him.

"Two more grief-stricken years passed. I shunned the world, keeping to the house and myself, with only my brother and Mrs. Thomas as companions. Then, one night about a month ago, I began to hear...*it.*"

Holmes opened both eyes and stared at her Ladyship. She returned his gaze, her eyes pleading.

"I heard a voice, Mr. Holmes. A strange whisper which filled my room nearly every night. Sometimes, it would moan in the ghastliest way. Other times, it would call my name. I tried several times to speak with the voice, but it would not answer."

"Did you reveal this to anyone?" Holmes asked.

"At first, I told no one. To tell the truth, Mr. Holmes, I doubted my own sanity and feared others would as well. Then, I thought of you. I hoped you would help me with my problem. I wrote you and Mrs. Thomas mailed the letter."

"She grew suspicious?"

Lady Bramstead nodded. "That evening, she confronted me in my bedroom. She asked why I had written you."

"And it was then she heard the voice?"

Lady Bramstead's eyes widened. "My goodness, Mr. Holmes. One would think you were present in the house that fateful night. Yes, to my great relief, she did hear it. And, for the first time, we both heard it speak. In a soft, yet clear voice, it said, 'seek the black key.' And, because she kept all the keys to the house, Mrs. Thomas hurried off to retrieve them. I waited for her in my room." She lowered her eyes. "If only I had gone with her."

"She did not return." Holmes said.

A single tear spilled down over Lady Bramstead's cheek. "I waited for over twenty minutes before I heard Harrison's voice from downstairs. He tried to keep me from her, but I pushed past him. When I entered the kitchen, I found the outer door ajar and Mrs. Thomas on the stone floor. The poor woman lay face down near the door, the ring of keys but inches from her fingers. I turned her over and—Oh, Mr. Holmes! Her face! I shall never forget her face." The lady closed her eyes and shook her head as though trying to purge the terrible sight from her mind. "It bore an expression of horror and dread such as I have never known."

Mrs. Hudson entered at that moment bearing a silver tray. She left it on the table and took her leave. The aroma of fresh tea filled the room and I rose to pour the lady a cup. She accepted it with a grateful nod and sipped. When she had sufficiently recovered, she continued.

"Harrison pulled me away from the frightful vision and took me to the sitting room. There I remained until the police arrived. Only then did I learn the extent of Mrs. Thomas's injuries. She had been attacked and suffered a grievous wound to the back of her head. I heard the constable remarking on how odd it was."

Holmes suddenly leaned forward in his chair. "Odd? How so?"

"He said there was little to no blood on the kitchen floor. Such a wound should have produced a copious amount."

Holmes leapt to his feet and began to pace before the fireplace. "Was anything missing? Had anything been taken?"

"Nothing in the house appeared to be missing, but I could not say whether any of the keys were. I found no black key on Mrs. Thomas's ring. If there had been one, the murderer may have taken it."

"And what of the voice?"

"I have not heard it since. Though, it may return this evening. Perhaps, you would be so good as to come to my home and delve into this mystery? I would be eternally grateful."

"Your problem is an intriguing one. And, if I may be so bold as to speak for the good doctor, I should say we both shall be glad to come."

"Indeed," said I. "I should not miss it."

"Thank you, both." She removed a ring from her finger and held it out to Holmes. "I am a wealthy woman, Mr. Holmes, but my brother has taken charge of my financial matters. I would rather our association goes without his notice. This ring contains a diamond my husband found upon his travels. It is worth several thousand pounds. I would like you to take it in lieu of a fee."

Holmes waved her hand away. "I've yet to perform my investigation, Lady Bramstead. I'm afraid I cannot accept a fee at this time."

The lady replaced the ring and rose to her feet. "Then, I shall be on my way. You have, no doubt, heard of my husband's ancestral home of Briarcliffe near Cranleigh?"

"I have. A venerable home which has stood since the days of Elizabeth I."

The lady smiled. "Then, you know where to find me." She rose to her feet.

"A minute, your Ladyship," Holmes said. "Your brother, was he fond of your husband?"

Lady Bramstead bit her lip. "Their friendship was a contentious one. Harrison was not happy with the match. He thought Richard too brash for me and it was his wish that I marry...another." Her brow furrowed at these words and a look of distaste affected her comely features. It vanished as she continued. "However, they seemed to have reconciled before my husband's departure and my brother was much affected by the news of his death."

"Are you still acquainted with this other man? The one your brother preferred."

"James Straff is one of our nearest neighbours and I see him from time to time. He moved into the house next door when Richard and I began courting."

"Did Straff know your brother before he took up residence in the house?"

"Yes. They had been at university together."

"Then, you knew him as well?"

"No. I met him at a party given by Harrison. Mr. Straff is a small, thin man with a face not unlike a rodent. He became rather infatuated with me and caused some embarrassing situations for Richard. They almost came to blows on several occasions. I did not see him much after we married. Only recently has he returned to keep my brother's company at Briarcliffe. I wish he had not."

"He has renewed his romantic attentions?"

She nodded a pained expression on her face. "I have tried to dissuade him from such pursuits, but he has not heeded me. Harrison has agreed to speak to him on my behalf. I hope he will be more successful."

Holmes nodded. "Will he be at Briarcliffe this evening?"

"No, he and my brother are here in London. They play cards at their club every Tuesday evening. Even though he has moved to the country, there are few things in the city Harrison has been willing to forego."

"You say your brother and his companion will be gone for the evening? Then we shall take the afternoon train. You may rest assured. He will not know we have been to Briarcliffe."

"Thank you, Mr. Holmes. I am grateful."

She took her leave and Holmes retreated to the fireplace. He took the cherrywood pipe from the coal scuttle and placed the stem between his teeth. Finding none of the dottles he usually kept on the mantel, he reached into the Persian slipper and pulled out a pinch of shag. This he placed in the bowl of the pipe and, having tamped and lit it with a match, took a deep draw. He breathed a ring of smoke about his head.

"In recent months, Watson, I have related to you some of my journeys as Sigerson, a Norwegian adventurer of some repute. During my travels, I had the pleasure of meeting Lord Bramstead. He was an interesting fellow with a rather large scar across the left side of his face. He said it came from the spear of a Somali warrior. Bramstead was clever, so clever Mycroft recruited him. I am sorry to hear of his demise."

"It was a sad time." I replied. "And all of London was in mourning. The country was still reeling from your disappearance at Reichenbach, and his death at such a young age was quite shocking."

Holmes glanced up at me, his expression puzzled. He seemed about to speak but shook his head and began to pace once more. At last, he disappeared into his bedroom and emerged moments later, dressed in his overcoat.

"Meet me at Charing Cross Station in an hour, Watson," said he. "We will be staying in Cranleigh overnight, I think. And be sure to bring your revolver. I've no doubt we may run into some devilry before we are through."

Before I could say another word, he had hurried out the door.

Holmes met me exactly an hour later, his face flushed and an eager gleam in his eye. We boarded the train bound for Cranleigh without a moment to spare.

I huddled in my overcoat as fields of white rushed past our window. The grey sky grew ominous, and a dull pain plagued me where the Jezail bullet had entered my leg so many years ago. Holmes leaned forward in his seat, offered me a cigarette from his case, and then lit his own.

"I wired the village constable before we took our leave," he said. "He confirmed Lady Bramstead's observation. There was indeed a decided lack of blood at the scene. They searched the house and found no corresponding stain."

"She was murdered outside then?"

"A search was conducted on the grounds as well, but nothing was found. Since there is no sign of a break-in, it is assumed the murderer entered the unlocked door and, finding Mrs. Thomas in the kitchen preparing to lock up, murdered her before she gave the alarm. He then fled through the door upon hearing the approach of Harrison Lettridge. That is the unimaginative theory of the country constabulary."

Holmes's face grew grave. "We are dealing with a particularly dangerous fellow here, Watson. Any man who would attack a woman in such a way possesses little conscience. You brought your revolver?"

"I did."

"Good." He leaned back in the seat. "After I wired the constable, I went to the Diogenes Club. Mycroft was quite interested in our little problem. Though, I'm afraid, it will not force him from the orbit he inhabits. He has, however, enlightened me and given a suggestion which may be of use."

"What was it?"

"He suggested I go looking for a priest."

"A priest? Whatever for?"

"I suppose I shall learn that once we arrive at Briarcliffe." He closed his eyes. "Be a good fellow and wake me once we arrive at the station, Watson. I've had precious little sleep since our investigation of the *Friesland* concluded and the rest will do me good."

I woke Holmes just before three, when we arrived at the station. After visiting the nearest inn, we hired a dogcart to take us out to Briarcliffe. It was not far from the village, perhaps a drive of fifteen minutes, though the chill did little for my old wound.

The manor stood on a hill, an imposing sight against the darkening sky. Its architecture did indeed reach back to those far off days of the sixteenth century, and Holmes seemed much interested in its history. He posed several questions to our driver, a man who eyed him suspiciously at first, but soon warmed when offered a half-crown for information.

"Lord Bramstead's ancestors weren't loyal to the queen," said he, in answer to Holmes's query. "It's well known their sympathies lay with the Catholics. They say many a priest was saved by hidin' here."

"I suppose the new inhabitants of Briarcliffe are aware of its history?"

"The lady's brother is. Been askin' questions up and down the village in past weeks. Him and that friend of his. Heard tell they were lookin' for a black key. But, in all my years, I've never heard of such a thing."

After our driver had left us at the front door and gone on his way, I turned to Holmes and said, "Lady Bramstead's brother must have heard the strange voice as well if he too is looking for the black key."

Holmes did not answer. His eyes roved over the walls of the first floor and the earth near the windows.

I rapped upon the door and it swung open. The lady herself stepped out to meet us.

Dressed in her customary black, but without her dark veil, Lady Bramstead quickly admitted us into the house. She carried a lamp in one hand, and her coppery-coloured hair gleamed in the light it cast.

"I have dismissed the staff for the day," she said as she led us inside. "We are alone in the house. Please, come this way."

We followed her through the well-furnished home and into the kitchen. Once there, she pointed to the floor near the outer door.

"Harrison found poor Mrs. Thomas lying here and, save for removing the body, nothing has been altered since."

"For that, I thank you," Holmes said and set to work at once. Pulling his glass from his pocket, he quickly dropped to the floor and examined the spot Lady Bramstead had indicated. He then rose to his feet and taking the lamp from the lady's hand, circled the room.

"It is as I feared," he said when he had finished. "Mrs. Thomas was not killed in this room. She met her end elsewhere in the house."

"How do you know this?" Lady Bramstead asked.

"First, the lack of blood. It is true a terrible wound would leave a large stain and yet, there is nary a trace upon this floor. Also—" He crossed the room and directed our attention to the floor near the south wall. "There are marks here, like those made by a door sweeping across the floor. I believe there is a hidden door here."

"Once again you have amazed me, Mr. Holmes," the lady said. "There is indeed a door. It leads to a secret corridor within the walls of this house."

She joined Holmes before the wall and, with the toe of her shoe, nudged a small stone near the bottom. They stepped away as the door swung outward.

"Does anyone else know of this passage?" Holmes asked.

Lady Bramstead shook her head. "I do not think so. Richard had closed the house upon the death of his father and did not open it until after our marriage. All the staff, including Mrs. Thomas, were hired then. Richard never revealed it to anyone but me. It was a secret between us, one I never intended to share."

"Where does the corridor lead?"

"Throughout the house."

"Does it pass your bedroom?"

"It does. But the voice could not have come from within it."

"You are certain?"

"Each time I have heard the voice, I have searched it. I never found anyone. Come. You can see for yourself."

Taking the lamp from his hand, she stepped into the corridor, and we followed single file.

The passage led us past several rooms and only once were we required to leave it.

"The ceiling is unsafe here," Lady Bramstead said, pointing to the crumbling stone overhead. "There was a fire in the room above sometime before Richard and I took possession of the house. He had intended to have it repaired but the opportunity never presented itself. We will detour through here."

She moved into a side passage and opened a wooden door. We entered a large and sumptuous sitting room, perhaps the most beautiful I have ever beheld.

Carpets from Persia covered the floors, and long velvet curtains flanked the windows. Two chairs and a settee stood near the centre of the room, and a piano stood off in one corner. A fire had been lit in the nearby fireplace, and several weapons were mounted above the mantel, including a handsome crossbow.

"An interesting piece of weaponry," Holmes remarked.

"My husband's," the lady said, her tone wistful. "He was a student of history as well as language and quite proud of that piece. He was the only one with strength enough to draw it back. Many men, including my brother and Mr. Straff have taken their turns, but none could shift it."

She took us past the piano to a tapestried wall. Once there, she pulled a silken rope which drew the tapestry back like a curtain, revealing a large wooden door. She turned the knob and we followed her through it.

Once again, we travelled down the stone corridor with Lady Bramstead in the lead. At one point, we happened upon a place where the passage branched off into three separate corridors. The left passage led into darkness, while the right ended at a stone wall.

"Where does this passage lead?" Holmes asked, pointing to the one before us.

"To the servant's quarters."

"And Mrs. Thomas's room?"

"Yes."

"What of this corridor on the left?"

"It leads to my bedroom. It is but a few feet from here. We will have to climb a few steps to reach it."

"And this on the right, leads only to a blank wall?"

"It has always been so."

"Why?"

"I do not know. Richard never said."

We continued to the left and soon arrived at a set of steps which took us up to another wooden door. The lady opened it and we stepped inside the room.

A large mahogany bed, a dressing table, a soft chair, and an ottoman greeted the eye as we entered. A full-length mirror, framed in gilt, stood in one corner of the room. Persian rugs covered the stone floor, just as they had in the sitting room.

"Do you see, Mr. Holmes?" Lady Bramstead said. "The narrowness of the passage left little place for hiding. The master of the voice could not have hidden from me every time I looked."

"Indeed," Holmes agreed. He took the lamp from her and turned to investigate the room.

"Where have you heard the voice?" he asked.

"There," she said gesturing to the left side of the bed. "The whispers seem to emanate from that place. Though, I could not tell you whether they come from above or below. They seem to be all around me."

Holmes crossed to the place and studied the space behind the headboard. The lamplight flickered, causing the shadows to cavort across the ceiling.

"I believe I have discovered the means by which the voice is heard," Holmes said. "There is a crack in the stone near the floor."

"How can that be?" the lady asked. "I have never seen—"

A loud knock suddenly sounded upon the door and a voice called out, "Penelope? Penelope, have you someone in there with you?"

"My brother," Lady Bramstead whispered.

"Into the passage," Holmes said to me. We rushed to the secret door and hid behind it. A thin crack between the door and the jamb afforded us full view of the scene which unfolded.

"There is no one here but me, Harrison," Lady Bramstead said as the tall, red-headed man entered the room. He bore an oil lamp of his own and the light flickered over his handsome features.

"What are you doing here in the dark?" he asked, his tone accusing.

"I had a headache and thought I might lie down."

Harrison Lettridge held the lamp aloft and quickly surveyed the room. "I thought I heard a man's voice in here." His piercing green eyes lingered on our hiding place for a long moment before turning away. "It appears I was mistaken."

"Of course, you were. Who would come to visit me? I know no one save you and Mr. Straff and I would never allow him in my bedroom. What a strange thing to say, Harrison."

"I suppose it was a trick of the mind." His look softened. "I am sorry, Penelope. Say you will forgive me."

"I will. Though, I must say I am surprised to see you. I thought you would be at the club with Mr. Straff this evening."

"We did go but found the weather too bleak. I thought we might return and keep you company."

"I would prefer to keep your company and not Mr. Straff's. Have you spoken to him?"

"I have not found the opportune moment. Would you rather I sent him home?"

"I would."

"Then, I shall do so. Come downstairs and I shall send him on his way."

The light faded from the room. I closed the secret door and then followed Holmes down the steps and into the passageway. We passed through the stone corridor, pausing only when we reached the blank wall.

"No, Watson, this way," Holmes said, taking my arm and pulling me toward the passage which led to the servant's quarters. "There is something in Mrs. Thomas's room I must see."

Moments later, we stepped through a wooden door and into a plainly furnished bedroom. The bed stood against the opposite wall, while a small table stood at the centre of the room. Several sheets of correspondence lay upon the table. All were addressed to Mrs. Lydia Thomas.

Holmes examined the sheets, then laid them back down and knelt beside the table. He drew his index finger across the floor and then pinched it against his thumb.

"Dust," he said. "A peculiar thing to see in the room of a housekeeper. I am thankful for it, however. It has left us many a clue." He moved the table aside and pointed to several footprints, then shifted his focus to the bed. He studied the pillow at length, then stood upon the mattress and examined what looked to be a hook in the wall.

"Move that table, Watson," he said. "Then, come help me move the bed."

I did as he asked and then, the two of us transferred the bed to the centre of the room.

"Look here, Watson," Holmes said. "This is where Mrs. Thomas met her unhappy end."

A rust-coloured stain covered the floor where the bed had once stood.

"She was attacked here, and the bed was moved to cover the stain. The murderer placed the table at the centre of the room, but he failed to clean the floor before doing so. You can see the marks where the bed stood and the dust which had accumulated under it. Such a ploy would no doubt confuse the country constabulary. It did not mislead me."

"Who would do such a thing, Holmes?"

"Someone who even now hides within the secret passages of this house. Come, Watson. We must hurry or a man's life, perhaps even the life of Lady Bramstead, will be forfeit."

We retraced our steps to the blank wall. Here, Holmes paused once more.

"Do you see anything remarkable about this wall, Watson?" he asked.

"It is strange that this branch of the corridor should lead to a stone wall. Also...the placement. It lies directly beneath Lady Bramstead's room."

"Capital, Watson! You have hit upon the point exactly. Have you ever heard of a Priest Hole?"

"I cannot say that I have."

"Like most of those who were secretly sympathetic to the Catholic faith, the Bramsteads built secret passageways and rooms into their homes. In these rooms, they could hide the priests who suffered persecution during Elizabeth I's reign."

"Then, this wall is part of a secret room?"

Holmes nodded. "We must find a way to gain entrance."

"What do you suppose we will find inside?"

"A prisoner."

I stood dumbfounded as Holmes held the lamp up to the wall and quickly inspected the stones at the bottom.

"It was his voice Lady Bramstead heard through the crack in her bedroom," Holmes said. "Last night, he escaped and hid himself in Mrs. Thomas's room. She found him in her bed when she came to retrieve the keys." He grinned up at me. "I found strands of a woman's hair on the correspondence, blonde hair. It certainly did not match the masculine strands of black I found on the pillow.

"His captors had come to the same conclusion as Mrs. Thomas and Lady Bramstead had. They came to Mrs. Thomas's room to take the keys and discovered their prisoner and the housekeeper together. One, the shorter of the two, attacked her from behind. They moved the bed to cover the stain, then carried Mrs. Thomas's body through the passage and into the kitchen to arrange their little scene."

"How do you know there were two men?"

"They left several footprints in the dust when they moved the bed. One man had a shorter stride than the other. His boots were smaller as well. I have no doubt the taller man was Harrison Lettridge. As to the shorter man, well, he and I are old friends. I knew him the minute Lady Bramstead described him."

He gave a little cry of triumph at that moment as a stone sank into the wall beneath his touch. The hidden door swung outward and I drew my revolver as Holmes entered the small room beyond.

In a wooden chair at the centre of the empty room sat a man with a black beard. His chin lay upon his breast, his eyes closed. Thick cords secured his wrists to the arms of the chair and his ankles to the chair's legs. We both hurried to his side, and he stirred as we untied the ropes which bound him.

"Who are you?" he asked, his speech slurred. A quick examination revealed he had been drugged, but the effects had already begun to weaken.

"I know you," he said to Holmes. "Do I know you?"

"Friends to Lady Bramstead," I answered. "Sit still, we shall have you loose in but a moment."

The man blinked and tried to rise from the chair, but the cords which held his wrists held him fast. He grasped hold of my arm and gazed at me with wide and haunted eyes.

"Forget me. You must find the one without a lock and touch the 36th. Find it now, before they do. If they find it first, they will kill her. They will kill us all."

He collapsed into the chair.

"He is raving," I said. "Suffering from the effects of the drug. Fear not, he will be right soon enough."

Holmes finished loosening the prisoner's bonds and rose to his feet. "We cannot leave him here. Take an arm, Watson. We will drag him if we must."

We took the unconscious man from the Priest Hole and up the passage which led to Lady Bramstead's room. There, we laid him upon the bed.

"The lady is in danger, Holmes," I said. "We must hurry to her aid."

"You are ever the white knight, Watson. The lady will be safe as long as we find the key first."

He fell silent, then suddenly cried out. "Ah! I have been a dolt! Come, Watson!"

He hurried back into the passage and I followed at his heels.

We arrived at the sitting room but moments later and found, to our surprise, two men waiting as we burst through the door.

Harrison Lettridge stared at us, his eyes wide with surprise. At his side stood a much shorter man with the face of a rodent. He drew a pistol as we entered.

A soft whimper caught my attention, and I glimpsed Lady Bramstead on the settee. A large, purplish bruise had begun to form on her cheek. I drew my revolver.

We faced one another as Lettridge stepped forward. "What is the meaning of this?" he blustered.

"Your game is at an end, Lettridge." Holmes announced. "We have freed your prisoner and the black key is lost to you."

Lettridge managed a weak smile. "You do not know where it is."

"I am closer to it now than you will ever be."

"Don't listen to him," the shorter man sneered. "He's nothing but a meddling busy body. You should have stayed at the bottom of that waterfall, Holmes."

"One cannot stay in a place one has have never been, Mr. Straff. Or should I address you by your right name? Igor Menloff?"

"Holmes?" Lettridge cried, trembling. "Sherlock Holmes? And he knows who you are! You said no one would know!"

"Quiet," Menloff commanded. "Don't show the white feather. We'll soon get out of this alright."

"I suppose you are an authority where courage is concerned, Menloff," Holmes retorted. "It takes very little of it to murder one woman and mistreat another." He turned to Lettridge. "I think you will find that treason against the crown exacts a much higher price than the gambling debts you owe, Mr. Lettridge. Better to turn yourself in now—"

"Don't you take another step forward," Menloff snarled at Lettridge. "You do and you'll find a hole in the back of your head."

"It's over, Menloff. We—no, don't!"

"Watch them, Watson!" Holmes cried.

Menloff trained his pistol on Lettridge and would have fired if Lady Bramstead had not thrown herself upon him. He struggled with her as Lettridge fled through the secret door on the opposite side of the room.

Menloff quickly gained the upper hand as Holmes and I rushed forward. He seized Lady Bramstead about the neck and shoulders.

"Stay back!" Menloff cried. "I will kill her. The sentence for one murder is the same as two and I've nothing left to lose. Just let me go."

"How do I know you will not kill her once you leave this room?" Holmes said. "Your word is worthless to me."

A wicked grin spread over the blackguard's face. "That is a chance you'll have to take. Let us make a bargain. You get the key for me and I'll let her go."

Holmes frowned. "Very well."

"Keep away from us, if you please," Menloff said. "That's it."

Holmes crossed to the piano.

"The black key without a lock is not meant for a door," Holmes said. "It is made of ebony and I must touch the 36th."

He touched the 36th ebony key on the piano. It made no sound, but a small panel above slid open. Inside the recess lay a packet of papers which Holmes withdrew.

"Bring those to me," Menloff said.

"You plan to sell them?"

"It is not your business whether I sell them or not."

"In the wrong hands, these papers could seriously compromise British holdings in the Sudan. Hundreds could die."

"That is not my affair. I've a commission I must satisfy and nothing more."

"Then...there is nothing more to be said. I will leave you with this thought: 'The blade itself incites to deeds of violence.' "

"Pretty words won't help you now, Mr. Sherlock Holmes. Hand the papers over or—"

Menloff trailed off, his face pale and eyes wide. He lost his grip on Lady Bramstead and slipped to the floor.

The bearded man stood near the fireplace, the crossbow in his hands. I hurried to Menloff's side and found the bolt buried in his back.

Lady Bramstead stared at the bearded man, the tears streaming down her cheeks. "Dear God!" she murmured. "Please...please...let this be true and not a dream."

The bearded man dropped the crossbow to the floor. Tears shone in his blue eyes and his voice wavered as he spoke. "It is no dream, Penelope."

"Richard!" she cried and rushed into his arms. "My love! Oh, my only love! You are alive! How? And how did you come to be here?"

"I will tell you in a moment, my love. Let me sit and catch my breath."

I helped Lord Bramstead to a nearby chair and poured him a glass of brandy from the decanter. He took it and after he had finished, began his amazing tale.

"The news of my death was erroneously reported," Lord Bramstead said. "I was wounded by a spear, it is true, but I did not die. The spear pierced my cheek and not my heart. I have always been in the employ of the Crown and when they asked me to feign death in order to infiltrate some of the most dangerous foreign organisations, I agreed. But on one condition. They were to release me after a period of two years and allow me to return to you.

"Many's the time I picked up my pen to write you, my love. But my work depended upon my secret. It drove me near mad when I learned what my absence had done to you.

"On the third of January, I was finally granted a leave to return to England and you. I came home to you first and hid the dispatches in the piano, intending to take them to London the next day. Unfortunately, I met your brother Harrison and the toad, Menloff, first. They tricked me into a drink and drugged me. In my intoxicated state, I revealed the location of the secret passage and the Priest Hole, but I did not reveal the location of the papers. They imprisoned and tortured me, keeping me drugged when neither could be with me. Yesterday, was the first time I found myself in my right mind. I tricked Menloff into leaving me and when he had gone, I attacked Harrison, knocking him to the floor. I escaped, but in my weakened condition, I could not even climb the steps to my wife's room. So, I made my way to Mrs. Thomas's instead. Would to God that I had not."

"Menloff killed her and they returned you to the stone prison," Holmes said.

Lord Bramstead nodded. "And there I remained until you and your friend found me. You removed me from my prison and helped me avenge myself upon my captor."

Lady Bramstead had gone quite pale during the descriptions of her brother's actions. She took her husband's hand and said, "Harrison will pay for what he has done, my love. I am sure of it."

Lord Bramstead squeezed her hand.

"I believe these are yours," Holmes said, handing the papers to Lord Bramstead.

"I cannot thank you enough," he said as he accepted them. "You have saved not only the lives of myself and my wife, but hundreds of lives in the Sudan."

"And you have restored my husband to me," Lady Bramstead added. "I offered you my ring before. I offer you five-thousand pounds now."

Holmes waved a dismissive hand. "My work is its own reward."

"I have heard those words before," Lord Bramstead said. He peered carefully at Holmes. "I am sorry for staring at you, Sir, but I feel as though I know you. Have we met?"

"In another life, Lord Bramstead. In another life. Will you remain in England long?"

"I am too well known here, I'm afraid, and too many know of my reputation. I prefer to remain dead to the world, and plan to live out my days in the south of France, if my wife is willing."

"I would travel to the ends of the earth with you," she replied. "I fear you will not leave my sight again."

"And you will not leave mine."

"I suspected the brother from the first," Holmes said, as we boarded the morning train for London. "Lady Bramstead feared and distrusted him, though she would never say it. She told me in other ways, however. Hiding our association from him and dismissing the servants so they could not tell him what she had done were but two of them. There were others."

"One thing puzzles me greatly," I said. "How on earth did you know Lord Bramstead was alive? And how did you know he was being held prisoner?"

"You provided me with the information about Lord Bramstead's death when you informed me, he had died shortly after I was supposed to have perished at the falls of Reichenbach. I met him two years after my supposed death, so I knew he was still alive. A quick visit to Mycroft confirmed this, as did the fact that Lord Bramstead had only just returned to England. He had planned to return to Briarcliffe before his disappearance, and Lady Bramstead had heard a voice which knew her name, ergo he must be a prisoner in his own home. I also knew that Lady Bramstead's erstwhile and clumsy suitor, James Straff, fit the description of a known foreign agent, Igor Menloff. This man appeared only when Lord Bramstead was present. He knew of Bramstead's true vocation and no doubt sought the company of his fiancé and later, his bride, in order to learn his secrets. Letteridge allowed him access to the lady and the house because he owed Menloff money."

"He would have sold his own sister," I said in disgust. "It is a shame he disappeared and was not captured by the police."

"I am not so sure he disappeared," Holmes said. "Lord Bramstead informed me, before we left this morning, that the crumbling ceiling outside the sitting room fell in last night. It is unlikely we will see Harrison Letteridge again. Have I cleared all of the points you found confusing?"

"There is one. The quote you spoke to Menloff before Lord Bramstead appeared, what was it from?"

"It was from Homer's *Odyssey*. I found it an appropriate quote at the time, Watson. Didn't you?"

The World Is Full of Obvious Things

Jon Courtenay Grimwood

Her Majesty was old by the time we met. Small, with a bun-like face and a round body swathed in widow's weeds for a man dead of a chill thirty years before. When she stood, I realised how short she was, a fact I'd already intuited from her thick heels, how straight she sat, and the fact her chair needed a dais to bring it to desk height.

She was barely taller than a child.

An Indian princeling rushed to pull back her chair, only to be brushed away. He pretended to sulk; she pretended to be angry. They looked at each other and smiled as the game was ended. He had dark and liquid eyes and couldn't have been above thirteen.

"You can go," Queen Victoria told him.

At the door, he turned to glare at me. I returned him the slightest nod and his face darkened. "He can be jealous," she whispered.

"He's served you long, Your Majesty?"

"He came as a small boy. A second son. They kill second sons, you know, sometimes. The second, third, and fourth. It helps to keep…"

She looked round the lavish railway carriage in which we sat and kept the rest of that thought to herself, although the way her eyes fixed on a fading photograph told me her family played its part.

He looked better in paintings and lithographs, her husband.

Taller, thinner, more decisive. In photographs, Prince Albert looked like a fussy clerk who'd been left in charge and wanted everyone to know it. It must have been a dream come true for him. A princeling from a minor German family selected to sit beside the most powerful woman in the world.

His death had nearly destroyed her.

In my earliest days, at the height of her isolation, I'd been retained to discover if the rumours of her-self murder were true. If, in fact, the Inner Household were hiding her suicide from the country and her family for fear of unrest, not to mention fear of the weaknesses manifesting in her heir.

I took my fee and told them she was alive but sulking.

"Did you know," the queen said, "in India, widows burn themselves?"

"Suttee."

"You know of it?"

"A painful way to die."

"There are drugs." She studied the photograph. "He would have disapproved. Traditions bored him. He liked new things, new ways."

London was littered with the results of what Albert liked. Theatres and museums, public lavatories, bridges, exhibitions, and concert halls. My friend, the colonel, indulged himself often. Watson's tastes are simple.

His ear not of the best.

It is my business to know what other people don't know.

Usually when I look, it's to discover who someone is. But the whole world knew this woman. The civilised bits of it, anyway. Her face was on coins, and her statues filled squares, parliaments, and city halls across the Empire.

I looked anyway.

Drunken, drugged, unwashed, and miserable...

Grubby clothes. Fingernails bitten to the quick. Her hair freshly dressed, but not washed recently enough to merit such dressing. She exuded an air of sadness, small spites, and regret. Her rings, unquestionably priceless, had sunk into her bloated fingers like wire round the trunks of growing trees.

Her pupils were huge. So huge, the light must hurt her eyes. Laudanum would be my guess. Opium dissolved in brandy. A heavy dose, too.

She handed me a folder. "I have a task for you," she said.

The boy in the photograph was young and pretty and spoilt by more than wealth and privilege. Not first in line, so not destined for the throne, and not a girl, so less likely to marry someone who'd inherit one.

"You've been told what to do?"

"Ma'am."

In the three weeks it takes me to make an infallible plan, I discover that another is doing the same, a man I know only by repute. He moves through the same streets, watches the same houses; some palatial, others substantially less so.

You will have heard me say already that if one eliminates all other factors, the one that remains must be the truth. He is good. So good, I decide the legends that have him walking through walls are true. All other factors having been eliminated.

One night, a few days after this realisation, I'm picking at the thought that Her Majesty might have set him the same task when I hear footsteps in the fog behind me and turn, instinctively twisting the amber handle of my cane. The slight click as its handle and shaft separate is enough to freeze my follower to stone.

His hearing is exceptional.

So is his ability to follow. We travel a long way this night through the streets of London, that sewer into which the idlers of the Empire drain. Grand houses turn to lesser ones and to warehouses and tar paper huts. Here, near the docks, we enter a world of opium dens, Tong lords, and peril as deep as the fog around us if the Penny Dreadfuls are to be believed.

It's a long time since I've believed anything so stupid.

This is simply where London's newest arrivals find a footing and discover they have to share it with drunks, dishonourably discharged sailors, opium addicts, and occasionally people like us, who pass through and hope to remain unnoticed.

But I've been noticed, and I watch him draw near.

Most days, I have Colonel Watson, my amanuensis, with me. Today, I have only my cape and cane, and this story must be mine to tell.

The first thing I must say is that reports lie. He has a shadow and quite possibly a reflection. The window of the ruined gin house next to us is too grubby to let me know if it's a reflection or an absence of fog I see.

He moves closer, smiling.

And I draw my sword stick with a slight swish that has him smiling even more. A glimpse of moonlight catches the silver blade and his smile falters.

"Yes," I say. "I've done my research."

I pat my pocket where a revolver rests and tell him it's a Beaumont-Adams, each round blessed by a priest, cut with a cross and washed in holy water. My rounds would be cut that way even if they weren't silver. The colonel is a traditionalist and finds habits he picked up in Afghanistan reassuringly hard to break.

"And I have done mine."

Producing a small glass phial, he tells me it's a 70 percent solution of cocaine. And promises me that it's an altogether more interesting stimulant than the morphine the colonel provides. In his country, he says, it's a tradition to give small gifts on meeting. But this is not the gift...

Putting the phial on the ground between us, his gaze never leaving my blade, he reaches inside his oversized cloak and produces a violin that catches the sullen light of the gin house window and shines like tortoiseshell. Even at a distance. Even without touching it I know what it is, who made it, and who for.

History doesn't record when it disappeared.

"In my country," he says, "we prefer..." He shrugs, with all the elegance of someone who has lived through centuries politer than this. "Perhaps, despite my reputation, it's simply that I prefer to offer rewards rather than threats."

"You have no country," I say.

He looks almost sad and glances around him, his face regaining its smile. "And you have this," he says. "Mud, grime, smoke, darkness."

"I don't live here."

"You live in London. The rest of it is little better."

Raising the point of my blade, I wait. It's either that or grab at the violin like a spoilt child. Maybe he knows how I feel. Maybe he's humouring me. He smiles approvingly whatever and I realise that for once, I've come across a mind as subtle as my own. It's well known there's nothing new under the sun, but he has centuries of experience where I have years.

He's seen bad things happen more times than me.

"Take this," he says.

The urgency in his voice makes me comply, and I look at the violin I'm holding and then back to the count, who is suddenly frozen. As said, my hearing is good, but his is better. Steps are approaching from both directions.

He looks at me.

I keep my gaze impassive and he smiles, his smile a little wider.

His eyes become the red of that dog on the moors. His shoulders tense like those of that beast in the seconds before it sprang. His hand flicks up, silencing me before I can ask if the hound was his.

That would make sense.

Certainly, more sense than the story I spun the colonel about mastiffs, stage paint, and phosphorous. A sweet man Watson, a brave man, but one too easily fooled by glib explanations, and not overendowed with critical capacity, imagination, or intelligence.

Cut throats come at us in both directions. Knifes dull in the fog, faces hidden behind filthy scarves, although I doubt they intend to leave us alive.

Twisting sideways to protect the violin, I take the first through his throat, my blade passing through the cheap wool of his scarf and the flesh behind. Blood flows and my companion's eyes flare as he reaches for one and bites out his throat as contemptuously as a terrier kills a rat.

They hesitate then.

And in the moment of their hesitation, my companion rips the throats from another two, and I pierce one through his heart from the front and another through his heart from the rear as he turns to run. I have as much a sense of fair play as the next man, no matter what the colonel mutters, but six against two without warning...

Besides, there's the violin.

Leaving the last of them to my companion, I watch the sullen swell of the Thames until he finishes feeding and the noises behind me cease. Then he's beside me, and before I can turn, he kneels at the river's edge to splash his face and wipe it clean.

I think of the wild hunt both of us have conducted across London for the last few weeks, at once both hunters and hunted, cat and mouse, time and about, through darkened squares and streets; but also through brothels and bars and drawing rooms with scarcely less bare flesh but a far higher price for the wares.

"In my country," he says.

I wait, knowing he will tell me whether I express interest or not, and already knowing what he intends to say. In his country, all the common expressions seemed to align with his interests. And we have, it seems, a common cause.

"Adversaries who fight together become friends."

"For life?" I ask.

He smiles, satiated enough to be amused at my mild mockery.

"Shall we go?" he asks.

And go we do. In my case, without looking back, in his, with a single wistful glance as if he wishes he could have the whole incident beside the warehouse from footsteps to sobs and silence all over again.

"You're not what I expected," he says finally.

I don't say anything. He doesn't expect me to. We walk together through darkness and he surprises me by asking if he can sleep out the coming day at my flat in Baker Street. Arriving home an hour later, I discover his case has just been delivered and carried up by Mrs. Hudson herself, my housekeeper having refused to let the urchin who delivered it through my door.

My new friend, if such he is to be, asks for the loan of a groundsheet, a dustpan, and a brush, and bids me goodnight as dawn is breaking.

"Will the count be eating with us, sir?"

"I doubt it." Seeing her frown, I add. "He's a foreigner. He'll probably prefer to keep to his own food."

"I'll clear a place in the pantry."

"I imagine he'll eat in town."

"Every meal?"

"I would think so."

Mrs. Watson wanders away, shaking her head at the profligacy of foreigners, while I return to that day's newspapers, all of them taken up, as they have been for weeks, with the Whitechapel murders.

"You think it's the Jews?" Mrs. Hudson asks.

"I very much doubt it."

"He wrote that it was the Jews."

"That's exactly why I doubt it. Everything he does is intended to mislead."

"Why would he do that, Sir?" she asks stubbornly.

"It's a game."

Seeing her shock, I add quickly. "You mustn't assume he's like you or me..." Although, of course, in part, he's exactly like me. And it is a he, I believe. For me, the answer, not justice, is the reward. I relish the challenge of unravelling mysteries and wonder that I didn't guess the connection before.

The count does whatever he does during the day and does it behind a locked door and windows so firmly draped they're still drawn when I return in the late afternoon from visiting the Yard, where they are as glad to see me as always. Which is to say not at all, despite my keeping my comments about their failings to an absolute minimum. The inspector admits, however—with protestations that they are on the edge of certain arrest—that his enquiries have come to nothing.

"Your friend is away, I hear?"

There is something in Inspector Lestrade's tone I dislike.

"The colonel's gone down to the country."

"And you have a new friend. A foreigner?"

"The count? Yes. I'll be presenting him at Court in a while. I'm sure his papers are in order. If that's what's worrying you?"

The inspector reddens.

I know he has men watching my apartment. I simply hadn't expected him get news of my visitor so quickly or throw his insinuations in my face quite so bluntly. I hope he is not going to prove to be a problem.

On my way out, I stop an urchin on the point of pick-pocketing a poor widow. I do so with a glance that stays his fingers.

"Look at her," I order.

He stares after the woman who was probably pretty before grief thinned her face and poverty took its toll on her health.

"What do you see?"

He stays silent.

"The mud on her heels says she walked here. Her tapestry bag swings too freely to have anything inside. Her hair is up and hidden in a hat to hide how filthy it is. Her wedding ring has been sold and the green on her finger suggests its replacement is brass. The rotting fabric beneath her arms says she has one dress and is wearing it... What did you think to take from her?"

"Guvnor?"

I sigh and give him sixpence and tell him to send me Jake. He doesn't ask which Jake because in his world, there's only one. The urchin has the wit not to ask my name, knowing Jake will know it already.

He hurries off through the crowd and stops only once to relieve a lawyer of his half hunter with a nimbleness that would impress a card sharp. The lawyer strolls up the steps and into the Yard, as self-satisfied as ever, without realising his timepiece is missing.

Dusk is falling by the time I return, and although the drapes are closed, they twitch and I can see gas light behind, a nice touch and a reminder of how artfully my new friend has taught himself to fit in.

I have supper, which is as sparse as it must be before a night like this. Then I reach for my violin and play an old Moldavian dance that draws the count to my door. "Come in," I say. And entering, he passes the threshold as lightly as he passed that of my apartment's front door.

He looks round and smiles approvingly.

"Your requirements are simple. Your thoughts..."

"Byzantine?" I say.

He sighs. "I miss the old days."

His tone makes me wonder how far back he means.

There's something appraising in his glance. He has the steady stare of someone used to dealing with matters of life and death. Someone who once settled them from a throne rather than dispensing justice outside a filthy warehouse beside sour water as he'd done the previous night.

"We're ready?" he asks.

"We're ready," I agree.

"I can do this without you."

I'm about to bridle when I realise, he means it as a kindness. All the same... "And I without you," I say.

He looks as if he wants to disagree.

From the half landing, he sees street lights and tells me London has changed. He misses the linkmen and the comfort of real darkness. This artificial light will stretch everywhere eventually. A time will come when even the darkest places of the world will fall. It's obvious the thought depresses him.

"So," I say loudly. "Where shall we eat?"

The count's gaze falls on a man lighting a gasper beneath the gas lamp and understands immediately.

"It's your city," he says.

"My club," I suggest loudly.

I hail a cab and horse shies at the sight of us, whinnies at the slash of a whip, and only stills when the pressure on its bit becomes too brutal to let it do otherwise. I tell the cabbie to take me to Brook Street, noticing he's Scottish, recently returned from overseas, very newly married and unwilling to return to the Highlands from which he originated. A London woman, then.

"Congratulations," I say. "I hope you're both happy."

He drops us on the Strand, where we catch a different cab. The second horse doesn't like us any more than the first and, having fought his beast with increasing ill temper, its owner lets us off at the river and trundles away relieved.

"You can cross?"

He can, although I notice he walks slowly, almost painfully, without once looking at the darkening water beneath Blackfriars bridge.

On the far side, smart houses are few and there's an air of decrepitude, a rising stink of latrines, sour cabbage, and cheap beef boiled for hours to make it tender. Those eating meat are the rich ones. Most of those who watch us pass live on potatoes or black bread; many look as if they barely eat at all.

"In here, dearie."

I shake my head and the madam's grumbles follow us down the street. The next time it happens, my friend says, "Perhaps later."

"Ah, you're foreigners. My girls like foreigners."

Somehow, I doubt it, but she lets us go without grumbling and shouts after us that she runs the best house in the street. The area gets poorer after that, impossible though it seems. A handful of men stare at us, hard eyed. They're the ones not already drinking in dens, betting on cockfights, or intent on getting themselves as drunk as possible. A docker jostles the count, after his wallet or looking for an excuse for a fight, and goes down, bent double.

The blow is fast, precise. The man's retching follows us for a while.

"We're close," the count says.

"How do you know?"

He smiles and I realise I've been wondering the entire way if this is a trap of some sort. The thought has been low level, bubbling beneath more important matters. There are weeks I sleep and weeks when sleep avoids me and night stretches out in an endlessly unfolding array of facts looking for a home.

This is where those facts have led me.

To the northern edge of Whitechapel. He will come this way.

I've followed and lost him so many times in the last few weeks that the decision that the only way I could trap him was to be there first made itself.

"Something wicked…"

"This way comes?" I looked at my new friend. "How does it feel?"

"For it not to be me?" He smiles. "How would I know? Feelings are not for the likes of us. I've killed what emotions I had, and I doubt you had any at the start. Now, you'd best wait over there."

I shake my head. But he's gone, and the filthy street is suddenly empty, and I realise I'm more alone than even I like. Twisting the handle of my cane, I free its blade from habit and put my back to a locked door for safety.

There are certain crimes the law cannot touch, and which therefore, to some extent, justify my intervention. Several such have recently been committed within short distance of this doorway, and one is still to come.

The night is muggy, and the noise of a cart being loaded comes from a knackers' yard behind. My club will be full of light and laughter, neither of which I'm ever expected to acknowledge. The late trains will be decanting revelers to the suburbs. The mail trains have left the north for the capital. The presses will be rolling in Fleet Street, huge mechanical monsters swallowing newsprint and spitting out papers that boys will heap into bundles and drop outside newsagents before dawn reaches us.

I am by no means a nervous man.

All the same, I will admit to a shiver when she appears at the end of the street in rags. Her face is pinched, her hair an unnatural yellow that clashes with her dress, which is red and reveals pasty flesh through its rips.

Her eyes are downcast in sadness or sullenness rather than modesty.

She looks up once and her eyes flare and, for a second, I see the count behind the glamour. Then he is the woman again, taking up his place in a doorway opposite where I hide in the shadow.

We hear footsteps, and as happened before, the count hears them first.

The man advancing through the fog is small and nondescript, dressed like a counting-room clerk in a suit so shiny at the elbows it almost shines. It is his chin that gives him away. It has that weakness found when close kin breed.

If the royal families of Europe were dogs, most would have been drowned at birth.

Behind him comes darkness, writhing and fluid. Smoke if smoke held fire at the centre instead of below. It glows with a sullen anger and sweeps its fingers against the wall, crumbling brick that is already rotten, blistering paint.

His shadow is more alive than he will ever be.

"Fancy a good time?"

The count's mimicry is so perfect that, for a heartbeat, I think the Madame who propositioned us earlier is back. The boy stops and his shadow hangs behind him, thicker than any smog that has ever enveloped this city. It is hard to do its stink justice. This is shit and sulphur, desire and decay.

Our century is nearly a decade from its end and already dead.

The boy must imagine he sees one of the wretched, the women driven by ill luck onto the meanest of streets. That is certainly what I see, a young woman soiled and sold and dragged down to disgrace by mistakes, misadventure or the simple and barbarous cruelties of life.

Behind the count, the bricks in the wall shift.

The boy's stare is too fixed to notice. Mortar trickles like tears and the houses shuffle themselves and suddenly there is another building in the gap. Older, darker. Red bricked and soot stained. As bleak as the look in the eyes of the women we saw earlier. As joyless as the pleasures on offer behind us.

The row stretches to let the new house in and the street closes and suddenly finds itself a blind alley. The squalid rookery up ahead, as rotten as brick can be and still keep standing, suddenly loses the underpass that passes through its middle, and gains a uniform façade of windows carefully watching nothing.

"Come on," the count wheedles.

The boy nods and his shadow gathers tighter, sullen as poison smoke, and acrid as damp soot. The air tastes so strongly of hatred and fear that it dries my mouth and leaves my tongue sour.

"In here," the count says.

"There." The boy points to the wall and a patch of shadow beyond.

Two men in suits wait up the street from us. They keep well back in the darkness and the way they watch their royal charge says they know already what is about to happen, having seen it happen half a dozen times before. There's a loyalty so blind that it can disregard murder if the disregarding it is wrapped in the virtue of vows and duty and keeping one's faith.

But an old faith is meeting an even older one and the oldest of evils.

It doesn't matter what these men see because they will never be able to say. In this age of rationality, they will lie to keep the ordinary ordinary, or run without looking back, and remake themselves halfway round the world where memories can be better forgotten.

The prince looks back and sees the street empty; the houses look as if they've always looked the way he sees them now, and, expecting no difference, the boy sees none and neither do those guarding him. There might be better a way to do this, but it is beyond me to find it: and if it is beyond me, then I can only think of one man it might not be beyond, and I have no intention of going to my brother.

What Mycroft knows of all this must remain unsaid. He wouldn't thank me for changing that, nor would I trust him to give me a straight answer. He is, in his way, as twisted by duty as those who guard the boy.

The young man reaches for his victim's yellow skirt and, in his hand, I see a knife, squat and practical. He drags it upwards hard and screams as his own belly opens and entrails fall like afterbirth. His two protectors hurl themselves forward.

Of course, they do.

And they stop as I throw back my cape and draw my sword cane.

One reaches into his jacket.

"Gentlemen..."

The confidence in my voice is enough to stop them.

They look to where their patron stands, rocking above a pile of his own entails, mouth open in a scream as fierce as it's silent. They watch the door to the house that slotted itself into position swing open. Bats pour out like wild smoke, enveloping the princeling and his shadow.

For a second, it's hard to tell shadow from bats. Then, the sullen glow at the shadow's heart fades, and so does the young man, toppling to his knees and sobbing at the sight of his viscera.

"Go," I tell them.

Glancing at each other, they look to what remains on the ground, then at the count, who now stands revealed. In their eyes, I can see relief. If not for duty done, then for duty that will never be needed again.

They turn, bemused to realise there's no way out of the circle of buildings, and freeze as the tunnel through the rookery reappears. That's not a route I'd choose, but it's the one the one the building offers and the one they take. Then the tunnel closes and the facades crowd in, and the count nods to me and a wall parts to let the two of us through.

An entire street disappears that night.

Since it was unnamed and those who lived in it were regarded as unimportant, no one who cared about important people or naming things noticed. It has long been my belief that the lowest and vilest stews in this city do not present a more dreadful record of sin than its grandest palace. That night confirmed it.

There is no grave, no marker, no record for the young man who died that night. A member of one of Europe's oldest and best-connected ruling families simply ceased to exist. The evil shadowing him still lives though.

The Case of the Missing Sister

Jan Edwards

Holmes frequently ridiculed my efforts as chronicler of our exploits and chose to ignore the fact that they were the reason he had become the most famous detective in these islands. But the lovely Miss Adler seemed to have disturbed his composure in that regard far more than any case we had previously tackled. I was mentally forming the best answer for this when Mrs. Hudson bustled in. "A letter for you, Dr. Watson," she trilled. "May I clear breakfast now?"

"You may, thank you," Holmes said when I did not reply.

I barely noticed her exit. The postmark told me all when that Scottish town had brought my family nothing but sorrow. I tapped the paper rectangle against my knee and stared into nothingness.

"Since you apparently know who the missive is from, and it plainly poses you a question, throwing it away unread would seem a pointless act, my dear chap."

I could feel Holmes's gaze on me, those piercing eyes glittering with curiosity and anticipation. He could deduce what I would only presume and had appeared to have already done so.

"You're right, of course, Holmes." Sliding my nail beneath the seal, I extracted the single sheet of paper and read quickly.

"Bad news?" Holmes enquired.

"Of the highest order," I replied. "I shall read it to you, if I may?" Holmes nodded his assent and I sat back to angle the watery April sunlight directly onto the page.

Dalleth House, Perthshire,

10th May 1888

My dear Uncle John,

Please forgive my presumption in writing. I've followed your exploits with Mr. Sherlock Holmes ever since cook brought your stories to my attention. You write with such humanity I am absolutely certain that you will help me, despite our never having met.

There is no delicate way to write this, so I shall be direct. My mother, your sister Elspeth, is missing. My father refuses to involve the police and does not know that I am writing to you now. You and I have never met, but I beg of you to set aside the past and help me find her.

I have taken the liberty of enclosing train tickets for yourself and Mr. Holmes, as well as a reservation at the White Stag Hotel.

With all good wishes and looking forward to meeting you very soon.

Your respectful niece,

Abigail Dalglish

Holmes held out his hand and I passed him the missive. He examined it minutely, turning the page over and back and peering at the envelope for a full minute. "A child with some strength of character to write so directly," he said.

"She must be more than twenty years old, so hardly a child."

Holmes inclined his head. "I was not aware you had a sister, far less a niece," he said at last. "But then, I know very little about your family."

"You deduced that my watch had belonged to my father and thence my elder brother." My hand strayed to touch the watch chain across my waistcoat, and I smiled at a small triumph. "Unlike you to miss a clue."

"You told me that you have no living kin in England."

"No living relatives *in England*." Even to my ears, my reply was churlish.

Holmes lit his pipe, wreathing his features in smoke to almost but not quite hide his amusement. "I do understand your reticence. We neither of us wish to be defined by our beginnings. My own brother is known to you only because he made himself known."

Holmes lowered his chin to regard me suspiciously. "Who has the honour of being your brother-in-law?"

"Alexander Dalglish. I was still a boy at school when he whisked our dear Elspeth away. It broke my mother's heart."

Holmes nodded slowly. "I am sorry," he said, with surprising gentleness. "Do you intend answering this *cri de coeur*?"

"My only niece?" I replied. "How can I refuse?"

"Then it is settled. If we leave immediately, we will make the one o'clock train." He rose abruptly, consulting his pocket watch and returning it to his waistcoat with a flourish. "Mrs. Hudson! My laundry, if you please!"

On our arrival at the White Stag Hotel, I signed the register while Holmes went to the guest dining room to secure a late supper. "Our landlord seemed reluctant to talk about Dalleth House," Holmes observed as I took my seat.

"Dalleth has a reputation," I replied. "Tales of death and ghosts."

"Is it right that Dalglish is an invalid and somewhat reclusive?"

"I'm no socialite, I'll own you that."

I jumped at the voice, but Holmes did not bat an eye, only tilted his head to regard the newcomer knowingly. "Mr. Dalglish?" he asked.

Dalglish ignored him and manoeuvred his wheeled chair further into the room. "What gave ye the notion to come here, John Watson?"

His voice was strong for an invalid of close to seventy years. And though his skin was pale and stretched tight over jutting bones, those deep-set eyes were shrewd and undimmed by age. This man had stolen Elspeth away and I had to wonder how. "I came to see my sister," I replied.

"Your family relinquished all right to her company," he said. "A binding contract."

"Made with my father, not me," I snapped.

Dalglish jutted his chin. "A wasted journey, then. You and your Mr. Holmes." He glowered at both of us in triumph. "Away with you."

My fists clenched. "I shall not leave until..." Dalglish's men, the term henchmen came to mind, moved between us.

Holmes donned a beaming smile, the one that charmed his clients but which I trusted the least, and said, "I am sure we can discuss this as civilised men."

"Leave," Dalglish snarled. "And do not return." He signalled with his raised hand and was wheeled away.

"Your family are far more interesting than I imagined," Holmes mused.

"How do you think he knew we were here?" I said. "I can't imagine Abigail would have told him."

"Doubtless he has informants all over the town." Holmes tamped his briar and relit it. "Tell me, did your family live here for long?"

"Just three years. Until my sister was married."

"Stolen by the laird? Theme of many a gothic novel." Holmes's features creased into a wry smile. "Did she go willingly?"

"You mean with Father's blessing? I'd always assumed she had."

Holmes nodded. "How acquainted were you with your brother-in-law?"

"No more than any schoolboy would be with the local squire." I drew on my pipe, barely tasting the sweetness of the rope-blend tobacco.

"Do you blame Dalglish?" Holmes asked.

"For what? I don't know what this 'agreement' entailed. I only know that when Elspeth married, we returned to Edinburgh. And that Father was a surgeon there until alcohol ruined both his steady hand and his professional repute." I scowled at him. "I joined the Brigade precisely because one does not require an illustrious sponsor to hack and stitch on the battlefield."

We sat silent for a while, the only sounds coming from the public bar across the corridor. It was Holmes who stirred first. "I'm honoured by your confiding in me." He leaned out to tap his pipe into the grate. "Tomorrow, we shall set about filling in the gaps in your story."

❦

Holmes was in fine form at breakfast and started on old game. "Well?" He flicked his gaze toward the only other diners.

"Two ladies of Edinburgh on a hiking holiday." I smiled. "There are no similarities between them beyond the plainness of their dress and quietness of manner, so not mother and daughter, nor siblings. The younger is a companion, perhaps? Or the elder a governess?"

Holmes applauded quietly. "Both accurate and wildly incorrect. Edinburgh when Stirling is the closer? I am impressed."

"Elementary," I replied. "I saw their entry in the hotel register."

"Bravo. But did you realise they are sisters of a different kind?" His brow furrowed. "Odd to see Anglican nuns without their wimples. Something is afoot."

I looked at the women curiously. "Elspeth once toyed with the notion of taking the veil."

"Yet in the end, she rejected Christ to marry a mortal man. Young women change their minds quickly and often. A strange breed." Holmes wiped his mouth on his napkin and laid both his palms on the table. "According to our host, your father's old practice changes hands often. The Kirk also welcomes new ministers rather frequently."

"Which you find odd?"

"Where a laird exerts patronage, it hints at his being unpopular. That may be useful. Now, if you have finished, we need to see the lay of the land."

We hired a small pony cart and toured the small town, and thence into surrounding hills. I wondered how much would be familiar to me. I had, after all, lived here for only a brief time and a long while ago. I was surprised at how much I knew.

"What are you hoping to find?" I asked, as we sat on a hillside overlooking the town.

"If your sister had been abducted for ransom, she would not be held in the town where she might be discovered, but close by." He gazed around us. "Yet we've seen few people, nor places where a genteel lady could be hidden."

"True enough," I said. There had been a few herders, and I thought we'd caught a glimpse of our hiking nuns just beyond the limits of the town, but, beyond those, our heather-strewn hills were a haven for grazing sheep and raptors circling lazily over the heights. The sense of isolation was something I did not miss, I realised. I had lived here for a time, but I had remained a city dweller by choice.

❦

The White Hart's bar fell quiet the moment we entered. "A warm day for spring." Holmes loosened his jacket and beamed at the publican. "Two malts, if you please. And take one for yourself."

"Most generous, sir."

Holmes looked around at the small number of men gathered in the gloom. "Would you care to join us for a wee dram, gentlemen?" he added.

They clustered around us as the landlord poured the amber fluid into dimpled tumblers, which they drained quickly before retreating once more like waves on the nearby loch.

One man of around my own age remained, watching me with a dry smile on his lips. "You're Dr. Watson's youngest bairn," he said.

"I am," I agreed. "Though my father passed away a long while ago."

"And your good lady mother, so I hear," he muttered. "We'll be drinking to her memory."

I held his gaze for a moment and nodded at the landlord to leave the bottle.

"McAllan," the man informed me. "Kenneth McAllan. You don't remember me?"

"No, I'm sorry. Do you live hereabouts?" I asked as I refilled his glass.

"Aye, I did, until just last year, but I've a shop away down in Edinburgh now. Wool cloth. That's the business to be in. Her Majesty has started a rare old want for the tartan. But you're no interested in that, are you?" He grinned and raised his glass. "To the Watsons. Not here for long, but who made their mark."

"They did." Holmes leaned in, welcoming conspiracy. "Shall we be seated?"

McAllan took the nearest chair and leaned back to gaze at Holmes and me. "There was quite a to do," he said. "When your friend here was a wee sprat."

I sensed Holmes come to attention, though to the casual observer, he did no more than recross his arms and draw deeply on his briar, making the tobacco hiss and crackle into a red heat. I only sipped at the whisky, rolling the peaty liquid roll across my tongue without replying.

"I knew your brother. Considered himself a cut above us village lads," McAllan continued. "It brought him nought but grief."

I sensed old sores behind the words, despite his deep chuckle. "I'm sorry for that," I said.

"For what? Were you your brother's keeper? No. he was master of his own fate."

"And Miss Watson?" Holmes asked.

"Ah, the raven beauty. Black hair and porcelain skin and eyes of deepest blue." McAllan nodded. "Small wonder she came to the laird's notice." He stared ruefully into his empty glass and I poured another libation. "Most generous." McAllan downed the third dram and smacked his lips.

"The wedding was sudden," I said.

"Your sister had a young gentlemen follower. Your father's assistant."

"Wallace Elgin?" I said.

McAllan poured himself another dram and sank it with less noise than before, his smile grimmer. "Your sister was set to marry, but none predicted her wedding the laird."

"Better prospects, perhaps?" said Holmes.

"If that was so, then it was a bitter choice. She almost died when the bairn came, and never recovered. Not been seen out and about for many a year." He sighed theatrically. "Miss Abigail grew up in a grand house that was full of nought but age and sickness, the poor wee thing."

"I knew none of this," I said. "Poor Ellie. What became of Elgin?"

McAllan screwed his lips into a thoughtful pout. "Back to Edinburgh, we supposed. Though I've not come across him, and I've asked. I liked the man." He finished his drink and stood. "Thank you for your hospitality, gentlemen. I'm away back to the Royal Mile tonight."

"Thank you," I said. "Most helpful."

Holmes watched him saunter away, and I knew that look. "What did you notice in his story?" I said.

"No firm deductions," Holmes replied. "I must visit the post office and you should remain here. Miss Dalglish will call this afternoon." He handed me a scrap of paper torn from a journal, on which was scrawled; "Uncle John. I shall call at four if that is convenient. Your niece, Abigail."

I looked up, angry that Holmes had not shown it to me straight away, but he'd slipped away, and I could do nothing but kick my heels.

Abigail did not arrive until after four, just a few moments after Holmes returned. When she arrived, for a moment the years slipped away and I was looking at Elspeth. The same fragile features. The same lustrous black hair caught loosely up on her head.

"Uncle John." She hurried forward and planted a light kiss on my cheek. "You cannot imagine how I've longed to meet my mother's family. And you must be Mr. Sherlock Holmes?"

"It is a great pleasure to meet you." Holmes bowed. "Please, do be seated."

"Thank you." She sat, arranging her skirts in a rustle of silk and I noted that her dress was the latest fashion. Isolated though this spot might be, she plainly kept up with the wider world. "You know why I've called you here," she said. "Father is a bag of contradictions, refusing to send for the police."

"Because he's unwell?"

"He's never *well*. Paralysed from the waist makes one fragile."

I exchanged glances with Holmes.

"My parents never lived as man and wife because of that and because my mother has long periods of—despair."

"She never displayed such as a young woman," I said.

Elspeth glanced toward the door and lowered her voice. "Recently, she's made several attempts to leave Dalleth House."

"So it's possible she's merely run away?"

Abigail shook her head. "There's nowhere her could go without money, and Father counts every farthing she has."

"He's controlling?" said Holmes.

"Always. I plan to leave Dalleth soon. My great-grandmother left me a fortune that I'm to receive on my twenty-fifth birthday."

"Which is?"

"In ten days." She looked down at her fingers, which she had been twisting all the while we spoke. "I would have gone a long while ago but for Father's grip on his purse. I wanted to take Mother with me. We'd go to Paris and Rome and Venice and so many places." Her face lit up and she leaned forward to touch my arm. "You don't think me frivolous?"

"Not at all. Every young person should see some of the world. You told your mother of these plans?"

"Obviously, I told Mother. Though I didn't know she understood. She's away with the wee people so much of the time." Her face fell. "My father keeps her subdued."

"Drugged?"

"Laudanum is prescribed to calm her. And her rooms are often locked, on the doctor's orders Father says. He treats her abominably." She bit her lip. "Father's parents were killed when their carriage overturned, and he was crippled. It left him bitter, they say. My father's grandmother raised him, and later me. But when great-grandmother died, my Aunt Katherine came to stay." She shuddered visibly.

"You didn't like her?"

"Few did. I've heard folk dub her the curse of Dalleth." Abigail sat a little straighter. "She passed away last autumn. One month short of her ninety-second year, and her mind still sharp as a blade."

"You speak very plainly," said Holmes.

"You find that unseemly?"

"On the contrary. I admire it."

"One small compensation of my upbringing by old women," she replied. "Aunt Katherine said that as the sole heir of Dalleth, I needed to be the equal of any man. We did not get on at all well, but she taught me much." She looked directly at Holmes, her expression holding a hint of challenge. "I cannot leave until I discover what has happened to my mother."

"As is right and proper." Holmes replied. "Daughters have a duty to their mothers."

"My father also demands a duty to Dalleth."

"That may change when my investigations are complete," he replied.

Abigail nodded, every fibre of her being to attention. "I wish I could believe it," she said. "Find my mother, Mr. Holmes. I beg of you."

A raucous laugh from the public bar drew her attention, and she rose quickly, pulling on her gloves. "I must return before Father wakes."

We watched the door close behind her before Holmes reached inside his coat and produced several pieces of paper. "I waited for answers to my telegram enquiries." He laid one sheet on the table with delicate precision. "From the Scottish Records Office. Abigail Beileag Caitlin Dalglish's birth was registered in May 1863. She is recorded as the daughter of Alexander Dalglish and in the absence of any male child, his sole legal heir." He chuckled quietly. "A.B.C.D. Someone had a sense of humour at least."

"It was said Dalglish could be perfectly charming when he chose," I replied. "Merely that he seldom chose."

"That must be the case. According to the garrulous Post Mistress, the wedding between Mr. Dalglish and Elspeth Watson occurred when your niece was already betrothed to Dr. Elgin."

"I don't..."

"There is more." Holmes laid down a second sheet. "Royal Medical Society. To whom Mr. Elgin has not paid the required fees since 1862, nor is there any record of his death." He drummed his fingers on the tabletop for a few moments, his thoughts lost somewhere deep in that gargantuan mind.

"Have you all the puzzle pieces now?" I asked.

"I await one final telegram." He slapped the flat of his hand on the oak surface. "For now, a hearty supper before a night-time excursion."

Dusk was falling as we took a circuitous route into Dalleth's park via a back way. I had not been here for twenty-five years, and then only for a mischief-night challenge. In the semi-dark, the pale stone of the mausoleum ahead of us shone as if lit from within, lending the round building an eeriness that someone of my profession should not feel. As I waited for Holmes to work his magic on the locked door, I kept a wary eye out for guards.

Holmes finally pushed open the doors and let the last pink rays of the day flood into the dank, dusty interior. Just inside the door was a small table with a lamp and matches. Once lit, we had a better view of two altar-tombs at the centre, which Holmes ignored as he made his way around the coffin sized niches in the walls. Some held stone sarcophagi. Others were sealed by ceramic covers, which were mortared into place and labelled with brass insets. He paused at last and read the final plaque aloud.

" 'Katherine Harriet Dalglish. 1798–1887.' The maiden aunt reached a venerable age. Here, take this, Watson."

He handed me the lamp and set about the cover with a broken block of stone until it shattered, revealing a black oak coffin, which was just as anticipated. The jumbles of bones and rag, crammed into the spaces at each end and poked into the gap above the coffin, were not. Human remains, darkly stained, but dead far longer than the single year since Aunt Katherine had been interred.

"The last resting place of Doctor Wallace Elgin," Holmes murmured.

"You're sure?" I stared at the sad remnants.

"As I can be."

"Then Dalglish..."

"Is a murderer," he agreed. "Aided by willing servants, I have no doubt." Holmes pulled at the rags, which shed grey dust as they crumbled around under his touch. "Charred," he said. "Somebody made an attempt to dispose of Elgin with fire before he was walled in with the old lady."

"But Dalglish is a cripple."

"He was a young man then, and as a medical man you must have observed those who have lost the use of their legs often develop greater strength in their arms. Also, his aunt would have been a sprightly sixty-five and doubtless more than capable." He paused suddenly, head cocked. "Listen. Dogs. We must leave." I pulled my pistol from my pocket, but he waved it away. "This is not the place to make a stand. Run, Watson. Run!"

We fled across the park, keeping to the shadow of trees while in the distance the yelping dogs and shouts of men came clearly to us on the night air. Our pursuers made first for the mausoleum where we knew it would not be long before the hounds picked up our scent.

Running had never been easy since an Afghan bullet had shattered my leg, but I arrived at the park wall only a few strides behind Holmes. I scaled the obstacle rapidly and soon stood gasping for air and racked with pain, but safe on the other side. I'd half feared the cart would have been stolen away, but it waited there, still. In moments, we were rattling toward the town and making good our escape. Holmes took us on a tortuous trail, pausing in several alleyways, but eventually, satisfied we had not been followed, urged the tiring pony out into open country once again, to stop at a small single-story croft house. I followed Holmes in full confidence that he at least knew who lived here. He hammered on the door which opened a crack, and a woman peered out at us.

"Mr. Holmes?" Her voice was low and measured.

"Good evening, Sister." Holmes placed the flat of his hand against the door's rough planking. "May we come in?"

"Of course."

Inside, a single guttering candle's illumination barely reached the walls. Holmes seated himself at the table without being asked and studied our two hiking nuns standing before us. "I am almost surprised you're still here," he said. "You would be far safer within convent walls."

"True enough," the older woman replied. "We were waiting for full dark to make our escape."

He nodded at the rucksacks near the far wall. "You intend going on foot, Sister..."

"Sister Mary Elena. And Sister Barnard. And yes, we know these hills. The weather is good, so we should make our first stop by dawn."

"With your new novice?"

Sister Mary Elena could not resist a glance at the loft ladder, where a pair of legs clad in brogues and plus fours had appeared. The figure who reached the floor and turned to face us was not a man, despite the clothes, but a slender woman of middle years.

"Elspeth?" I breathed. "Ellie?"

"Hello, John." She smiled, and it was the young woman I remembered who ran forward to embrace me. "So good to see you," she mumbled into my jacket. "I never thought I ever would."

"Nor I you. But where are you going?"

"First to Stirling," she said, "And then to the mother house in York."

"But your husband..."

"...is a monster. I will not go back to him. Don't ask me to."

"A murderer also," said Holmes.

Elspeth turned to him. "You know?"

"We found Elgin's remains," Holmes replied.

"Poor Wallace." Her face fell for a heartbeat. "Such a long time ago. I've been little better than a prisoner since then. I only survived by becoming a little mad. Even a man like my husband shies away from harming an imbecile."

"Abigail asked me to find you," I said. "She thought you'd been kidnapped."

Elspeth frowned and shook her head. "Don't tell her where I am. Not until I'm safe behind the walls."

"But she's your child. A Watson."

"And a Wallace by blood. But a Dalglish in every legal way. Alec wanted an heir but didn't want some local servant's offspring. When he heard I was with child by an educated man..."

"How did Dalglish know?" I said.

"He paid the doctor's stipend and for that he demanded to know everything," said Holmes.

"My father?" I took Elspeth by the shoulders. "Our own father told Dalglish you were pregnant?"

"I rather imagine Father confided in him as an anxious parent without any idea of what Alec had planned."

I nodded. "Guilt. It killed them all," I said. "One way or another."

"But all in the past," she said. "I have a fresh life planned."

I gave her another hug. "As a nun? Exchanging one locked fortress for another? Surely..."

"Never make the mistake of assuming that nuns are unworldly." Holmes laughed. "The business of evil, after all, is their raison d'etre. Is that not so, Sister?"

"Ellie was my childhood friend." Sister Mary Elena placed a protective arm around Elspeth's shoulders. "That is how we arranged all of this. I will care for her, Dr. Watson. You will be able to visit. Ours is not a closed order. But now," she picked up one of the bags. "We must leave. If you've discovered poor Wallace's bones, then the search will be all the more deadly."

"Yes go," said Holmes.

"We should go with them." I took Elspeth's hand to hold her back.

"No, Watson, we need to hold the line whilst these ladies melt away into the heather."

"Goodbye, John." Elspeth whispered. "For now. I shall send word when you can come to see me."

"Goodbye, Ellie, and take care."

The trio hurried out into the dark without a backward glance. And Holmes, highlighted in the faint shaft of light spilling from the doorway, watched them go. "Bring the conveyance to the front, Watson," he said.

"Won't that be easily spotted?"

"Indubitably. A flame to draw deadly moths." Holmes peered into the dark, strangely calm and far more pleased with himself than I thought he had the right to be.

We waited with pistols to hand for no more than twenty minutes before a small carriage with a pair of outriders came to a halt a few yards past the gates. Then the noise of wheelchair on the pathway came clearly and the door opened.

"Alexander. Very late for you to be out." I looked beyond him to Abigail. And beyond them to the burly ghillies. "Abigail," I said. "Why are you here?"

"Because I ordered it." Dalglish snarled. "Now where is my wife?"

"Gone." Holmes edged closer to me. "Beyond your reach."

"My wife is unwell," Dalglish said. "She needs the protection of her family."

"In the way you protected her from Wallace Elgin?" Holmes asked. "It was his bones we found resting with your aunt, was it not?"

"What?" Abigail said. "How can that be?"

I looked to Holmes and back to her, wondering if she was so innocent as she appeared.

"Nothing for you to worry over, my dear," Dalglish snapped. "Aunt Katherine's remains are quite alone now." Dalglish produced a dirk and pointed it at my head. "Elgin had no right to come to Dalleth. No more than you, John Watson. I've a good eye with a throwing blade."

"So you admit you secured Elgin's silence with his death?" said Holmes.

"He'd not been missed. Never once has anyone come looking," Dalglish sneered.

"Until tonight." Holmes raised his voice. "Have you heard enough Inspector McLevy?"

"I have." A thick set man, flanked by burly policemen, stepped from the shadows. "Alexander Dalglish, I'm arresting you for the murder of Wallace Elgin."

Dalglish grabbed the wheels of his chair to back away. "It wasn't me." His voice rose to a shriek like a beast caught in a snare, though one of Holmes's making. "T'was my aunt."

"No, Father. You're going nowhere." Abigail grabbed the chair firmly, and our eyes met over Dalglish's screeching form. "Enough now."

"We'll take him, Miss." Inspector McLevy signalled to his officers to take charge and turned to Holmes. "A neat little bundle you've handed me. I had wondered why you wanted this place watched this night. But I should have known there would be an end game. Thank you for your telegram message. Mr. Elgin's family will be glad to lay their missing son to rest."

"I should have been hard pressed to prove his guilt without his confession in your presence," said Holmes.

"His kind can never help themselves," the inspector replied. "Now, if you'll excuse me?"

I looked for Abigail, but she held up hand up from a distance. "Thank you," she mouthed before stepping into her carriage. I would have followed her, but Holmes hauled me back.

"She needs time," he said. "And you've already done what you came here to do. You've found your missing sister."

The Case of
the Terrified
Tobacconist

David Stuart Davies

On returning to Baker Street one morning in the autumn of '95 after a visit to my bank, I was alarmed to hear the sobs of a distressed woman emanating from our sitting room. I raced up the stairs and, with some apprehension, entered to discover a young woman bent forward on the chaise longue, weeping into her handkerchief, her frame shuddering with strong emotion. Holmes was sitting in his usual chair by the fire opposite her, coldly and calmly viewing this fit of hysterics like a scientist observing an intriguing experiment.

"Ah, Watson," he said casually, "you arrive at a propitious moment. As you will observe, my client is somewhat overcome. Perhaps, with your usual soothing bedside manner you would be kind enough to administer some brandy as a restorative."

I gave my friend a steely glance. Sherlock Holmes could at his best lack empathy and at his worst could be an unfeeling brute.

The lady accepted a glass of brandy and sipped it gently as she made a great effort to bring her emotions under control.

"Thank you," she said, drying her eyes.

"I am Dr. Watson," I said. "A friend and associate of Mr. Holmes."

"This is Mrs. Edith Daubney, and she had a strange domestic problem which has brought her to my door, but as yet, I have not learned the full nature of it due to the lady's distress." Holmes passed this information to me as though she were not in the room.

I laid a comforting hand on our visitor's arm. "Perhaps, Mrs. Daubney, if you could bring yourself to explain your dilemma, Mr. Holmes and I may be able to help you."

"Thank you, sir," she said softly, dabbing her eyes once more. "I apologise for my unseemly display of emotion but...I am at my wit's end."

"I understand," I said gently, casting a glance at Holmes, and added with some force, "*We* understand."

Holmes leaned forward, selected his cherrywood pipe from the rack and, tamping it with shag, proceeded to light it. "Pray give us the facts, Mrs. Daubney," he said, amid a billowing acrid cloud of tobacco smoke.

"My husband's gone," she said after a pause, her voice finding strength and volume.

"He has left you?"

"In a manner of speaking. Please do not misunderstand me: he hasn't abandoned me for another woman or anything like that. He's left because he was too terrified to stay."

"Why was he terrified?"

She shook her head. "I do not know."

"Give me more details, please. I cannot make bricks without clay. Tell me all about it."

Mrs. Daubney took another sip of brandy and began her narrative. "I have been happily married for three years. My husband Samuel runs a tobacconist shop in Praed Street. It's his pride and joy. He has always wanted to own such an establishment since he was a boy. Then, as fortune would have it, he managed to set one up a few years ago after an uncle left him a considerable amount of money in his will. This was six months before we met. We married shortly afterward. It's a nice little business that provides us with a comfortable living. We live above the premises. Our life is quiet and contented. That was until yesterday. That was when my world was turned upside down."

Holmes laid down his pipe and leaned forward with interest. "Do go on."

"It was our routine of an evening that after the shop closed for the day at seven o'clock, Samuel would retire to the parlour and partake of a glass of sherry while reading the evening paper. I would be in the kitchen preparing our supper. Last night, while I was busy getting the meal ready, I heard my husband cry out as though he was in great pain. When I rushed through into the room, I saw him, his features twisted in an awful grimace. He was running his hands furiously through his hair as he paced up and down in a frantic manner. 'No, no, no,' he kept crying out, with such a look of terror on his face as I have never seen before.

" 'What on earth is the matter, Sam?' I asked, moving toward him.

" "It's all up,' he cried. 'All up. My life is over.'

"I could make no sense of it and when I tried to comfort him, he brushed me aside. 'Leave me,' he said, his voice a hoarse strangled croak. 'For heaven's sake, leave me alone.'

"I tried to reason with him, to get him to tell me what had brought about this terrible change, but he would not say, shaking his head vigorously. In the end, he just ushered me out of the room and locked the door.

"To tell you the truth, I did not know what to do. After an hour or so, I knocked on the door and asked if he was going to come to bed, saying a night's rest would ease his distress. He just replied that I was to leave him alone. What else could I do? I can tell you, Mr. Holmes, I spent a restless and wretched night. It was only as the sky lightened toward dawn that fatigue overtook me, and I slept. As a result, I rose quite late and hurried to the sitting room. The door was wide open, but there was no sign of my husband. I called out his name, but there was no response. I went down into the shop in the hope that he had opened early but that was not the case. The place was in darkness with the shutters down. My Samuel was nowhere in the building. He had...disappeared." Her voice wavered once more and I thought that she may well start crying again, but with a great effort, she overcame her emotions. Her eyes remained damp and her features taut with anguish, but the tears did not flow.

"Can you help me, Mr. Holmes? I am beside myself with worry. What can have happened to him?"

"It certainly is a pretty problem. You have no idea what caused him to behave so oddly?"

"None whatsoever."

"And before he entered the sitting room, he seemed his normal self."

"Yes, he even made a little joke about the fact that we were to have rabbit stew for our supper. 'Not rabbit again,' he said, with a smile. 'You'll have me hopping about with long ears soon.' "

Mrs. Daubney gave a brief brave smile at the memory.

"Have you any notion as to where your husband might have gone? Does he have premises elsewhere? Does he belong to a club in the city?"

Mrs. Daubney shook her head resolutely.

"Are his parents alive or does he have any brothers or sisters?"

"Samuel was an only child and his parents have passed away. He always said that he was quite alone in the world."

Holmes turned and stared at the flickering flames in the grate for a moment and then jumped to his feet. "Very well, Mrs. Daubney, your problem interests me greatly. Let us grasp the nettle. The first thing I must do is to visit your home."

The tobacconist shop, quaintly named A Smoke in the City, was in a small run of three shops on Praed Street—sandwiched between an ironmonger and a pawnbroker. As we entered the premises to the accompaniment of the tinkle of the shop bell, we were overpowered with the exotic smells of numerous tobaccos which infused the air and assailed our nostrils. Holmes gazed at the various packages and pouches that filled the shelves. As an avid smoker, this must have seemed like an Aladdin's cave to him.

He stood for some moments, breathing in the atmosphere before moving behind the counter. "Your husband carries many foreign brands, I see," he observed, scanning the stock. "Especially French shag, cigars, and cigarettes."

"Yes," said Mrs. Daubney. "He loves Continental brands, and they sell well. He takes regular trips to Paris to make his selections for our stock."

At Holmes's request, Mrs. Daubney directed us upstairs to the sitting room. Once there, he asked her if she would check the till in the shop and any other place where money would be kept on the premises, while he carried out his investigation of the chamber. I knew it was his method of getting the lady out of his way, thus gaining privacy for his examination of the room. In the instant she had gone, my friend dropped to his knees and reached under the table, retrieving a newspaper. He held it aloft with a cry of satisfaction.

"Is that important?" I asked.

"It is vital. I am convinced that this paper contains the key to the mystery."

"How so?"

"You do not see? We are told that until Daubney came into this room last evening for his habitual read with a glass of sherry, he was acting quite normally, jovial even. Moments later he had begun raving and tearing at his hair. What had prompted this dramatic change?"

"That newspaper?"

"Yes, my dear fellow. Or to be more precise: something that he read in this newspaper. Something so shocking that it chilled him to the marrow."

"It is *The Westminster Gazette*, is it not? I read that last night and saw nothing of a sensational nature in its pages."

Holmes gave me one of his icy smiles, which usually indicated that I was missing the point. "Of course, nothing to you, but something very personal to Samuel Daubney."

"What could that be?"

"I have no idea, but I will when I have studied the paper thoroughly."

At this point, Mrs. Daubney returned, her face paler than ever. "I have checked the till and the small safe we keep in the storeroom. All the money has gone."

"It is as I suspected. Your husband is making a desperate bid to disappear."

"But why? Oh, heavens why?"

"I intend to find out. I promise you that I will get to the bottom of this mystery. Now, do you have a photograph of your husband that I could borrow?"

Without a word she went to the bureau and retrieved a carte de visite of her husband and handed it to Holmes. I glanced over to look at it and saw a well-built man with a large bushy beard which appeared prematurely grey. It spread across his face with a heavy moustache like some alien growth. It was both amusing and rather intimidating. It certainly clouded his natural features.

Holmes slipped the photograph into his coat pocket. "I thank you for this. I am sure it will assist us in our enquiries. However, for the moment, I think I have learned all I need to know from my visit here. We will leave you now in order to carry out our investigations elsewhere. I will return this late evening with, I hope, some news to impart."

We returned to Baker Street and Holmes spent the next hour scouring the pages of *The Westminster Gazette*. At length, he sat back in his chair and gave a long sigh.

"No success, eh?" I observed.

"On the contrary, I think I have put my finger on item that caused Daubney's distress, and it isn't good news."

He folded the paper, passed it to me, and with his long index finger, indicated a paragraph in the Stop Press news section.

It read:

ESCAPE

Wandsworth Prison. In the early hours of this morning it was discovered that the prisoner, Edward Bell, was missing from his cell. A thorough search of the prison proved fruitless and it seems that Bell had managed to escape the confines of the institution in a laundry van. Bell was serving an eight-year sentence for robbery with violence. He was involved in the City & County Bank robbery in 1892.

"What can this story have to do with Samuel Daubney?"

Holmes tapped his forehead. "There are facts and notions floating around in here that are not fully formed yet, but if my instincts are correct... Watson, make a long arm, will you, and reach for my criminal file for 1892. I have vague memories of the City & County Bank job. I wish to refresh my memory on the matter."

I did as he asked and Holmes spent another half hour in study, before he placed the file down at his feet. "This case will not end happily. There will be more tears for Mrs. Daubney, I fear."

"Would you kindly elucidate," I said, somewhat tartly. I felt that, not for the first time Holmes was holding back information which would allow me to form my own theories concerning the mysterious disappearance of the terrified tobacconist.

Holmes leaned back in his chair and steepled his fingers. "I think of myself as an artist, Watson, and in this instance I am in the process of sketching in the structure of this dark work of art in readiness for painting the finished picture. I have certain details in place and where facts are vague, I have etched in my surmise. I apologise if all this seems fanciful, but it will, I hope, explain how I have reached my theory which I feel assured is the correct one. In Daubney, we have a gentleman who has set up a successful tobacco shop a few months before he meets and marries his wife. He tells her that he was able to fund such a venture because of an unsuspected windfall from a rich uncle, and yet he claims to have no kith or kin. He lives a quiet life, but then becomes distraught and panic stricken one evening as a result, I deduce, by something that he read in the evening paper. Having scrutinised this edition closely, the only item I can see that may have the power to bring about this dramatic effect upon him was the piece concerning the escaped convict, Edward Bell. Reading up on the case—the City & County Bank robbery—it seems that the felon Edward Bell had an accomplice who assisted him in the venture. This fellow, a Stephen Dawes who worked at the bank, provided Bell with all the essential inside information in order for him to carry out the robbery. However, once the deed was done, Dawes and the stolen loot disappeared, and an anonymous note was passed to the police giving details of Bell's whereabouts."

"So Bell was imprisoned, and Dawes slunk into the shadows of obscurity."

"Indeed."

"And you believe that Dawes is in fact our Samuel Daubney."

"I do. A change of name and identity, and with the money, he is able to set up himself in legitimate business, a respectable tobacconist shop. Stephen Dawes becomes Samuel Dawson—same initials. He grows a prodigious beard to change his appearance and disguise his comparative youth. Now, he feels safe and content that his old cohort is in gaol for many years."

"These are slender threads, Holmes."

My friend gave me a bleak smile. "Oh, I agree, but the premise fits the facts. Remember that one utterance Mrs. Daubney heard through the door last night: 'My God, he means to destroy me.' Surely, he was referring to Bell. His old partner will be hellbent on revenge now. Daubney knew that it wouldn't be long before Bell tracked him down. Daubney knew he had to escape. His comfortable life was in ruins. He must save his skin."

"If you are right, his life is in danger."

"Yes. That is how I see things."

"But where is Daubney now?"

"I hope we may discover that later this evening when we take an excursion. You will come with me?"

"Need you ask?" I said.

Holmes beamed. "I am always happy to have you by my side on these occasions, but I think it would be wise if you carry your pistol with you."

At ten o'clock that evening, we were rattling through the darkened streets of London in a Hansom cab en route to Victoria station. As usual, Holmes had been circumspect regarding the nature of his plans. It was a frustrating foible of his that he liked to keep his cards close to his chest until the last moment. However, as he settled back in the cab, he relaxed and explained the purpose of our excursion. "I believe that when Daubney read of Bell's escape from prison, he knew that the game was up. He had no option but to flee before Bell discovered his whereabouts and carried out his revenge with the inevitable outcome."

"Murder," I said.

Holmes nodded gravely. "And so Daubney had to slough off all the trappings of his comfortable life, including the security of his marriage in order to save his own skin. He had to escape. To leave this country—to find a safe haven abroad. Today, we learned that he was a frequent traveller to France on business. Surely, this would be his escape route. Once in Europe, he could easily find refuge. My Bradshaw informs me that today's departure of the Continental express leaves from Victoria this evening at eleven thirty. I have great expectations that our friend Daubney will be attempting to board it."

Some moments later, our cab drew up outside Victoria station, one of the great railway cathedrals of the metropolis. As we alighted, I saw a familiar figure standing by one of the columns by the entrance. I recognised those sharp inelegant features. It was Inspector Lestrade.

"I thought it appropriate that we include the official police in our night's adventure. I sent a telegram to Lestrade outlining events and requesting his assistance. If all goes well, an arrest will be necessary," said Holmes, giving a wave of acknowledgement to the inspector who was accompanied by two uniformed constables.

"I hope this is not going to be a wild goose chase, Mr. Holmes," observed Lestrade sourly as we shook hands.

"I am quite sanguine that you will end up with a prize fish in your net before the evening is over," said Holmes he withdrew the photograph of Samuel Daubney from his pocket and held it up for examination by Lestrade and his colleagues. "This is the fellow we're after," he said.

"Blimey, that's a beard and a half," cried Lestrade.

"A singular visage indeed. It should make our task of identifying him somewhat easier."

"You don't think he'll have shaved it off to alter his appearance?" said Lestrade.

Holmes shook his head. "No, to do so would reveal his features as they used to be—giving him the face that Bell would immediately recognise. His old face, as it were. As bearded Daubney, he has a chance of remaining anonymous."

"If you say so, Mr. Holmes," said Lestrade glumly.

"Now, according to Bradshaw the Continental leaves from platform five. The carriage doors remain locked until thirty minutes before travel." He consulted his pocket watch. "It is ten forty now, so we have just over fifteen minutes to spot our man."

With some haste, we made our way to platform five. We passed through the ticket barrier with ease thanks to Lestrade's credentials and the presence of the two bobbies. The concourse was already fairly crowded with passengers milling around with their luggage, waiting for the train doors to be released.

Holmes suggested that the two uniformed officers remained by the barrier in case Daubney, realising the game was up, tried to make a bolt for it while Holmes, Lestrade, and I patrolled the platform in search of our quarry. We walked slowly through the throng of passengers, each of us searching the faces for our man. There was no one in view who had a beard of such fulsome growth.

"Are you sure that it isn't really a wild goose chase after all?" said Lestrade with weary sarcasm.

Holmes did not reply, but I could observe a flicker of uncertainty in his eyes. Perhaps he, too, was having doubts.

Moments later, two guards moved down the train, unlocking the doors, and passengers began to board.

"He must be here," muttered Holmes, more to himself than to us.

Lestrade did not respond.

Within less than a minute, the platform was almost empty. I was beginning to think that on this occasion that my friend had been wrong in his convictions. Then suddenly at the end of the platform, from a trolley piled high with travelling trunks, there emerged a crouching figure. As he began to make his way surreptitiously toward the train, his face was illuminated briefly by the gas lighting, and we all saw a white frightened face framed by a large grey beard.

"That's our man!" hissed Holmes, but before we were able to make a move, another shadowy figure raced past us toward Daubney with a grotesque guttural cry which echoed to the steely rafters of the station. As this figure grew near to Daubney, he raised his hand, which held a knife with a long savage blade which flashed brightly in the gaslight.

"It's Bell!" cried Holmes rushing forward, but he was too late. The knife had already struck a violent blow and Daubney crumpled to the ground with a gurgling moan. Bell struck again before Holmes was able to drag the assailant off his victim and with Lestrade's help, managed to restrain him. I knelt down by the wounded man, and I knew instinctively that I could be of no assistance: the man was breathing his last. Blood gushed from his chest wounds and a crimson stream dribbled out of his mouth. He tried to speak, but nothing emerged but a frothy gargling sound. Within seconds, the eyes took on a static glassy look and the life oozed out of Samuel Daubney.

"Is the blackguard dead?" cried Bell, his eyes flashing wildly.

"Yes," I said harshly. "You have succeeded in murdering him."

Bell gave a strange high-pitched mirthless laugh. "Praise be. All those years I spent in that dirty cell dreaming of this moment. To get my own back on that conniving, cunning devil who sent me up the river."

"You'll hang for this," said Lestrade, snapping a pair of handcuffs on Bell.

"I don't care. I have achieved my ambition. It was my hatred of the man that kept my spirits alive for three years. I knew I'd be content to go to my grave if I could do for him. And I have." There was another bout of wild laughter. "I can go to my maker content in the knowledge that I got my own back on that devil Dawes." He smiled grimly as he gazed down at the bloody corpse.

"Well, Mr. Holmes, it was an unusual night's adventure."

"Indeed. Not quite how I hoped it would end. Daubney was a felon, but he hardly deserved to die as he did. But at least you have recaptured Bell, and he certainly will pay dearly for his actions."

"The seed of evil was in both of them," observed Lestrade.

"You may be right, Inspector. If that is the case, there but for the grace…"

❦

It was nearing midnight and we were seated around the dying embers of the fire in our Baker Street rooms. Earlier, we had left Lestrade and his constables to deal with the business of removing the corpse and arranging for Bell's transfer to a cell in Scotland Yard. He had now become quite docile and accepted his arrested with equanimity, offering no resistance whatsoever.

Meanwhile, Holmes and I had undertaken the unpleasant task of informing Mrs. Daubney of her husband's death. She took the news bravely. There were no tears this time, just a pale, strained expression.

"I have had a long day on my own to mull matters over," she said, "and somehow I knew in my heart of hearts that I would never see Samuel again. The way he acted last night, his terror and wild behaviour somehow told me…" She gave a grim smile and I observed a steely glint in those moist eyes that suggested she was determined to cope with his deceit and her tragedy.

Holmes, who is never comfortable in these circumstances was heartily relieved when we were able to leave. I felt terribly sorry for the lady, but somehow, I believed that in time she would rise above her loss.

Back in our quarters, I had hardly finished pouring out a brandy and soda for us when Lestrade called for a postmortem of the case. Holmes was able to fill in all the details of the matter.

"How did Bell know where to find Daubney?" The Scotland Yarder asked.

"Mrs. Daubney told us that her husband had always dreamed of owning little tobacconists since he was a youngster. No doubt he'd talked about it often. Presumably, he had told Bell that he hoped to fund such a venture with the spoils of the bank robbery. Bell would have checked out any new tobacconist shop to open since he went into prison and narrowed his search down to A Smoke in the City, Daubney's emporium. When he turned up there today and found the shop closed, he no doubt put two and two together and worked out that Daubney had read of his escape from prison in the newspaper and was aiming to disappear. The easiest means to get well away was to travel to the continent. The most convenient way was to catch the late-night Continental express."

Lestrade nodded sagely as though he would have reached the same conclusion. "Well, time I was home and in bed," he said draining his glass. With a weary sigh, he rose and retrieved his hat from the rack. "I'll bid you both goodnight." He paused at the door. "Another successful investigation, eh, Mr. Holmes?"

"Not quite, Lestrade. I would have much preferred Daubney to have spent some time in gaol for his sins rather than ending up in the morgue."

After I had retired for the night, I could hear the melancholy strains of Holmes's violin floating in the air. It was his way to come to terms with life's disappointments.

With regards to Mrs. Daubney, after an appropriate period of mourning, she opened the shop again, and I believe it became a successful venture.

About the Editor

MAXIM JAKUBOWSKI is a London-based former publisher, editor, writer, and translator. He has compiled over one hundred anthologies in a variety of genres, many of which have garnered awards. He is a past winner of the Karel and Anthony awards, and in 2019 was given the prestigious Red Herrings award by the Crime Writers' Association for his contribution to the genre. He broadcasts regularly on radio and TV, reviews for diverse newspapers and magazines, and has been a judge for several literary awards. He is the author of twenty novels, the latest being *The Louisiana Republic* (2018), and a series of *Sunday Times* bestselling novels under a pseudonym. He has also published five collections of his own short stories. He is currently Vice Chair of the Crime Writers' Association.

www.maximjakubowski.co.uk

About the Authors

ROSE BIGGIN is a writer and performer living in London. As well as fiction, she writes as a theatre academic. This is her second story featuring the indomitable Irene Adler: the first thrilling installment can be found under "The Modjeska Waltz" in *The Adventures of Moriarty*. www.rosebiggin.uk.

MATTHEW BOOTH is the author of *Sherlock Holmes and the Giant's Hand* and one of the authors contributing to *The Further Exploits of Sherlock Holmes*. Matthew was a scriptwriter for the American radio network, *Imagination Theatre*, syndicated by Jim French Productions. He was a regular contributor to their series *The Further Adventures of Sherlock Holmes*. Matthew is the creator of former criminal barrister and amateur detective Anthony Rathe, who appeared in a radio series produced by Jim French Productions. Rathe now appears in *When Anthony Rathe Investigates*, published by Sparkling Books.

KEITH BROOKE's first novel, *Keepers of the Peace*, appeared in 1990. Since then, he has published eight more adult novels, six collections, and more than seventy short stories. His novel *Genetopia* was published by Pyr in February 2006 and was their first title to receive a starred review in *Publishers Weekly*; *The Accord*, published by Solaris in 2009, received another starred *PW* review and was optioned for film. His most recent SF novel, *Harmony* (published in the UK as *alt.human*), was shortlisted for the Philip K Dick Award. Writing as Nick Gifford, his teen fiction is published by Puffin, with one novel also optioned for the movies by Andy Serkis and Jonathan Cavendish's Caveman Films. He writes reviews for *The Guardian*, teaches creative writing at the University of Essex, and lives with his wife Debbie in Wivenhoe, Essex.

JON COURTENAY GRIMWOOD was born in Malta. He grew up in the Far East, Scandinavia, and the UK. He has written for *The Times*, *The Telegraph*, *The Guardian*, and *The Independent*. Two times winner of the BSFA Award for Best Novel, he's been shortlisted for the Arthur C. Clarke, the British Fantasy Award, the John W. Campbell, and Le Prix Montesquieu. He writes as JCG, Jack Grimwood, and Jonathan Grimwood.

DAVID STUART DAVIES is the author of eight Sherlock Holmes novels and *Starring Sherlock Holmes,* which details the detective's film career. David's three successful one-man plays, *Sherlock Holmes: The Last Act* and *Sherlock Holmes: The Life & Death*, have been recorded on audio CD by The Big Finish. *Sherlock Holmes: The Final Reckoning* premiered in Edinburgh in February 2019. David is the author of other works of crime fiction including seven Johnny Hawke novels—the latest being *Spiral of Lies*. Other recent titles include *Sherlock Holmes: The Instrument of Death* and *Oliver Twist & the Mystery of Throate Manor*. David is a Baker Street Irregular, a member of The Detection Club, and edited *Red Herrings*, the monthly magazine of the Crime Writers' Association for twenty years.

O'NEIL DE NOUX is a New Orleans writer with forty-one books published and over four hundred short story sales in multiple genres. His fiction has received several awards, including the Shamus Award for Best Private Eye Short Story, the Derringer Award for Best Novelette, and the 2011 Police Book of the Year. Two of his stories have appeared in the Best American Mystery Stories anthology (2013 and 2007). His latest book is *12 Bullets*, a police thriller. He is a past vice president of the Private Eye Writers of America. Website: www.oneildenoux.com.

JAN EDWARDS is a UK author of many novels and short stories in horror, fantasy, mainstream, and crime fiction, including *Mammoth Book of Folk Horror and* several volumes of the MX *Books of New Sherlock Holmes Stories.* Jan is also an editor with the award-winning Alchemy Press, including *The Alchemy Press Book of Horror Vol 2* (2020). Jan is a recipient of the Karl Edward Wagner Award (BFS) and won the Arnold Bennett Book Prize for *Winter Downs* (first in her World War II crime series The Bunch Courtney Investigations). To read more about Jan, go to: janedwardsblog.wordpress.com.

RHYS HUGHES has been a published author for the past thirty years. His books include *Worming the Harpy, The Truth Spinner, Tallest Stories*, and *Mombasa Madrigal*. He graduated as an engineer and currently works as a mathematics tutor. He divides his time between a poky old apartment in Britain and a farm without electricity in Kenya.

NACHING T. KASSA is a wife, mother, and writer. She's created short stories, novellas, and poems, and cocreated three children. She lives in Eastern Washington State with her husband, Dan Kassa. Naching is a member of the Horror Writers Association, Head of Publishing for HorrorAddicts.net, an assistant at Crystal Lake Publishing, and an honorary member of The Trained Cormorants of Long Beach. You can find her at nachingkassa.wordpress.com.

ASHLEY LISTER is the author of more than fifty books and countless short stories. He has lectured in creative writing for more than a decade, writing and running a broad range of courses. He recently completed his PhD in creative writing where his thesis considers the relationship between plot and genre in short fiction. www.ashleylister.co.uk.

CATHERINE LUNDOFF is a Minneapolis-based, award-winning writer, editor, and publisher. Her recent stories and articles are available or forthcoming at the *LMHPodcast*, *Fireside Fiction*, *American Monsters Part 2*, *Queer Voices*, *The Cainite Conspiracies: A Vampire the Masquerade V20 Anthology*, and the SFWA Blog. Her books include *Silver Moon*, *Out of This World: Queer Speculative Fiction Stories*, *Unfinished Business: Tales of the Dark Fantastic*, and as editor, *Scourge of the Seas of Time (and Space)*. She is the publisher at Queen of Swords Press. www.queenofswordspress.com.

KEITH MORAY is a doctor and novelist. He is the author of the bestselling Inspector Torquil McKinnon Mysteries, cosy Scottish crime capers set on the fictional Hebridean island of West Uist, and of a new series of historical crime thrillers, all published by Sapere Books. He also writes Westerns under the penname of Clay More and is a member of the Crime Writers' Association, International Thriller Writers, and Western Writers of America, and is a past vice president of Western Fictioneers. He lives in England within arrow shot of a ruined medieval castle, the setting for a couple of his historical crime novels. His website is keithmorayauthor.com.

MARK MOWER is a long-standing member of the Crime Writers' Association, the Sherlock Holmes Society of London, and the Solar Pons Society of London. He has written numerous crime books, including *A Farewell to Baker Street*, *Sherlock Holmes: The Baker Street Case-Files*, and *Sherlock Holmes: The Baker Street Legacy* (all with MX Publishing).

LAVIE TIDHAR's most recent novels are *By Force Alone* (Tor) and *The Escapement* (Tachyon). He is the author of the World Fantasy Award winning *Osama* (2011), the Jerwood Fiction Uncovered Prize winning *A Man Lies Dreaming* (2014), the Campbell and Neukom awards winning *Central Station* (2016), and many others, including children's book *The Candy Mafia* and graphic novel *Adler*.

BEV VINCENT is the author of over ninety short stories, including appearances in *Alfred Hitchcock's* and *Ellery Queen's Mystery Magazines*, *Cemetery Dance* magazine and two MWA anthologies. His books include *The Road to the Dark Tower* and *The Stephen King Illustrated Companion*. He recently coedited the anthology *Flight or Fright* with Stephen King. His work has been nominated for the Edgar, the Stoker (twice), and the ITW Thriller Awards, and he is the 2010 winner of the Al Blanchard Award. He lives in Texas, where he is working on a novel. Learn more at bevvincent.com.

Mango Publishing, established in 2014, publishes an eclectic list of books by diverse authors—both new and established voices—on topics ranging from business, personal growth, women's empowerment, LGBTQ studies, health, and spirituality to history, popular culture, time management, decluttering, lifestyle, mental wellness, aging, and sustainable living. We were recently named 2019 *and* 2020's #1 fastest growing independent publisher by *Publishers Weekly*. Our success is driven by our main goal, which is to publish high quality books that will entertain readers as well as make a positive difference in their lives

Our readers are our most important resource; we value your input, suggestions, and ideas. We'd love to hear from you—after all, we are publishing books for you!

Please stay in touch with us and follow us at:

Facebook: Mango Publishing

Twitter: @MangoPublishing

Instagram: @MangoPublishing

LinkedIn: Mango Publishing

Pinterest: Mango Publishing

Newsletter: mangopublishinggroup.com/newsletter

Join us on Mango's journey to reinvent publishing, one book at a time.